D1520172

Grace Falling Like Rain

Grace Falling Like Rain
Readers' Comments

The following are just a few of the comments of some of my first readers:

From Clara Jo Horton, Cotulla, Texas, library director and voracious reader that I had asked to proofread the manuscript:

"Okay. Just finished the book about two hours ago. Have to tell you, I was all prepared to be only 'proofreader- interested' in it -- you know, [since it's] not my usual preference in fiction and all; but, Donna, I found myself being eager to get back to it when I had to leave it! I liked the story, and I liked the morals, and it flowed, and it had humor, and it sounded real...

"I found a wonderful turn of phrase that you wrote that just made me see what is really an abstract idea. Loved it! After having been with the Indians for a few days, you wrote about 'how fragile the line was from hand to mouth.' Awesome. Phrases and images like this are one of the reasons I read a lot."

Bill Cotulla, South Texas rancher, said the book made him think of my writing as a female Elmer Kelton. I take that as a huge compliment!

Carmen Oliver, a fellow writer from Round Rock, Texas, said, "I've read the entire manuscript and it was awesome, truly awesome. A real page turner..."

Mary Jan Jenkins, Curriculum Director in Alice, Texas, called me right after she finished the story. She said she was hooked from chapter one and couldn't stop reading excerpts to her husband, Robert, who had grown up cowboyin'.

Karen Thomison, high school educational assistant in Hutto, Texas, stuck her head in my office within an hour of receiving the story and said, "I've been in the library and just read the first chapter. I can't put it down. You know what I'm going to be doing tonight!" And she stopped by again leaving work and told me she was making her husband drive to the football game that night so she could read the book. Later, her husband asked if he could read it, and Karen said she caught him reading it during one of the Astros play-off games. "And we're huge Astros fans!" she said.

Rita Beights of Pilot Point, Texas, called me at work to tell me that I'd made her miss her nap that day because she couldn't put the book down.

Carolyn Hinojosa of Hutto read the book as a high school senior. She told me it was now her favorite book, and she couldn't wait for the sequel. She's now in the U.S. Marine Corps—hoorah! And I *will* track her down when I've finished the sequel.

Male and female readers from ages sixteen to their nineties have read and enjoyed this story, so I'm hesitant to categorize it in a particular genre. It is definitely historical fiction, though, and woven throughout are noble themes of love, forgiveness, and grace in the midst of serenity, danger, laughter, and tears— much like life.

Enjoy the ride!

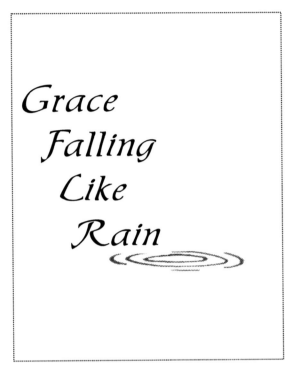

Grace
Falling
Like
Rain

Donna Van Cleve

Two Story
Publishing House
Hutto, Texas

Grace Falling Like Rain
Published by
Two Story Publishing House
P.O. Box 482
Hutto, Texas 78634

Copyright ©2006 by Donna Van Cleve
www.donnavancleve.com
Email: donna@donnavancleve.com

Publisher's Cataloging-in-Publication Data

Van Cleve, Donna C.
    Grace falling like rain / Donna Van Cleve
    240 p. cm.
    ISBN 0-9787937-0-6   ISBN 978-0-9787937-0-8
    1. Frontier and pioneer life—Fiction. 2. Kidnapping—
    Fiction. 3. Apache Indians—Fiction. 4. Texas—Fiction.

                        2006906874

On the Cover: *Muddy Waters*
by Bill Owen, member of Cowboy Artists of America
Used with permission
Visit his website at www.billowenca.com

*For my parents, Jim & Isla Casey,
who have demonstrated
unconditional love & support
throughout my life—
You are what I aspire to be when I grow up.*

*For Van, my son & globetrotting hero—
Thank you for your help in this endeavor.*

*For my late mother-in-law, LaVane,
a beautiful & gracious lady
who taught me so much,
& who, like a character in this story,
loved her grandchildren fiercely.*

Acknowledgments

Thank you, Vanessa, Van, and Jonathan for your part in this.

Thank you, Jenna, for insisting that I print out the story chapter by chapter so you could read it. Your eyes were the first to see it, and you gave me the courage to press on in order to share it with even more folks.

Thank you, CJ, for your sharp memory & eyes—you're the best!

Thank you, Christy, for your enthusiasm and encouragement for my writing efforts.

Thank you, all you early readers in Cotulla, Hutto, Baghdad- Iraq, Pflugerville, Crosby, Corpus Christi, Houston, Alice, Pilot Point, Three Rivers, Arlington, Round Rock, San Antonio, Taylor, & Norman's Crossing for your encouragement & wonderful comments about this story—even in its roughest stages!

Thank you to a most gracious couple, Bill and Valerie Owen, for the privilege of using *Muddy Waters* on the cover collage. Please check out Bill's outstanding artwork at
http://billowenca.com/lithographs.htm
and even more amazing bio at
http://billowenca.com/about.htm

And especially—thank you, God, for your amazing, life-changing grace anyone can receive through your Son, Jesus Christ.
John 3:16

&
Proverbs 3:5-6

Chapter 1

The young couple stood together on the riverbank. His rugged face smiled as he looked down at her. She held his hands, strong hands—hands that could handle a stallion or gently caress a newborn colt. She lifted her face to his and closed her eyes in anticipation of a tender kiss.

Suddenly the ground gave way beneath his feet, and she felt his hands wrenched from hers. She screamed as he slid into the river; the strong current carried him away from her. She tried to follow along the riverbank, but branches and thorns grabbed her clothes. Entangled, she watched helplessly as his face slipped from her sight. A cry started deep within her and begged to be released...

"Alexandra! Wake up, sweetie!"

Allie sat up in bed, blinking her eyes. Aunt Sister sat beside her, patting her arm.

"You were dreaming again, honey. I thought you were over those nightmares long ago."

Allie wiped her eyes. "I'm sorry, Aunt Sister. I hadn't thought about him in so long. I don't know why it came back."

"Maybe it's because you're going home soon, and it's opening up old wounds."

Allie thought for a moment. "The dream was the same, but it was different, too. Miguel was there on the riverbank, but for some reason his eyes were... blue."

"See there, you're already forgetting what he looked like," Aunt Sister said. "Now go back to sleep and let me get some shut-eye. We have a busy day ahead of us."

1

"I love you, Aunt Sister," Allie said as she hugged her aunt and snuggled back under the bed sheet. "I'm really going to miss you when I go home."

"It's going to be awfully quiet around here soon," her aunt smiled as she paused at the door, "but we'll survive somehow."

Dawn broke with the sound of dishes clattering and heavy steps on the stairs. Uncle Junior maneuvered around in his world with the grace of a stove-up buffalo. Allie stretched in bed and grinned at the familiar sounds she had become so accustomed to hearing every morning this past year. It was odd how neither her aunt nor her uncle went by their given names of Elizabeth and Charles. Their childhood nicknames had grabbed hold and followed them into adulthood.

It grieved her now to recall a snide remark about their names she had made in anger not long after her arrival. They were so patient and forgiving, seeming to understand the frustration and pain she was going through. Her parents had insisted she come live with her aunt and uncle over a year ago because of a forbidden relationship with a young Mexican man.

Miguel and Allie had met secretly for some time, but eventually it became known. The town was in an upheaval over it, but Allie thought she was strong enough to handle it. That is, if she had been the only one involved, which unfortunately was not the case. Her family suffered the most for her sake. Men would stop her father on the street and confront him about it, sometimes threatening bodily harm. Women made ugly remarks and gossiped openly around her mother in the local businesses. Her younger brother found himself constantly defending her honor, usually through fistfights, even among his friends. It tore her family apart, and she knew she had to do something.

Allie's parents never told her directly that they disapproved of Miguel. They believed that God created all men equal and taught their children this principle, but they were concerned about the pain their daughter would have to endure if the relationship continued. Miguel's family was educated and prosperous, but his parents also disapproved of the friendship.

Miguel and Allie considered running away together, but they both deeply cherished their families and felt the cost would be too great to go against their parents' wishes. So Allie agreed to go live with Aunt Sister and Uncle Junior in northeast Texas until... well, she wasn't sure of that part.

During the first couple of months, Allie had the same recurring nightmare of Miguel falling in the river and being swept away from her. But after a while the nightmares disappeared. Maybe it was because she began to realize that much of the feelings she had for Miguel was respect, and the danger of sneaking around to see him added to the excitement of the relationship. But no matter when or where she met him, Miguel remained a gentleman. They usually talked more than anything else when they were together. They shared their dreams in life and idealistically wished away the divisions between the two cultures.

Sometimes Miguel would kiss Allie, although he did not have the dubious honor of being the first to kiss Alexandra Blake. Billy Clarkson held that title, as forgettable as it was. When Allie was younger, she used to fret over her first kiss and was concerned enough to ask her mother about it one day.

"But what do I do when a boy kisses me, Momma?"

"It'd better not be any time soon, Allie," she warned teasingly.

"No, but if you're supposed to shut your eyes, what if we bump noses, or completely miss or something?"

Her mother laughed. "Don't worry about it, honey. It'll come naturally."

And after Billy kissed her quick on the mouth behind the church one Sunday, she had walked halfway home before she realized she had been kissed—her first kiss. The only thing she could think of was *big doodle-ee deal*. Billy's kiss was not that impressive, but later on, Miguel's was.

After the town learned of Allie and Miguel's relationship, many of the young men Allie had known all of her life would try to get fresh with her. They assumed since she was friendly with a *meskin*, as they referred to him, she had to have acquired loose morals. One particularly sorry specimen for the male gender had the gall to tell her that if she was so desperate to have a beau, he would gallantly let her have him. She simply answered that if he were the last man in Texas, she would rather keep company with a skunk than with him. When all of his friends laughed and chided him about it, she proceeded to insult the whole group by saying that Miguel had more integrity and manners than all of them combined.

They did not laugh at that.

Allie was now eighteen years old and would start the trip back home tomorrow. She could not wait to see her family, but there wasn't much more she was looking forward to in Dalton. Most of her friends were married and having babies, and the prospect of finding a husband she could respect back in her hometown was fairly dim. Most would probably have little to do with her anyway. She had crossed a line—invisible, yes, but most definitely in place. She was tainted goods even though her virtue was still intact.

What made it even more difficult was for Allie to learn recently in a letter from home that Miguel had become engaged to a beautiful young lady from Mexico. The talk around town said that his family had made an arrangement with her family years ago. But Allie knew Miguel well enough to know he would not follow through with it if it was merely an arranged marriage. She knew he would have to have some feelings for her. She hoped he was happy, but she also dreaded the moment she might encounter them in town. She determined to avoid that for as long as possible.

Her mother had gently broke the news about Miguel in her last letter. The only other person that sent her a letter that year was Uncle John. He really wasn't Allie's uncle, but rather her father's best friend. She had known him her entire life and was as close as a daughter to him. He had lost his wife and baby during childbirth, and he never remarried. Allie knew little about his wife Sarah except that she was beautiful, evidenced by the portrait hanging in his parlor. Uncle John swore he would never love another in his lifetime.

Most would say John Stockton had suffered more than his share of sorrow in his life, and it all came within one year's time—the same year his wife died. Just before Allie was born, a small group of Apaches had taken John's only sister and her youngest son in a raid on their newly built home in Central Texas. Allie's church prayed for almost six years for their safe return, and over the years many had lost hope of ever finding them alive. But no one would suggest out loud that John take them off the prayer list.

Everyone said it was a miracle that God finally allowed them to be found and returned home. John wept openly and praised the Lord as he told the church the wonderful news before he set out to see his only remaining sibling and her son Johnny, named after his uncle. Allie remembers only one thing about that worship service. It was the only time she ever saw Uncle John cry. When she was older, Allie decided she would add Uncle John to her list of kin and would always remember him on holidays and his birthday. He was too good of a man to be left alone.

Allie knew, too, that Uncle John adored her, and that he would lasso the moon for her if he could. It was he who covered the cost of the trip and accompanied her to Aunt Sister's home across the state, insisting he had business in nearby Dallas. Allie's parents ran the local newspaper office back home in Dalton, and her father took pride in the fact that he never missed a publication of the weekly newspaper in his twelve years as editor and owner. John's gracious offer to escort the Blakes' headstrong daughter out of harm's way kept her father's record intact as well as his pride, since he couldn't afford the fare. And John would also bring her home under the ruse of more business in Dallas, Dalton would hear. Allie hoped to slip back into life unobtrusively, but she knew that things would never be the same.

Allie had made new friends in Munford, but wasn't bosom buddy close to any of them. She saw her married cousins every so often when they would visit their parents, but she had little in common with them since they were busy with their businesses, homes, and children. Her uncle ran a thriving blacksmith shop and livery stable along with his eldest son, who planned to take over the business someday. Uncle Junior also owned some horses he kept at the livery and ran a few head of cattle on another son's place outside of town. Her aunt was content to keep house, garden, and sew, and Allie learned all about canning and drying vegetables and fruits before the year was out.

She single-handedly took over the feeding of the animals around the place, which included dogs, hogs, chickens, and a milk cow. It took a while, but she finally mastered the art of milking Beatrice, to Aunt Sister's relief. Until then, Allie thought she would squeeze those teats off before a drop of milk ever came out. A tomcat also roamed around the place, but Allie was told to not feed him so he would continue to keep the mice and rat population down. Tom usually had to bring his catch to the porch to show it off before he ate it, which disgusted Allie. But she learned that the sooner she praised him, the sooner he would dispose of the carcass.

Allie participated in Aunt Sister's sewing circle, too, and helped complete numerous quilts over a period of months. She felt especially proud to bring home a beautiful quilt for her own bed. Aunt Sister let her pick out the colors from the scrap bag and also the pattern to use. Allie couldn't decide between the Pincushion or the Star of David patterns, but finally chose the latter. She jokingly told Aunt Sister she would place it in her *hopeless* chest back home, but inside she felt like the description would prove accurate.

Time slowed to a crawl the first couple of months she spent with Aunt Sister and Uncle Junior, but the more Allie found to do, the faster time sped by. Over a year had passed before she knew it, and tomorrow morning she would board the stage with Uncle John to head home. Her mother's letter said he would come for dinner tonight, so Aunt Sister and Allie worked hard to prepare a special meal. She knew he loved roast beef with gravy, and they fixed side dishes of buttered potatoes, carrots, and green beans—the best of the past season's garden canned by Allie's own hands. And for dessert, peach cobbler. It took all of Allie's will power to keep from pinching off a corner to taste before dinner. She would be sure to point out to Uncle John that his investment in her for all this time away from home would not return void.

Allie and Aunt Sister prepared everything down to the last detail. They even set out the best china, and Allie had picked a beautiful assortment of flowers from her aunt's garden for the center of the table. Uncle Junior thought that went a bit far, but Allie wanted the evening to be special for her dear friend.

Allie took a quick bath in the washroom and dashed upstairs to finish getting ready. She decided to wear her white linen and lace dress with the cameo brooch Uncle John had given her for Christmas several years ago. This dress would be the last item of clothing placed in her trunk before closing it tonight. She set aside several other sturdy outfits to be packed in a smaller bag for the overnight stops on the way home.

Allie brushed her long brown hair and used a silver barrette to clasp it up and away from her face. She pinched her cheeks and studied her reflection in the mirror. Some said she looked like her mother, but others said she walked like her father. Allie wasn't sure if that was good or bad. She used to be a tomboy with her brother in her younger days, but had become quite comfortable in her role as a young lady in recent years. People used to comment on her pretty face, but that was before her friendship with Miguel. Allie would have felt like a leper in town if Miguel had not regularly convinced her otherwise. He told her that her heart was just as beautiful as her face. He will never know how often she pulled that memory out and turned it over in her mind during the times she felt bad about herself.

Allie dabbed on some *smell-good*, as her father called it, and stepped back from the dresser mirror. She practiced one of her best smiles, and immediately chastised herself for vanity and primping. As she reached the door to her bedroom, she heard a loud knock downstairs.

"I'll get it!" Allie hollered, and grabbing up her dress, ran very unlady-like down the stairs. She reached the front door and swung it open with arms wide.

"Uncle Joh..." she stopped mid-word, looking into the bluest eyes she had ever seen. It wasn't Uncle John. She put her arms down quickly.

"Uh, howdy, ma'am," the blue eyes said.

"I'm sorry," Allie said as she shook her composure back into place. "I expected someone else. Do you need to see my uncle?"

"No, ma'am," the blue eyes replied. "John Stockton sent me in his place. He's waiting for us at my parents' home not too far from Waco, and we'll all travel back to Dalton together."

"Oh." Allie wasn't sure what else to say.

"I know you're disappointed, but after we got to my folks' house, Uncle John came down with something that wouldn't let him travel too far from the privy... uh," he cleared his throat, a faint red crept up his cheeks. "I mean, he wasn't feeling well and asked me to go on ahead and bring you back."

"I hope it isn't anything serious," she said, noting the sudden change of direction in that last sentence.

"I'm sure he'll be fine," the blue eyes assured her. "He's as strong as a bull."

"I'll get to see him soon." Allie said as she stood there awkwardly for a moment.

Her aunt and uncle walked up behind her.

"Well, are we going to make him stand out there on the porch all evening, sweetie?" Uncle Junior said.

Allie smiled a crooked smile, the red now creeping into her own cheeks. "Where are my manners? Please come in. I am so sorry, uh... what is your name?"

"Justin Taylor."

"Nice to make your acquaintance, Justin Taylor. I'm Allie Blake."

"Alexandra is her given name," Aunt Sister piped in.

"And this is Charles and Elizabeth Spafford, otherwise known as Aunt Sister and Uncle Junior."

"Pleased to meet you," Justin said as he shook Junior's hand.

"Supper's on the table—I hope you're planning to stay for dinner, Justin," Sister said as she took him by the arm and led him captive toward the dining table. "We cooked enough for an army."

"Something sure smells good," he said, smiling. "I don't think I could leave now if I wanted to."

Aunt Sister giggled like a sixteen-year-old. Allie's eyes widened when Uncle Junior chuckled and then winked at her.

Justin was stealing Aunt Sister's heart from right under Uncle Junior's nose.

The meal was a resounding success. Justin sealed Aunt Sister's approval after having seconds of everything and thirds when it came to compliments on her cooking. The conversation was quite enjoyable, too. Justin said he had moved down to Dalton nine months ago to run the cattle operation for John and seemed to find a lot of satisfaction in his work.

Allie studied him a little closer during the meal. His sandy-colored hair was untamed; he had several days' growth of facial hair, and his skin was tanned from the sun like he spent a lot of time outdoors. His face had a brooding, almost hard expression when he wasn't smiling. His hands were rough and callused. She had no idea how old he was, maybe mid-twenties, but it looked as though life had not been easy on him. His piercing blue eyes seemed to look straight through to her thoughts when he met her eyes. She found herself avoiding them, feeling more comfortable talking to his nose or mouth or chin.

After dessert, the men went to the porch while the women cleared the table and washed the dishes. Junior offered Justin a chaw of tobacco, but he declined, saying he never could spit worth a damn.

"It'd end up dribblin' down my chin and onto my clothes. And what's the use of chewin' if you can't spit decent?"

Junior laughed. "Well, there's definitely some skill to it, though the Missus doesn't appreciate my talents in that capacity."

The two began to talk cattle.

"Well, what do you think about him?" Aunt Sister said after the men left the room.

"About what?" Allie said, feigning ignorance as she gathered the plates.

"I think he's quite handsome," Aunt Sister continued. "I wonder if John Stockton really *was* sick."

"Aunt Sister!" Allie said, blushing. "Of course he was sick! What are you talking about?"

"Maybe he intended to spark a little interest between the two of you."

"Ssshhh! He'll hear you. I don't even know this man! I can't believe you would think such an improper thing," Allie scolded. "You know Uncle John would've been here if he could. I'm surprised he let him come on without him. He must really trust Justin. And I noticed he charmed the

8

stockings off of you at the dinner table. And in front of Uncle Junior, too!"

"Well maybe Junior needs to be reminded every once in a while that he's lucky to have such a wonderful wife—at least others appreciate my talents."

Allie laughed, shaking her head in agreement. "I have to admit, though, it is going to be an interesting trip home. For some reason, I'm not dreading it in some ways as I was before."

"Ah ha! You'd better behave yourself on the way home," Aunt Sister teased, and then paused. "Home…" she said as her eyes filled. She turned around to face the dishpan. "Oh, sweetie, we're going to miss you somethin' fierce. I sure have enjoyed your company these past months."

Allie hugged her tightly from behind.

"You and Uncle Junior mean so much to me, and you've helped me in more ways than you could ever know. I'm never going to lose touch with you—I promise," Allie said, kissing the back of her head.

"Now go on and take those two handsome fellers a cup of coffee, child. I'll be out shortly."

Allie walked out on the porch just as Uncle Junior told Justin to go cancel his room at the hotel and bring his stuff back over to the house to stay.

"This is a three bedroom house, and we only had five kids. I didn't think about how big it would be after all the kids left home," Uncle Junior explained. "So we have plenty of room for you."

Allie handed them their coffee, smiling at her uncle's remarks.

"Thank you, ma'am," Justin nodded to Allie. "But I wouldn't want to impose."

"Sister'll be highly put out with you if you don't stay here tonight," Uncle Junior said. "John Stockton wouldn't have had a choice either, son. Now don't argue with me; my mind's made up."

Justin grinned. "Well, I sure wouldn't want the Missus to get on my case, especially if there's an opportunity for another meal in this house."

"Then it's settled," Aunt Sister spoke from the doorway, about to burst with pride from that last remark. "Go get your things, young man."

"Now you did it," Allie said to Justin as he handed her his cup. "Aunt Sister may never let you leave this house."

"Might not be such a bad thing," Justin said over his shoulder as he walked off.

* * *

It seemed like Allie had just shut her eyes when she heard heavy footsteps on the stairs, followed by another set of boot steps—lighter, though. That had to have been one of the reasons she had a hard time getting to sleep last night.

Justin Taylor.

She liked the sound of that name. If Uncle John thought highly enough of him to manage his cattle operations, he must be something special. She wondered if he knew anything about her past. Surely not, or he wouldn't have been so polite and charming around her last night. She figured it was only a matter of time before someone would break the news to him after returning to Dalton, though. She had better not entertain any thoughts about him if she wanted to avoid another big hurt.

She got up and made the bed, and then dressed in her traveling clothes: a gray skirt, white blouse, and matching gray jacket with black trim. She braided her long hair into a single strand and rolled it into a bun at the base of her neck, holding it in place with several combs. She grabbed her flat-crowned, black felt hat and went downstairs to help Aunt Sister with breakfast. Justin and Uncle Junior were nowhere in sight.

At Allie's inquisitive look, Aunt Sister explained, "They're feeding the animals for you this morning so you won't have to get dirty before you go."

"Oh, Aunt Sister, I'm so sorry! That's my responsibility, and I've already forgotten it," she said apologetically. "I can't believe I didn't at least make the effort this morning."

"We didn't expect you to, sweetie. We know you're excited about going home."

"Well, what can I do to help you in here?" she offered, hanging her hat and jacket on the hall tree.

Allie helped Aunt Sister put on a breakfast feast that had rarely, if ever, been seen in that house. Uncle Junior's mouth dropped open when he saw the dining table.

"Now why don't you ever cook like this for me?" he demanded to know.

"Well, if you showed a little appreciation every now and then, there's no tellin' what all I'd do for you," Aunt Sister chided with a feigned sternness. "Have a seat here, Justin. How 'bout some biscuits?"

"I do appreciate you, dear. You know that," Junior defended himself.

"It'd be nice to hear it every once in a while," she said, heaping mounds of scrambled eggs onto Justin's plate.

"But why do I have to tell you somethin' you already know?" Uncle Junior said as watched her spoon grits into a bowl for Justin.

"Junior, pass Justin the ham and bacon," she ordered.

Justin and Allie kept their eyes downward, trying their best to keep a serious expression on their faces.

"Well, I do appreciate you, Elizabeth," Junior said with the enthusiasm of a whipped puppy. "And you're the best cook in this county. Everybody knows that."

Sister stopped in mid-stab. Her heart melted. She walked around the table and put her arms around Junior.

"That's one of the nicest things you've ever told me, husband," Sister said. "Now, was that so hard?"

He shook his head, no.

"Well, how 'bout an apple pie for supper tonight?"

Junior smiled. He was back on his throne.

After breakfast, Allie excused herself and slipped outside. She had forgotten to feed the animals, but wasn't about to forget to tell them goodbye. Feeding them every morning for over a year had earned them a spot in her heart, whether the feeling was mutual or not. The dogs followed at her heels to the barn where she touched 'ol Beatrice on the head as she continued to munch on her hay for milking. She would take herself out to the pasture soon, and bring herself back like clockwork tonight for milking.

"Goodbye, Beatrice."

Allie walked outside to the chicken coop, keeping an eye out for Mean Mortimer, the young black rooster who spurred her only when her back was turned. She even tried to trick him at times by turning her back to him and peeking over her shoulder, but that bird always seemed to know when she was watching him. One time she tried that trick while she unknowingly stood in a red ant pile. Mortimer paid no attention to her until the first ant stung her leg, and she turned her head to look down at her feet. He immediately flew up and hit her in the back. That rooster made her so mad she chased him all over the backyard. The memory brought a smile to Allie's face.

"Goodbye, chickens."

Uncle Junior's huge sow, Big Gal, remained content in the mud hole while Allie talked to her. For months she thought her name was Big Al and finally asked her uncle why they had named her such a masculine name when she was so obviously female. Uncle Junior had a big laugh about it. Big Gal was a prolific breeder and had given birth to a litter not long after Allie arrived. Baby pigs looked so cute with their pink snoots and little high-heeled hooves. Allie made the mistake of naming each one of them, which led to tearful separations when the time came to fill the smokehouse or sell some to townsfolk. She decided she would never get that personal with any animal that had the potential of ending up on a plate somewhere, including her own.

"Goodbye, pigs."

Tom was nowhere to be found, but that was normal. He showed up when he felt like it—not when someone called him. She smiled when she thought about him bringing up the next carcass for her to praise and wondering where she was.

"Goodbye, Tom, wherever you are."

The three dogs each received a hug and a leftover biscuit from breakfast.

"Goodbye, you sweet dogs. I'm going to miss you the most."

Allie walked quickly back to the house, knowing she would probably never see any of them again. As she wiped a tear from her eye, she saw a movement in an upstairs window. It was Justin watching her. Embarrassed that she had been caught being sentimental about a bunch of silly animals, she lowered her head and dashed into the house.

Uncle Junior brought the buggy and horse around from the barn to take Allie and Justin to the stage office. Justin carried Allie's trunk down the stairs, and Allie walked out with the smaller bag.

"I'm going to have to say goodbye to you here, sweetie, since there's not enough room in the buggy for all of us," Aunt Sister said as she walked arm and arm with Allie.

"Well, maybe it's best that way so I won't squall in front of everybody on the stagecoach," Allie said as she started to cry.

Aunt Sister hugged her. "Now don't you start that, or you'll have me going. And it's not very pretty when I get to wailing!"

They laughed through their tears. Aunt Sister handed her a kerchief of goodies for the road.

"For Justin, I presume," Allie snorted.

"Well, ladies, we have a stage to catch, and it's not going to wait for us," Uncle Junior said from the buggy seat.

Justin waited to help Allie into the buggy, and climbed in beside her. They still hadn't made eye contact since he had seen her from the window.

"I love you, Aunt Sister!" Allie said as the buggy pulled away from the house. "I'll write you often!"

But Aunt Sister could only nod her head and wave; her dishtowel covered her nose and mouth as if to keep a dam from bursting.

At the stage office Justin handed an envelope to Junior to take care of the tickets inside while he unloaded the luggage and helped re-load it onto the stagecoach. Allie stood outside the door waiting for her uncle.

A couple of disheveled men walked by, and the first one paused before stepping into the office. The stench of alcohol and stale smoke made Allie involuntarily step back.

"My, my, what have we here?" the older one said, looking at Allie.

"Come on, Burt," the younger one said. "We don't have time for this."

"If she's going to be on the stage, I think I'm going to enjoy this ride," the older one said as he leered.

The younger one pushed him through the door and tipped his hat to Allie.

"Sorry, ma'am. Burt enjoyed himself a little too much last night, and it hasn't completely worn off yet," he apologized quietly for his friend and stepped inside.

Allie didn't know what to say. She noticed that Justin had stepped away from the stagecoach toward her, his blue eyes glaring at the doorway.

"It's all right, Justin," Allie felt compelled to say when she saw the intensity in his face. "I'm used to it," she said before she thought, and then regretted it immediately.

Justin looked surprised at her, and then a different expression altogether swept over his face.

What was it? Allie asked herself. *Pity? Disgust?* Then it was gone.

He knows! She thought with remorse. For the second time that day, she lowered her head to avoid his eyes and turned away.

Uncle Junior walked out with the tickets and handed them to Justin. He turned to Allie and gave her a bear hug.

"Big Al's going to miss you," he teased as Allie slapped his back. "And I guess I am, too, missy."

"Thank you for everything, Uncle Junior," she said as she kissed him on the cheek. "I love you."

"You take care of yourself, young lady," he said as he helped Allie onto the stagecoach.

"Walk with me, Justin," he said as he motioned toward the buggy. He climbed in and turned to face him. "I don't know what you've heard about Allie back in Dalton, but they don't come any better than that little girl. You take good care of her, you hear?"

"You have my word, sir," Justin said as he shook Junior's hand. "I appreciate your hospitality, too."

"Yeah, you sure spoiled my wife with all those compliments, son. I'm going to have to go back and get plumb romantic with her ever once in a while!" Uncle Junior chuckled. "Take care of yourself." He turned and spoke to the horse. "Giddy-up, Sassy."

Allie introduced herself to an older couple sitting on the opposite side of the coach. She sat there wondering what Uncle Junior said to Justin when the crude man she had encountered earlier boarded the stagecoach. To her chagrin, he chose to sit beside her.

"Well, hello again."

"I'm sorry, but this seat is already taken," Allie said firmly.

"I don't see anyone sitting here but me."

His sidekick climbed in, noticed the seating arrangement, and shook his head.

"Burt, why don't you sit over there next to the window by that nice gentleman, and I'll sit by the window over here."

"I'm perfectly happy where I'm sitting, Pete. And I'd much rather sit by this pretty young thing than that old goat. It makes losing our horses last night in that card game a little more tolerable," he said as he put his arm around Allie.

"Please remove your arm," Allie said through gritted teeth.

"Sir, where are your manners?" the elderly gentlemen said. "That is no way to treat a lady."

"Who asked your opinion, old man? I'd mind my own business if I were you."

"Come on Burt." Pete reached for Burt's arm. "Don't start anything."

Burt pushed him into the seat next to the elderly couple.

"Now, where were we," he said as he turned to face Allie.

"Nowhere to be exact," she said angrily, rising from her seat to leave. Burt grabbed her arm and pulled her back down.

Mr. Benjamin started to stand when Justin stuck his head in the coach. Allie was surprised to see a smile on his face. What was humorous about this situation?

"Good morning," he said to the group. "Beautiful day, isn't it?"

Silence greeted him.

"By the way, sir," he said as he continued smiling, "you're sitting in my seat."

Burt glared at him, sizing him up, and incorrectly assumed Justin's good nature meant he faced a greenhorn.

Justin stepped up into the coach and stumbled clumsily, dropping several coins at Burt's feet.

Burt acted on instinct, leaning over and grabbing at the coins with both hands. Before anyone knew what happened, Justin grabbed Burt's head and slammed his face into his knee, making a sickening crunch. Justin threw him out the door and face down in the street before Pete could react.

Justin had no smile on his face when he held out his hand in warning to Pete.

"I have no quarrel with you, but your friend is going to take the next stage. And if I were you, I'd advise him to learn some manners before he steps onto a stage with ladies present. You can stay with him or come on with us. It's your choice."

Pete hesitated for a moment before he stood. "I'm truly sorry, ladies, for the trouble Burt caused. Dadgumit, I don't know why I put up with him." He sighed and shook his head before he spoke again. "He's the only friend I've got, so I guess we'll both take the next stage."

He started out the door when Justin handed him a pistol. "It belongs to your friend. You might ought to hold onto it until we're out of sight."

Allie never even noticed he had stripped Burt of his weapon. Justin started to step out to tell the stage drivers what had happened, but one of them stopped him and said they already knew. They looked at Burt moaning on the ground and grinned at Justin.

"Thanks for saving us the trouble," one of them said as he climbed up the side of the stagecoach and grabbed the reins.

Justin found the last coin and settled in his seat, not too close, but not too far from Allie. She didn't know if she shook more from anger or fear.

15

The elderly gentleman reached across and offered his hand to Justin. "My name's Walter Benjamin, and this here's my wife Gladys. You did a fine job handling that situation back there."

Justin nodded and shook his hand. "Thank you, sir. I'm Justin Taylor."

"Pleased to meet you, Justin. I thought I was going to have to jump up and whip that scoundrel myself," the older man said.

"Thank heavens you came along when you did because my Walter would've done just that. I've never seen him so angry," Gladys declared. "Are you all right, Allie?"

Justin looked at her for the first time since he had climbed into the stagecoach. Her face looked a little pale, and she was visibly shaken, but she nodded her head, yes, and smiled, not trusting herself to do or say anything more for a moment.

Justin was surprised at the overwhelming sense of protection he felt toward Allie. He touched her hand and reassured her.

"Everything's fine. As long as you're with me, I would never let anyone—"

She nodded in understanding and placed her fingers on his mouth, refusing to let him finish the sentence lest his expression of concern unravel what little thread of control kept the tears from falling. She wanted to be stronger than that. She had to be before she returned to Dalton. She would return home with her head held high, dignity intact.

What a way to start the trip home, she thought to herself. She took a deep breath and looked at her fellow passengers. She smiled again and chanced speaking.

"I'm fine, thank you. I couldn't be in better company," she looked at Walter and Gladys, and then at Justin, "or better hands."

But he was reeling from the sensation of her fingers on his lips. He prided himself on his instinct and ability to read a situation, but that touch completely blind-sided him.

And for some reason, he could smell Aunt Sister's biscuits.

Chapter 2

The first day on the road proved to be quite pleasant after the jolting start at the station office that morning. Allie enjoyed visiting with Mr. and Mrs. Benjamin, who were on their way to Waco to visit their youngest daughter. She had recently given birth to her fourth child—grandchild number sixteen, they had proudly announced.

The stagecoach stopped and changed horses at a ranch around noon, and the rancher's wife treated the travelers to a tasty beef stew and cornbread. Not long afterwards the stagecoach was off and running again, and inside, four heads nodded in their seats. It seemed to be a comfortable routine for Mr. and Mrs. Benjamin to lean into each other and nap, but Allie was embarrassed that she could not hold her eyes open. On one particular downhill slope, she would have slid completely off the seat if Justin hadn't caught her in time.

"I'm sorry," she said. "I just didn't get much sleep last night, and after that wonderful meal back there, my will power isn't holding up too well."

"That's all right," Justin said. "I'm having the same problem myself."

He scooted back into his corner and leaned against the wall. Allie did the same on her side, and felt less guilty about relaxing and resting a bit.

Later when she opened her eyes, she noticed Mrs. Gladys was sideways. She smiled, thinking it was charming to see a couple at their age snuggle that way. Then with a shock, she noticed Mr. Benjamin and the rest of the coach was sideways, too. She sat up with a start when she realized she had curled up on the seat with her head on Justin's thigh.

"Oh, my goodness!" she said as she turned every shade of red possible. "I would never have been so bold to use you as a pillow if I were conscious. Why didn't you wake me up and push me back over to my side?"

"I knew you were tired," Justin said, and then grinned, "and besides, it was easier to keep you from falling off the seat every time we hit a bump."

Allie felt obligated to explain to the Benjamins that she did not make it a habit of curling up and sleeping on any man she happened to be sitting near.

"Don't give it a second thought, dear," Gladys said, smiling.

And Justin thought he had demonstrated a tremendous amount of self-control.

Early in the evening the stagecoach pulled into the station where the passengers would spend their first night. The proprietors had converted a small abandoned army fort into a thriving number of businesses that brought new life to the tiny community that had originally grown up around the fort. The barracks had been turned into small guest rooms for stage passengers or any other travelers who could afford the modest price for a room. Passengers from another stagecoach heading north had already checked in for the night. It appeared to be even busier than a year ago when Allie and Uncle John came through.

Justin and Mr. Benjamin unloaded the overnight bags for the group and went to find the proprietor. Allie and Mrs. Benjamin took in the view from where they waited. The station property led down to a river shaded by massive trees. Allie recognized the familiar sounds of a blacksmith shop nearby. She hadn't even noticed it the time before, but after being around Uncle Junior's business the past year, she saw this one with a new appreciation. It looked like they not only repaired wagons there, but built new ones as well. She could see a number of horses in the livery stables, and in the fields beyond were brood mares and some of their young.

The men returned and led the women to their respective rooms. Allie's room was situated protectively between Justin's and the Benjamins' rooms. Justin placed her bag right inside the door.

"They said supper's in forty-five minutes, so we'll meet out here and go together," he told her.

"Thank you, Justin."

Allie stepped inside the room. It was clean, and although the furnishings were sparse, they were adequate: a double bed, a mirror above a small dressing table and chair, a row of pegs on the wall for hanging her hat and clothes, and a commode with a wash basin and pitcher on top. She walked over to it and opened the lower doors to make sure, *yes,* a chamber pot was there. She was relieved to know she would not have to use any outdoor facilities where she might have to contend with creeping, biting, stinging, flying, or spraying critters.

Allie sat down and tested the bed, and then jumped up to check the bedclothes for cleanliness and any small bedmates. All clear. She picked up the feather pillow and sniffed. The pillowcase smelled like it came right off the clothesline. She took off her jacket, shook it out, and hung it on the back of the chair.

She sat down and leaned back on the bed to shut her eyes for just a few minutes. After a bit she heard a door slam and thought more time had passed than she realized, so she got up and washed her hands and face. Looking in the mirror, she straightened the flyaway hairs as best as she could and dug around in her bag for her smell-good. She took out her clothes for tomorrow, shook them out and hung them on the pegs, and decided to don a black quilted vest instead of her gray jacket for supper tonight.

Allie wasn't sure if forty-five minutes had passed, but she stepped outside anyway. No one else was there yet, so she walked down to the livery where the pens of horses were. She could still see the rooms from where she was and checked every few minutes to see if anyone had come outside. She stepped up on the lowest fence board and propped her head on her arms on the top board. She loved watching animals, especially horses, although she wasn't much of a horsewoman since her family only used a buggy or wagon occasionally when they had to go further than across town. Otherwise, they walked.

She had always lived in town, although some of her closest friends lived on ranches during her growing up years. When the few opportunities to go horseback riding came up, she chose the gentlest old nag since she had little experience handling a horse. She had nothing to prove to anybody about speed or dexterity atop a horse. She felt like she accomplished something extraordinary if she didn't fall off or get lost in the brush when everyone else rushed on ahead.

She closed her eyes and listened to the familiar sounds of the livery, and it immediately took her back to Uncle Junior's. She smiled, remembering...

"You ride much?"

19

Allie 'bout jumped off the fence when the voice broke into her thoughts.

"Whoa, girl!" Justin said, steadying her as he climbed up beside her.

"I didn't hear you walk up," Allie said, clutching the fence.

"I'm sorry. I didn't mean to startle you," he said, smiling.

"That's all right—I was thinking about Uncle Junior's livery." She looked back at the horses. "They sure are beautiful animals, aren't they?"

She sighed and continued. "But I'm not much good with them. I bet you are since you take care of Uncle John's cattle."

"I can't remember a time in my life when I wasn't riding a horse," Justin said thoughtfully. "I can teach you if you'd like when we get back to Dalton. Uncle John wouldn't mind at all, I'm sure."

Allie smiled at his reference to *Uncle* John. "I'd like that, but only if you'll go easy on me. I've had friends try to teach me things the hard, fast way, and it just made me want to avoid it altogether."

"Some friends they were," Justin said. "I'd take it slow with you, Allie. I promise."

"Uncle John's taught me some things about horses—like their colors," Allie said. "I didn't realize they weren't the names of the normal colors like brown and red and tan that I learned growing up."

She pointed to a tan-colored horse. "That one there is a buckskin dun, and that other one with the black mane, tail, and line down its back is a line-back dun, and that splotchy one over there is a dappled gray, and that reddish brown one is a..."

"Bay or a chestnut," Justin said.

"You already know this stuff, huh," Allie said, feeling a little embarrassed.

"Not all of it—there's still a lot I need to learn about cattle, too, but Uncle John's a good teacher."

There he went again with the *Uncle John* bit, Allie noticed. "You know he's not my real uncle, don't you?" Allie asked.

Justin nodded yes.

"But I wish he were. I think I'm closer to him than my own father."

"You know him much better than I do, Allie, although I know that he's a good man," Justin said as he glanced back at the rooms. "I see the Benjamins have just stepped outside. Guess we'd better catch up to them."

They found the dining room filling quickly. At least a dozen other people were eating supper with them. The simplicity and organization of the operation impressed Allie. Everyone lined up and served themselves from a long table where an assortment of food was placed. It reminded her of church dinners on the ground, but this was inside. The owners could get by with less people having to work and serve in the dining hall that way. They let everyone eat their fill, and good-naturedly told the group if they didn't eat it all up, it would be served for breakfast the next morning.

The atmosphere was congenial, the food was good, and Allie was glad they stopped here again on the way. After supper, one of the guests pulled out a fiddle and began to play. Mrs. Benjamin leaned over to Allie.

"I hope this morning's incident doesn't ruin your thinking about people in general, Allie. This here's the typical behavior of most of the people Walter and I have encountered when we've traveled."

"Yes, ma'am," Allie said. "I realize that."

But what Allie also knew was that she had seen bad behavior in too many of the 'good' folks, too, especially in the area of determining the value of people by their skin color. That seemed to bring out the worst in people. But now wasn't the time or place to mention it, so she just smiled at Mrs. Benjamin as they listened to the music.

After a while, Allie asked her traveling companions if they would like to walk down to the river before dark. Gladys declined, saying they went to sleep with the chickens, and giving Allie a sly wink, she and Walter bid their goodnights.

Justin offered to walk with her, and she was glad he did. Otherwise, she would not have gone by herself. And to be honest, it was Justin she really wanted to accompany her. Gladys recognized her intentions and graciously refused the invitation. Walter and Justin hadn't a clue.

Allie knew that conventional rules stated that a proper young lady should be chaperoned at all times and should never be alone with a man. But from the time she was little, it was in her nature to question any rules or traditions or social etiquette. And if the reason for any of them came up short of justifying its existence, she either rewrote it with a dose of common sense, or disregarded it entirely. Some might call that rebellion, but Uncle John always told her he liked how she thought things through for herself and didn't blindly follow the social expectations of young ladies of her day.

When it would never enter her friends' heads to even look at a young man of a different skin color, Allie looked beyond the social stigma and saw the person. And she happened to see Miguel very clearly one day in Cranfill's General Store when she asked if he could reach a jar of peaches from the top shelf. She remembered the pleasant surprise on his face when he saw that her eyes showed no fear or disdain for him. Eventually she threw all the rules of genteel courtship out the window when curiosity bloomed into friendship, and then to romance. But respect always remained between them, no matter what the town gossips conjured up about them.

And even now Allie knew she was treading on thin ice when it came to her feelings. She had warned herself not to get interested in Justin, but she just couldn't help it. She hoped it wasn't a desperate attempt of her pride and emotions to latch onto someone before she made her appearance in Dalton. His expression at the station that morning also concerned her, and she wanted to find out just how much he knew about her past.

Allie and Justin walked down to the river's edge and watched the last moments of the sunset.

"Look at the clouds," Allie said. "My mother used to tell me they were fingers of violet and deep blue reaching out to touch the last remaining light of day."

"Waxing poetic, are we?" Justin said as he looked at the sky. "But you're right."

"You try it," Allie said.

"I don't talk poetry," Justin said.

"Then don't think of it as poetry," Allie said. "Think of it as just looking at things a little differently."

She looked around and said, "Describe the trees."

Justin said without hesitation, "The trees have big trunks and lots of leaves."

Allie snickered. "That is really bad."

"Bad?" he said. "But it's the truth."

"Right, but sometimes we need to look at things in a different way— this time really look at them, but don't think of them as trees."

Justin took a few moments to look at the trees again in the fading light.

"The shadows and moss make the trees look ghostly, but the fiddle music drifting down keeps them friendly."

Allie clapped her hands. "That's good! And you said you weren't poetic."

"I'm not, and don't you dare tell anybody I am," Justin said, propping his boot on a root growing above ground.

"Now these are real trees," Allie said as she leaned against one of the massive trunks.

"Good-sized trees grow along the Nueces River, too," Justin pointed out, already defensive of his new home. He leaned down and picked up a flat stone.

"I know, and I love Dalton. It's home. But these rolling hills and tall trees are beautiful to see."

"Uncle John thinks the brush country is the prettiest place in Texas," Justin added, skipping the rock across the water.

"Justin, you don't have to call John Stockton '*Uncle John*' just because I do. It sounds rather silly when you say it," Allie chided him, amused at his copying her.

Justin turned and looked at her with disbelief.

"But he really *is* my uncle, Miss Know-it-all," Justin gave it right back to her.

It was Allie's turn to look at him in surprise.

"But how can that be? He doesn't have a nephew named Justin. There's one named Matt and the only other nephew that I know of is named Johnny," Allie said, looking at him suspiciously. "Just who do you think you are?"

"Justin John Taylor," he replied. "Uncle John's the only one who calls me 'Johnny' since he was so proud that I was named after him."

"Oh, my goodness," Allie said as her eyes widened. "Then you're the little boy our church prayed for when I was a little girl! But you're all grown up!"

"Time tends to do that," Justin said. "Look at yourself. You're not a little girl anymore."

"I guess Johnny will always be a little boy in my mind," Allie said. "Was it a horrible time for you in captivity with the Apaches?"

"Yes, or maybe no—it was hard, but it was all I really knew, and… I'd rather not talk about it, if you don't mind."

"I'm sorry," Allie said, unsure of what to say. Thinking he must have been tortured or something worse, she found herself observing him closer for scars or signs of mistreatment.

"Don't look at me that way," Justin said. "I've had enough of that since I came back." He turned and started walking back to the inn.

"Justin, I'm sorry," Allie said, catching up to him. "I didn't mean to offend you. I know what it's like to be an outcast, but for me, it was in my own hometown."

Justin stopped and looked at her. The same look she saw that morning swept across his face again, but she understood it this time. It wasn't pity or disgust. He knew exactly what she was feeling—he had experienced it as well.

"I'd returned to my hometown, too," Justin said. "Everyone was so glad to get us back at first, but then they'd have little to do with us—my brother especially, like we might make them dirty if we touched them. School was a nightmare that first year, and I had a lot of catching up to do, which made it doubly hard with the way everyone acted toward us. My parents ended up sending my brother and me to a boarding school for several years. It wasn't much better, but at least it was only five years for me. My brother had to endure it for eight years."

"Why would your parents send your older brother with you?" Allie asked.

"I meant my half-brother, Jimmy, the only brother I knew for five years of my life," Justin answered. "Momma wouldn't come home without him; neither would I. But looking back now, it might've been better to have left him."

"Why would you say such a thing? Your own brother..."

"*Half* brother..."

Justin watched her face as it dawned on Allie that his half brother was half Indian—that his mother had lived as a wife to her captor.

"It wasn't her choice," he answered her unspoken question, "but I didn't understand that for a long time. I don't remember much of my life before with my real father."

Allie could see the pain in his eyes, and she knew there was much more than he was telling her.

Justin was quiet, lost in his own thoughts as they walked slowly back to their rooms.

"I shouldn't feel a bit sorry for myself in my situation," Allie said, feeling obligated to fill in the gap left by the silence. "Have you heard the stories about me?"

"Some, but Uncle John told me more about you than anyone."

"Good things, I hope," Allie said, smiling, and then more seriously, "and most importantly, the truth?"

24

"You're more deserving to be his kin than me," Justin said. "You've done things for him like a daughter would do, and he's said nothing but kind words about you. He warned me after I arrived that I might hear some unflattering stories and to pay no mind. Most folks quickly learned to not talk about you around John Stockton if they didn't want to get whipped. I think folks assumed I would react the same way, so I didn't hear much."

"But you did find out why the town disowned me, didn't you?" Allie asked apprehensively. "Does it bother you knowing that about me?"

"Have you already forgotten who you're talking to here?" Justin said. "If nothing else, I'm a little envious of this Miguel fellow now that I've met you."

Allie blushed as she smiled, and noted that Justin even knew Miguel's name. "You've been so nice to me, I thought for sure you knew nothing about my past. I wish it could've been different."

"Are you ashamed of what you've done?"

"No, of course not! I'll never regret my friendship with Miguel. I just feel bad that my family suffered for my sake."

"Do you still have feelings for him?"

"Yes, but I think it's more respect for him than anything else. I hope he's very happy with his future bride." Allie paused. "I can't say I'm looking forward to the first time I run into them, though. That might be a little awkward, and I'm sure it'll give the town more reason to gossip about me," Allie said, suddenly weary of the subject.

Justin suggested they turn in for the night.

"We wouldn't want the Benjamins to enjoy another day of seeing you waller all over the stagecoach tomorrow from lack of sleep, now would we?" He began walking at a fast pace as it dawned on her what he said.

Allie growled and ran up to punch him in the arm before he got to his room.

He was laughing, and she couldn't keep a stern face if she wanted to.

"Justin John Taylor, you just wait until I catch you at a weak moment."

"That moment will never come," he said with a confident smile. "Goodnight, Alexandra Blake."

He leaned over and kissed her on the cheek and walked to his room.

Allie stood there stunned at what had just transpired. And she wasn't thinking about Billy Clarkson or even Miguel this time.

It also occurred to Justin as he closed his door that Allie had just caught him at a weak moment, and she didn't even know it. He couldn't resist kissing her goodnight.

"Dadgummit. How'd that happen? You'd better straighten up, Justin, and slow down or she's going to turn tail and run from you," he said to himself.

Dawn was breaking, and Allie lay in bed hoping for a few more moments of sleep before hearing Uncle Junior's heavy boot steps tromping down the stairs. Then she remembered where she was, and with a twinge of sadness realized she would not be hearing those familiar sounds any more. She could hear movement in the rooms bordering hers, so she thought she had better get up and get going before someone knocked on her door.

Allie took a washcloth bath the night before, so getting ready took little time. She dressed in a plaid skirt with a pale blue blouse and the same black vest she wore for supper last night. She shook out and folded her dusty clothes from the day before and packed them in her bag. She brushed her thick hair and quickly braided it into a single strand to the right side of her face, leaving it down this time.

Allie smiled at the thought of the Dalton Ladies Home Club chattering about the audacity of her wearing any style other than her hair up in a bun at her age. She took another look around the room, donned her black hat, picked up her purse and bag and stepped outside, turning back to close the door.

"I'll take that for you."

Allie jumped again at the voice behind her.

"How do you always manage to sneak up behind me without my ever hearing you?" Allie asked.

"Good morning to you, too," Justin tipped his hat and reached for her bag. "Old Indian trick," he said under his breath.

She looked at him, not sure how to take that comment, but she saw that he had a smirk on his face.

"Oh, my," she sighed. "This is going to be a long day. You'd better watch your back, Taylor." *And your heart, too,* she thought to herself.

The Benjamins joined them at the breakfast table. Allie was mindful of Justin's wisecrack the night before, and only ate a biscuit with her cup of coffee, which most would argue against calling it that.

"How 'bout a little coffee with that milk and sugar, honey," Mr. Benjamin teased.

Allie grinned. "I love the smell of coffee, but I can't drink it for some reason. Maybe one of these years I'll learn how."

Gladys patted Allie on the arm. "Pay no mind to Walter, dear; a spoon could stand straight up in his coffee."

"When do you think we'll get to see Uncle John?" Allie asked Justin.

"We'll probably get to Waco around four o'clock, and he's supposed to meet us there with a buggy. It's about an hour and a half to my parents' home. We'll come back early Monday morning to catch the next stage. My parents are repeating their wedding vows tomorrow afternoon, with a meal and a social afterwards. Hope you don't mind."

"No, not at all. It sounds wonderful," Allie said. "But I didn't pack a dressy dress for a party."

"What about that white one you wore back at your uncle's?" Justin asked, remembering every detail.

"It *is* at the top of my trunk. Don't let me forget to slip it out when we get to Waco. I won't need to take my trunk to your parents' home, will I? Do you think they'll let me leave it at the station office until Monday?"

"I don't think the horses could make it home having to haul us *and* that trunk, too," Justin teased. "We'd have to stop and put them out of their misery."

That earned him another punch.

The Benjamins and Allie settled into their familiar seats in the coach while Justin was becoming more efficient at handling the luggage than he ever wanted to be. A lady with two rambunctious young boys boarded the stage, and Allie thoughtfully moved to the other side to sit next to Mrs. Benjamin. When Justin stepped in, there was no other place to sit other than squeezing in beside the two little tornadoes. Allie faced him with a wicked smile as the Benjamins made the introductions for the group.

After an hour or so of misery for Justin, she began to feel sorry for him, well, for all of them, to be truthful. The young boys spent much of their time wrestling on the floor and kicking everybody's legs. Their mother kept asking her children if they wanted a spanking in front of everyone. They ignored her. When the children started fighting over a couple of small tin soldiers, the mother threatened to throw the toys out the window. The children acted as if they didn't hear a word she said.

After the tenth empty threat, which again caused no change in the boys' behavior, Justin grabbed one of the soldiers and threw it out the

27

window. That shocked the children into silence, and then they commenced to bawl at the top of their lungs. Their mother was just as shocked.

"That was one of their favorite toys!" she shouted over the wailing. "How dare you do that!"

"Well, why did you keep threatening to throw it out the window if you never intended to do it?" Justin asked. "No wonder they don't mind you when you don't mean a word you say."

"Well, I never!" she said, trying to console her screaming children.

Justin leaned down in their faces and said, "If you two don't sit down, shut up, and behave yourselves for the rest of the trip, I'm going to throw another toy out the window." The look he gave the mother told her not to open her mouth. He looked back at the children. "And you know *I* mean what I say."

The children sat down on the floor and did exactly what Justin said. The mother's mouth gaped open at the children's immediate obedience, but she remained silent. The rest of the group made a collective sigh of relief.

After a while, one of the little boys climbed onto the seat beside Justin and asked him if he was a cowboy.

Justin answered him, "Yes, I am. Are you?"

"Nope, but I'm gonna be a cowboy when I grow up."

"Me, too," the younger one chimed in.

"Do you know what a cowboy does?" Justin asked.

They shook their heads, no.

Justin proceeded to tell them all about cowboying. Allie was amazed at the change in the demeanor of the children. By the time the stagecoach pulled in to change horses at the next station, those little boys thought Justin had hung the moon.

After everyone unloaded to stretch and eat a bite, the mother told the group goodbye—that this was their stop. Justin suddenly found both of his legs being hugged fiercely by the two little boys. He ruffled their hair, not quite sure how to react to their displays of affection.

Their mother extended her hand to him and simply said, "Thank you."

"How did you do that?" Allie asked as she watched them walk away.

Justin shrugged his shoulders, "I'm not sure."

"I thought I'd gotten you good, Justin, by making you sit over there with those hellions. But you seemed to handle yourself quite well. I can't believe you had the nerve to chunk a toy out the window."

"It was that or a kid," he replied, "and it was a tough choice."

Allie giggled.

The afternoon ride to Waco was a pleasant respite after the storm.

Allie knew they had to be getting close to Waco. She prided herself in the fact that she dozed off not once on the trip that day, although there were a few times after the noon meal that her eyes kept crossing in the struggle to keep them open. She kept pinching herself in the tender area on the inside of her upper arm to stay awake.

On the way Justin told her a little about the rest of his family she would soon meet. His older brother Matt was married to Catherine, and they had three sons. Justin's sister Jenny was the second born, and she was married to Marcus. They had two sons and a daughter. Justin said his other brother Jimmy may or may not be there, but gave no explanation why. He also told her about Faith, an orphaned Indian girl who also came back with them after their rescue. His mother, Julia, had taken care of her since she was about three years old. Justin said that Faith and Jimmy were around the same age because they were born during the same year.

Justin didn't know the exact day Jimmy was born since they had lost track of time in captivity, but his mother said he was born in the spring. After their return home, she chose two days during the year for Jimmy and Faith to celebrate their own birthdays. It never occurred to Allie for someone not to know their birthday. She realized she took a lot for granted growing up in a stable and loving family.

Allie learned that Justin's parents would celebrate thirty years of marriage, although six of those years were apart. She could not imagine how difficult it must have been for Mr. Taylor to lose his wife for all that time, not knowing if she were alive or dead. And it had to have been even harder for him to try to pick up where they left off with the knowledge that she had lived, even though unwillingly, as another man's wife and even bore his child. She wondered what happened to Jimmy's father.

Allie also wondered how Justin felt about his Apache father—surely he had to have had some feelings for him as young as he was when he was taken, and then to have lived with him for six years. She wondered what Justin was like when he came home, and how hard it must have been for him to readjust to life in the white man's world. She had heard stories of captives who never could adjust to their previous lives, even after a much shorter time in captivity than Justin had been. Some even ran away from their birth families to go back and live with the Indians. She was glad

Justin had been rescued before coming of age and going on raids to steal from and murder the enemy—the Texans.

Allie thought about Justin having to get to know his real family all over again. She wondered what it was that enabled him to adjust. By all accounts, he should be torn between two worlds. But all these thoughts remained in Allie's head. Justin told her very little about his own experiences, and she didn't want to intrude on what may have been painful memories.

The stagecoach slowed down for the toll as it approached the massive suspension bridge crossing the Brazos River into Waco. Justin had been fascinated with this architectural marvel ever since he first saw it five years before on one of his many trips to Waco. He had heard claim that it was the first single-span suspension bridge west of the Mississippi. He craned his neck as far as he could out of the window. The sound of the wheels clattered a whole different song passing over the bridge.

"Allie, can you see the river from your side?" Justin asked.

No answer.

Justin turned around to see Allie sitting in the middle of the seat right next to him with her eyes shut and fists clenched in her lap.

"Allie?"

"Just tell me when we're on the other side," she said in a strained voice.

"What's the matter? Are you sick or something?"

"No, are we across yet?"

"Almost."

"Allie, you're as white as a ghost, dear," Mrs. Benjamin said. "Are you afraid of this bridge or the river?"

"Both."

"But we were standing near a river last night, and it didn't bother you."

"That was different—are we across yet?"

"Yes."

She opened her eyes and took in a big breath. "A bridge can collapse, and that river is huge and you can't see how deep it is or how fast it's running."

But before Justin could say anything else, it was Allie's turn to stick her head out of the coach window to look down the street for Uncle John.

The stagecoach continued on Bridge Street to its destination at the stage stop hotel.

Allie immediately spotted John Stockton on the boardwalk in front of the hotel. He carried himself with such authority and stood a head taller than anyone else around. His stern expression went completely soft when he saw Allie waving at him in an unladylike fashion from the window of the stagecoach coming down the street. She jumped out almost before the coach stopped rolling and ran and threw herself in John's arms. He swung her around several times before finally putting her down.

The Benjamins and Justin laughed at Allie's boisterous reunion with John Stockton. At the same time, though, Justin felt a pang of envy at the attention Allie gave his uncle, or was it the other way around? Maybe it was both.

"How's my little girl? Let me look at you." John said, holding her at arm's length. "I don't think I'm going to be able to call you 'little girl' any more."

"I think Aunt Sister's cooking has pushed me over into the 'big girl' category, Uncle John," Allie said. "But you can always call me your 'little girl.' Justin said you weren't feeling well earlier. Are you all right?"

"I'm much better, thank you," John said. "Hello, Johnny. Looks like you've taken excellent care of our Allie here. Hope she didn't give you too much trouble."

"It was pretty tough at times, but we managed," Justin said, grasping his uncle's hand in a firm handshake and ignoring Allie's friendly glare. "I'd like you to meet our traveling companions, Walter and Gladys Benjamin. This is my uncle, John Stockton."

"We've heard quite a bit about you," Walter said as they exchanged handshakes and pleasantries.

Justin went to unload the baggage as Allie hugged the Benjamins goodbye, and Uncle John walked her to the buggy.

"Well, what do you think of my nephew?"

"I should've recognized the similarities between the two of you, but it didn't dawn on me who he was at first. I really embarrassed myself last night when I got onto him for calling you *Uncle John*," Allie said. "I thought he was calling you that because I did. And then I kept putting my foot in my mouth when I realized he was the little boy our church prayed for all those years ago. I didn't handle that conversation too well."

"It doesn't look like he's bothered too much about it," John said. "He's a good man, Allie. He had a rough go of it early in his life, but he

31

hasn't let it destroy him. In fact, it's made him stronger. Can't say the same for his half-brother."

"I don't know anything about Jimmy," Allie said. "Why didn't you ever mention him to us?"

"When I came to visit Julia and Johnny soon after their return, I met two young Indian children I thought were orphans that she had brought back with her to raise; that is, until I saw his eyes. Then I knew immediately that Jimmy was Julia's child. It almost destroyed the family when it became publicly known. Jimmy has been a constant reminder to my brother-in-law of the hell his family has been through, and Jimmy's suffered for it. Not physically, mind you, but emotionally. It was just easier to send the boys off to boarding school.

"And the brother Jimmy grew up idolizing, he now resents because he thinks he can never be what Johnny is in the white man's world. Nor does he have a secure place in Julia's family, either. He's stuck in-between, not really belonging to either culture. And it didn't help that Jimmy saw his own father killed by the group of men that rescued them, which included Matthew Taylor. I'm sure Jimmy didn't understand what happened until he was older, but he's never forgotten it. Johnny was off hunting and didn't witness it, thank the Lord."

"Oh, my heavens. I knew there was so much more to it than what Justin told me, but I didn't dare ask," Allie said. "That is so sad."

"Don't mention any of this to him," John warned her, "and don't pity him. He's doing just fine now. Just accept him for who he is right now."

"I seem to recall asking him to do the same for me in my situation," Allie said thoughtfully. "And what I feel about him has nothing to do with pity."

John raised his eyebrows and opened his mouth to say something, but Allie interrupted.

"Oh! I almost forgot! I need to get a couple of things out of my trunk for the anniversary party tomorrow. I'll be right back."

Allie ran into the hotel lobby and found Justin in the storage room grunting and groaning over her trunk.

"It's not *that* heavy!" Allie said. "You almost let me forget."

Justin turned around with the white lace dress folded neatly in his hands.

"No, I didn't."

Allie smiled and took the dress. "Thanks—I don't know where my head is right now. I think I'm going to need a couple more things, too," she said as she opened the trunk and grabbed another outfit. "Well, I might need one more," and grabbed another.

Justin looked at his own clothes, wondering why she might need more clothes this weekend—he had packed only one extra shirt for the whole trip, and that was at Uncle John's insistence.

"Let's go. Uncle John doesn't like to be kept waiting," Allie said.

The ninety or so minutes to the Taylor home went by as fast as Allie and Uncle John caught up on the past year. She had received one letter from him since she had been gone, and was lucky to get that one, he told her. It was brief and to the point and primarily about the ranch and his cattle. She did recall his letter mentioning that he had visited his sister on the way back from delivering Allie to her aunt and uncle's home last year. He wrote briefly that he had some plans for Johnny, but Allie never made the connection with Justin until she so adeptly embarrassed herself in front of Justin last night.

Justin was content to handle the reins and listen. He also had his own thoughts to contend with since it had been some time since he had been home, too. Even though his mother had continued to talk to Justin about his real father during their years of captivity, it had taken several years for him to learn to accept and feel comfortable around Matthew Taylor. But that had never happened for Jimmy. In recent years Jimmy began to disappear for long lengths of time, never telling anyone when he decided to leave or where he was going. A few incidents with alcohol showed he could be very volatile and unpredictable, and the family began to look forward to those times he disappeared, although no one expressed that aloud.

Justin had loved him so when they were growing up. He felt like he had raised Jimmy as much as his mother had, teaching him to ride and hunt and fish. Jimmy was his shadow most of the time after he was old enough to go with him. He even taught Jimmy how to defend himself, having learned it the hard way through the years. But something began to change drastically between them during the first few years after they were rescued and brought home.

Justin always tried to include him at school or around town, and later at the boarding school, but Jimmy looked too much like his father to be accepted by anyone. Justin could better protect Jimmy at the local school where everyone was in the same room. But at the boarding school, the age difference kept them in separate classes and sleeping quarters, and Justin wasn't always around to take up for his brother. But in the times he could, other students mocked Jimmy about Justin's defense of him. He began to withdraw into himself more and push Justin away, and eventually became resentful of any offer of help by his brother.

Uncle John's words broke into his thoughts.

"...and Matthew has been grooming Matt to take over the farming and ranching operations eventually, so I thought it might be a good time to nab my namesake to take over my cattle operations. It'll all be his some day, so he might as well learn to take care of it now," Uncle John was telling Allie.

"Could you repeat that last part again?" Justin asked.

"I wondered if you had heard a word I said," John said, smiling.

"Are you serious?" Justin said.

"I had my will changed last week. I'd rest easier knowing my life's efforts would be in good hands. These past several months have convinced me of that," John continued. "I'm mighty proud of you, son."

"I don't know what to say, but I'll do my best for you, sir," Justin said, moved by his uncle's gesture.

An unfamiliar, but welcome feeling coursed through Justin's thoughts. It felt like a path and definite direction was opening up before him, and it felt good. For some years Justin wasn't sure where he belonged, especially since the bulk of his father's property would go to his older brother Matt. His father didn't believe in dividing up the land among the children to dwindle away through each generation to smaller and smaller properties that eventually could not support a single family. It would not take many generations to lose the Taylor legacy, so he wanted to establish some legal guidelines that would insure that the property remained intact long after he was gone.

Matthew Taylor had moved his young family to Texas from Illinois after inheriting a substantial amount of money from his grandfather and eventually, his own father. He patterned his estate plan after his own family, where, like Justin, he was not the firstborn son, either. No land tied him to Illinois—he could go to Texas and build his own legacy for his family.

For Jenny and Justin, he had provided trust funds for them to receive at age twenty-five. Marcus and Jenny had used hers to start a mercantile store in the small community, which Matthew Taylor established some twenty years before. For many years, area residents grouped together to send a wagon to Waco every month for supplies that they were not able to grow or provide for themselves. Then the demand increased the supply wagon's trip to twice a month, and eventually weekly. It had been a dream of Marcus' for some time to establish a store locally since he had driven the supply wagon for several years and knew what the people needed throughout the different times of the year. And because of that knowledge, their new store prospered.

Justin had two more years before he came into his trust, but he had given it little thought since his father told him about it the year before when his sister turned twenty-five. He had worked hard alongside his father and brother the three years following his return from boarding school. He enjoyed getting to know them again, and the family had experienced a peace and unity for the first time since Julia and Justin had come home.

But the atmosphere changed immediately when Jimmy came back. He was fourteen by then. For a while Matthew Taylor's donations to the school above and beyond tuition, room and board glossed over problems they had with Jimmy. He matured faster than his peers and was close to being full grown. The last straw for the administrators was when Jimmy took the quirt away from his math teacher in the middle of a whipping and refused to return it. Jimmy didn't hit him with it, but the teacher swore that the look on his face said that the next time he would. The school said they could not teach a child who would not be disciplined, and if Jimmy struck a member of the staff, they would be forced to file charges. Mr. Taylor instructed the school to send him home, and an uneasy ambiance settled over the house.

Justin knew that his father had assured his mother that Jimmy and Faith would also receive a modest fund at the age of twenty-five, but it was not legally binding. Matthew wanted Jimmy to show some evidence of responsibility and maturity before receiving his, and he had a long ways to go in Matthew's eyes.

Allie knew nothing about Matthew Taylor's trust funds for his children. Based on the time spent with Justin so far, she assumed he came from humble stock. She thought Uncle John was mighty generous to name Justin as his heir. Maybe that would make up for some of the heartache he had experienced in his life.

It was almost six o'clock in the evening when Justin drove the buggy through the main street of the small town. The community was picturesque, surrounded by cultivated fields soon to be harvested. A white church steeple rose above the rooftops off the road a ways, and the newly painted, two-story Kimball Mercantile Store drew Allie's eyes to the big picture windows in front, creatively arranged with all sorts of merchandise.

"Marcus' and Jenny's," Justin nodded toward it when he saw Allie staring at it. A couple of dozen houses, several other businesses, a livery and blacksmith shop, and a small, but stately brick building in the center of town made up the rest of Matthew Taylor's town from what Allie could see.

"It's beautiful," Allie said. "What did your father name it?"

"At first he named it Taylor, for some odd reason," Justin said facetiously. "Then after he brought us back home, he changed the name to *Grace*, Texas."

"What is that brick building over there?" Allie asked as they passed by.

"My father plans to make Grace the county seat some day, so he built that in hopes of eventually becoming a courthouse. Until then, it's the school and community building. The school used to be in the church," Justin said. "My father had a lot of dreams for this town, and it probably would be much more prosperous today if he hadn't spent so much of his time and money looking for us all those years."

"Money well-spent," Uncle John added. "Your father is a very determined man, and he would never have given up searching for you and your mother. I'm grateful he didn't. He loves you both very much."

"I know, and I'm glad now that he found us," Justin said. "And I know you had something to do with that, too, and I can't remember if I ever thanked you."

"You had a tough time those first few years back, Johnny. I'm just glad you came home."

Justin looked at Allie and then turned his head forward again. "Well, there it is, Allie—my humble home."

She gasped when they cleared the trees.

Chapter 3

*A*llie looked back at the way they had come through town, and it now seemed obvious that the street was merely a long roadway leading up to the Taylor's beautiful three-story red brick home. A huge staircase led up to a porch on the second floor that ran the entire length of the house. Allie could see that the bottom floor was partially below ground level. The roof of the porch created a balcony for the third floor. There were more out buildings in the back, but Allie could not take her eyes off the manor house.

Allie had never seen a house like this except in books and was surprised that Justin had even lived in such a place. He seemed content in whatever surroundings he found himself during the past two days. She realized how simple and plain Aunt Sister's home must have been for him, and she cringed remembering how they tried to be so impressive using the fine china that evening. Her cheeks blushed with embarrassment thinking about Uncle Junior insisting Justin save his money and come stay with them since they had all that extra space with a three-bedroom house.

Justin watched her response. She seemed uncomfortable. He thought most women loved pretty houses. Florine had a fit over it when she came to visit. Did Allie see something offensive about it? He looked back at his home to try to see it with new eyes.

The road split in front of the house and circled around a flower garden. Justin hadn't pulled the buggy to a complete stop before a passel of children and young adults came tearing out of the house and down the expansive stairs.

Justin stepped out of the buggy and little ones surrounded him, clamoring for his attention. The adults stood back, smiling as they watched him greet the children. Allie noticed no sign of awkwardness around this bunch as Justin knelt down and hugged every one of them, calling them by name. She wondered how long it had been since he had been home.

"What's the matter, Allie?" John broke into her thoughts.

"The matter? Nothing's the matter."

"I know you better than that," he said.

She glanced at him and looked back toward the house where Justin hugged his siblings now in front of the stairs. John helped her out of the buggy.

"I didn't know the Taylors were so well off."

"Should that bother you?"

"Well, no," she paused, "but I'm not sure I'll fit in here."

"Alexandra Blake," he scolded her, "the Taylors have never put on airs toward anyone or made them feel beneath them. You won't find anyone more accepting or loving than my sister and her family."

Allie dropped her head—she felt even worse now that she had pre-judged them.

"You're right, I'm sorry."

John squeezed her shoulders. "Come on, let's go meet this rowdy bunch—I think Justin's forgotten all about us."

Allie looked up at John and smiled as they walked to the steps. From the midst of the crowd someone grabbed her hand and pulled her forward. It was Justin.

"Everybody, I want you to meet Allie Blake. Allie, this is everybody."

"Oh, Justin," one of the women said as she pushed him aside. "Hi Allie! I'm Justin's sister Jenny, and this is my husband, Marcus. And two of those little boys wrestling over there and the only little girl in that pile of kids are ours."

She hugged Allie as she said, "I'm so glad we finally get to meet you. We've heard so much about you."

Allie was surprised by that remark, but at the same time was touched by her openness and friendliness. Jenny introduced her to her brother Matt and his wife Catherine and their sons, and finally, to Justin's parents standing by the front door.

Allie faced the couple and clasped Matthew's extended hand.

"Hello, Allie. Welcome to our home," said Matthew. He had a commanding presence and seemed more aloof than the others, although

Allie didn't feel put off by it.

"Thank you so much, Mr. Taylor," Allie replied. She turned to Julia. Justin's mother was taller than she expected, and her hair was completely silver. Life had carved deep lines in her face, but she was still beautiful—especially those eyes. Justin's eyes.

So that's where they came from.

Julia, like Jenny, pulled her close and said, "We're so happy to meet the young lady my brother thinks so much of."

Allie embraced her fully. Julia kept her arm around her shoulder and turned around to introduce her to a lovely young woman who had been standing behind Julia.

"Allie, this is Faith, my youngest daughter."

Allie smiled and shook her hand. "I'm so happy to meet you, Faith."

Faith smiled shyly and nodded her head. Julia led them both inside as she told the others to come on in for dinner.

"I thought you were never going to get here, Uncle Justin," said one of the little boys.

"I'm glad to know I was missed," Justin said.

"No, we're starving, and MeeMaw wouldn't let us eat until you got here!" he said as he and several of the cousins took off giggling into the house.

"What?! Why you goobers…"

Everyone laughed as Justin chased the boys through the house.

Allie turned her head and caught Uncle John's eye, speaking volumes with her own. He winked back and smiled, knowing her thoughts exactly.

The entry was a wide hallway lined with wood paneling and doors. Allie could see that two double doors on the left opened to a large parlor. The doors on the right were closed. Julia led them straight ahead to a wide stairway that led up to the third floor, but split on each side going down to the first floor. Julia said that the left hand stairs led to the kitchen, so they took the stairs on the right that went to the dining room. When they reached the bottom of the stairs, she told Allie that a hallway, a bedroom, and large pantry separated the dining room from the kitchen.

Julia led the family into the dining room. Allie had never seen such a large room for eating in a house. It looked big enough to have a dance if the furniture were pushed up against the walls. A long rectangular table that could easily sit twelve took up the center of the room. A shorter table and smaller chairs were nearby, obviously set for the children. Several smaller round tables filled the back corners of the side of the house that was below ground level. A huge fireplace was centered in the long wall, and several rockers and small tables gathered around it. It looked like the family spent a lot of time in this big room with its cozy clusters. Another pair of double doors opened to the outside in the wall facing the stairwell. Allie could see some kind of porch and more tables, as well as a nearby garden.

A horrific scream and a loud crash rose above the chatter and laughter. Allie jumped and looked toward the kitchen.

"Don't worry, Allie," Jenny said, "Justin probably snuck up on Vestal."

"He's good at that," Allie laughed, relieved. "Who's Vestal?"

"She's been with our family since before we arrived in this territory."

"Vestal's one of the reasons we hang out here at the big house all the time—her butter horn rolls are the best," Marcus added.

Justin came dancing through the door with Vestal laughing and scolding him at the same time.

"She thinks Justin can do no wrong, that boy," Julia laughed, and to the entire group she said, "Everyone take a seat. Jenny and Catherine, come help Vestal and me bring the serving dishes in."

Allie offered to help, but Julia wouldn't hear of it.

"Tonight, you are our special guest. Tomorrow, we'll put you to work."

Allie laughed, "All right, Mrs. Taylor, if you insist."

"I do, and everyone calls me Julia. Now sit over there by Justin, and try to keep him in line for us. Sweetheart," she said to a grandson, "scoot on over to the other table and let Allie sit there. You'll have plenty of time to see Uncle Justin while he's here."

The meal was simple and delicious, consisting of smoked ham, green beans and new potatoes, baked squash, and egg custard for dessert. And Allie couldn't help herself—she had three of Vestal's butter horn rolls swathed in butter, and even added honey to the last one. Allie was convinced that she had met Aunt Sister's match in culinary skills.

The conversation proved even more enjoyable than the food, which was no slight on Vestal's cooking. Allie felt an immediate rapport with the Taylors. The house, although impressive, melted into the background around this family. Allie felt as if she had known them all of her life.

The older children asked to be excused from the big table, and the younger ones at the other table followed suit. The noise level decreased significantly as they ran outside to play.

"Just for a little while, kids!"

"Don't wander too far—it's getting dark!"

"Don't slam the door!"

Allie smiled at the familiar orders spoken by most parents, including her own not too many years before.

Julia turned to Allie and said, "John told us you play the piano, Allie."

"Yes, but I'm a little out of practice since I haven't been around one this past year."

"Could I ask a big favor of you?"

Allie nodded, with an inkling of what was to come.

"Would you consider playing the piano for our ceremony tomorrow?" Julia asked. "Matthew and I would really appreciate it."

"Isn't there someone in town you'd rather have play?" Allie said. "Someone from your church, perhaps?"

That remark was punctuated with several groans at the table.

"Well, Mrs. Mamie Wilkins is our regular pianist, but bless her heart, her eyes and ears aren't what they used to be," Julia explained, "and most times folks can't even recognize what she's playing in order to sing along."

"We've just learned to tolerate her playing and try to sing over it," Marcus added, "but I'm afraid the Lord himself must plug his ears during our song services."

Allie laughed. "I'm not sure I'd sound much better."

"John's told us otherwise, so Julia won't let you off the hook that easy," Matthew said.

"Well," Allie paused, looking between Julia and Matthew Taylor, "it would be an honor to play for you."

"Wonderful!" Julia beamed at Allie, and then at her husband.

"It's going to be a splendid day tomorrow," Julia said as she reached for Matthew's hand. He smiled back as he lifted her hand to his lips and gently kissed it.

Allie noticed for the first time that Julia's left hand was withered.

"Do you have music picked out?" Allie asked, trying to keep her eyes on Julia's face instead of her hand. "And is there some place I can practice? I don't want to embarrass myself and you, too."

"I'm sure that won't happen," Julia assured her, "but yes, I do have the sheet music here, and you're welcome to go over it on our piano in the parlor. In the morning, Catherine or Jenny can take you by the church to practice on that piano, too, if you'd like. I know each piano has a different feel to it, so I think you would be more comfortable practicing on the actual one you'll be playing tomorrow afternoon."

"You play the piano, too," Allie said, knowing that a pianist would recognize that each piano plays differently.

"Many years ago," Julia said, "but I've had to let it drop by the wayside."

"Mom used to play beautifully when I was a little girl," Jenny said. "I've missed that."

"There have been too many other important matters to deal with through the years," Julia brushed it off, slipping her hands under the table.

"Yeah, like me," a new voice entered the conversation.

Allie looked around to see a young man in the doorway. His dark hair reached his shoulders, his skin—a dark olive. A sullen expression marred his otherwise handsome face. The room quieted immediately.

"Jimmy!" Julia jumped up and walked around the table. "Where have you been? We've been worried about you. Are you hungry?"

"Nowhere, and no," Jimmy replied without looking at his mother. He was looking around the room, briefly pausing on Justin's face, then stopping on Allie's.

"Adopt a new daughter since I've been here, Mother?"

Allie felt Justin tense up next to her. Everyone seemed ill at ease.

"No, Jimmy, this is Allie Blake," Julia continued, ignoring the snide remark, "and you remember your Uncle John. They're traveling back to Dalton together."

"Hello, Uncle John," Jimmy said, then leaning closer to the table, he whispers loudly, "Isn't she just a bit young for you, Uncle?"

"Shut up, Jimmy," Justin said quietly.

"Oh, hello, big brother." Jimmy acted like he had just seen him for the first time. "A little on the touchy side about this one, eh?"

Matthew pushed away from the table and stood. "That's enough, Jimmy. If you can't show any better manners to our guests than that, then leave."

Jimmy grunted disgustedly, "That'll make you happy. Right, *Father*?"

"Jimmy," Julia intervened, "we've told you not to come here when you've been drinking."

"So the true son returns home and gets the fatted calf," Jimmy said as he looked at the table and buffet, "or fatted pig, I see, and the prodigal returns and is kicked out again. I don't think that's how the story's supposed to go, *Father*."

This time Justin and John both stood up as Matthew started around the table.

"You ungrateful…"

Julia stepped between them.

"Leave, Jimmy," she said quietly, but sternly.

Jimmy threw his hands up and backed toward the door.

"I'm going, dear family," Jimmy said with feigned affection in his voice. "It was a pleasure to meet you, Allie, and welcome to Grace. You won't find much of that around here." And he slipped out the door.

Faith stood and walked around the table.

"Faith!" Julia's arm reached out toward her.

But Faith, who hadn't said a word all evening, followed her brother out the door.

Allie didn't know what to think. Julia turned and faced the wall to regain her composure as Matthew put his arm around her.

Catherine leaned over and squeezed Allie's hand. "I'm so sorry, Allie," she apologized quietly as Uncle John and the younger men talked among each other.

Jenny exhaled as if she had been holding her breath the whole time. "We're at our wit's end about Jimmy. We usually don't have much of a problem with him until he starts drinking, and then he's absolutely insufferable. Mom and Dad have been more than patient with him, and yet he provokes Dad to the point where it makes him lose his temper."

"And then Jimmy throws the Bible back in his face to pile the guilt higher," Catherine added.

Julia walked over to Allie. "I want to apologize for Jimmy's behavior, Allie. There's no excuse for that, and I'm so sorry you had to witness it."

"Please don't worry yourself about it," Allie said. "I'm fine."

"I've tried everything I know to do with Jimmy, and nothing seems to help. I'm afraid Matthew won't put up with his behavior much longer."

Jenny said, "We've all tried, Mother, and we're tired of walking on eggshells around him."

"Well, we don't need to burden Allie with our problems," Julia said.

"We just need to keep praying for Jimmy—that God will change his heart," Catherine said.

Julia changed the subject. "Let's clear the table and head to the parlor. I'd like to show Allie the sheet music she'll be using tomorrow."

"Mom, Catherine and I will help Vestal. You go on upstairs with Allie. We need to round up the kids and head home soon, too."

The ladies were glad to focus on something more productive, and the somber mood lifted. Matthew and John were deep in discussion by the door to the garden. Marcus, Matt, and Justin stood nearby.

Justin caught Allie's eye as she headed toward the stairs; his blue eyes showed remorse. Allie smiled back to reassure him she was all right. She determined within her heart to do what she could to make this weekend special for Justin's parents. Their lives were still haunted by remnants of the past, especially the one named *Jimmy*.

In the parlor, Julia uncovered the piano keys as Allie sat down. Allie played the *C* chord, and ran through several scales while Julia found some sheet music. The piano sounded a little tinny.

"It hasn't been played or tuned in years," Julia explained. "We haven't had a piano tuner out here in quite a while. The piano at the church is newer, though, and sounds a little better."

She handed Allie the music.

"These are a couple of songs I used to play when I was your age. Do you recognize either one?"

"I love Bach's *Jesu, Joy of Man's Desiring*, but I'm not familiar with this one: Pachelbel's *Canon in D*." Allie said as she played the first line with only her right hand.

"That's close, but it's smoother, more flowing," Julia said.

Allie tried it again, this time with her left hand, too.

"Like this." Julia reached down with her right hand and played an octave higher along with her. "Yes, you're getting it."

As they reached the end of the page, Allie couldn't help but comment. "You play beautifully, Julia."

Julia quickly pulled her hand back.

"I haven't played in years," she said. "I haven't even thought much about it until I started planning this anniversary ceremony. But I knew Mamie couldn't play these pieces, so I had picked out a couple of simple hymns for her. I am so pleased you'll be playing instead."

"Does Mrs. Mamie think she's playing the piano tomorrow?" Allie asked. "I wouldn't want to hurt her feelings."

"Mamie won't mind—she's probably forgotten about the whole ceremony. Did I tell you her memory's not what it used to be, either?"

Allie laughed. "No, but that goes along with her eyes and ears."

"Well, I'm going to check on things downstairs. Feel free to play as long as you'd like. It's been a while since this house has heard those piano keys sing."

Julia stopped at the double doors, "Oh, and do you know *Amazing Grace?*"

"Yes, our church in Dalton sang it almost every Sunday."

"Catherine will be singing it tomorrow. Would you mind accompanying her, too?"

"Not at all."

"That's one of my favorite hymns," Julia said as she walked back over to Allie and hugged her. "I am so glad you're here."

"Me, too," Allie said.

She turned her attention to the music, determined all the more to play her best for Justin's parents tomorrow.

After a while, Allie heard voices in the hallway. She stopped playing when Uncle John and Justin walked into the room.

"Don't stop," Uncle John insisted. "It's been too long since I've heard you play."

"Don't you dare laugh if I hit some wrong notes," Allie said. "And that goes for you, too, Justin."

"Yes, ma'am," Justin grinned as he and Uncle John sat down in a couple of armchairs nearby.

She played through both songs again, and then thought she should save the rest of her practice on those particular songs for the church piano. She looked at some other music Julia had brought to the piano and chose to play Beethoven's *Ode to Joy,* another favorite of hers, as well as a few hymns.

Before she had finished, the parlor was full of Taylors. She played *Sweet Betsy from Pike* and *Shenandoah,* and several joined in singing. Vestal's voice bellowed above the rest of them.

Everyone laughed and clapped when Allie finished with a rousing version of *Yankee Doodle* she was able to play by ear.

"It's been too long since we've had music in this room," Vestal said, dabbing her eyes. "It's good for the soul, and it's so good to have Justin home."

Justin put his arm around her. "It's good to be home, Vestal."

Marcus and Jenny said they had to get home and finish some work at the store. Matt and Catherine rounded up their boys to head to their house, also on Taylor property, but down the road further.

"We'll have to finish our chores in the dark," Matt said, "but it won't be the first time."

"Or the last, I'm sure," Catherine said. "We really enjoyed the meal and the company, everyone. Allie, can you meet me at the church around nine in the morning? We can go over my song."

Allie assured her she would be there. Another round of hugs, and everyone left that was leaving. This was the huggin'est family Allie had ever been around.

And she loved it.

Julia led Allie upstairs to one of the two bedrooms facing the front of the house, both of which opened to the balcony, along with double doors in the hallway. Windows could be opened at the top of the stairs to make a cross breeze through the upper floors.

Julia told Allie if she needed anything during the night that Faith would be right across the hall. Allie had seen her come into the parlor when everyone was singing, but hadn't seen her since. Justin and Uncle John would be in the remaining two bedrooms on the third floor. Julia and Matthew's bedroom was one of the rooms downstairs across the hall from the parlor.

Julia explained that when the house was built, Vestal insisted the Taylors put her own room next to the kitchen, claiming she would rather not climb those stairs unless she absolutely had to. Most of her work centered around the kitchen, dining area, garden, and laundry/bathhouse near the big house, so she was happy to have the bottom floor to herself.

Julia said she would check on Justin's room to give Allie a few minutes to gather her things before she took her out to the bathhouse.

Allie looked around her bedroom. She had never seen a prettier room, much less spent the night in such. The walls were papered in a pale green and pink floral print. The bedspread was a brocade in a darker green than the wall. She ran her hand across the silky, embossed fabric as she leaned up against one of the tall posts of the four poster bed. Allie noticed that the head of the bed had several more pillows than one person could comfortably use, and then realized some were just ornamental. Allie had never seen anything but quilts on a bed, along with a couple of flattened feather pillows that usually had little quills sticking out of them.

The furniture in the room was dark like her mother's mahogany dresser back in Dalton. And the roomful of furniture matched. Allie had never seen that before, other than Uncle John's dining room set, which had belonged to his wife Sarah. Most of the furniture in Allie's home and Aunt Sister's house were hodgepodges of hand-me-downs and handmade items.

Allie unpacked her bag and slipped her outfits on wooden hangers in the wardrobe before gathering up her night clothes and other items to go to the bathhouse.

Julia stepped into the room. "Are you ready? I know you're probably looking forward to a hot bath after that long trip. I hope we haven't completely worn you out this evening."

"No, I've enjoyed myself immensely, but a hot bath does sound nice."

Julia walked Allie out to the bathhouse. This was a new experience, too. Baths at home and Aunt Sister's usually involved filling a No. 3 wash tub in the kitchen where water could be easily heated. This bathhouse was separate from the manor house. Allie learned that it was the first house the Taylors built soon after they arrived in Texas. They lived in it until the big house was completed, and then the bathhouse became one of Vestal's domains.

Vestal must have heard Julia and Allie coming because they found her pouring scalding water into a large bathing tub as they walked into the room.

The walls were a whitewashed board and batten with a huge fireplace on one end. Julia said that they used to heat water for washing clothes and baths in the fireplace, but they eventually purchased a woodstove to do the job. The tub was situated in the middle of the wall opposite the door and not too far from the woodstove. Drapery could be pulled around the area for privacy. A toilet closet stood in the far corner and another door led to a smaller room. A large table and a few chairs were situated in the big room for Vestal's laundry work. Allie recognized all the containers and tools for canning food here, along with shelves of a variety of canned fruits and vegetables from the garden. A quilt frame hung from the ceiling, and cloth and sewing needles and thread filled several baskets.

"When the weather's cold, we just put a tub in the corner of the kitchen and hang a sheet so we don't have to leave the house to take our baths," Julia said. "But during the summer, we really enjoy this room."

"I can see why," Allie said.

"Well, Vestal and I will leave you to your bath. Take all the time you need, Allie," Julia said.

Vestal added, "There's plenty of soap and towels on the chair beside the tub."

"Thank you both," Allie said. "This is wonderful. I hope I don't fall asleep in the bath water."

They said their goodnights and closed the door to the bathhouse. Allie was alone in the room, but she still pulled the curtain around the tub area for modesty's sake. It also helped block the breeze coming in through several windows.

The bath *was* wonderful, but Allie knew she shouldn't dawdle. Someone else was bound to be waiting for a bath, too. Back at home she or her mother had the luxury of being the first to use the bath water; her brother and dad followed. Bath water used only once was an extravagance. Allie quickly washed her hair and scrubbed every inch of her skin to get the travel dust off.

Although there were plenty of linen towels folded on the chair, Allie used only one to dry her hair first, and then her body. She had been taught to use no more than one towel—anything more than that was wasteful, and laundry chores were hard enough without creating more unnecessary laundry to wash.

Allie quickly pulled her cotton nightgown over her head to block the chill of exposed skin. But she froze when she heard the sound of something brushing against the outside wall behind her.

Chapter 4

*A*llie turned to face the wall. It was solid—no windows along here She heard nothing else, but still shivered, trying to shake off the feeling that she wasn't alone.

You're being ridiculous, Allie Blake, she told herself. *It was probably just a branch brushing up against the wall.*

She quickly gathered her belongings without bothering to brush out her tangled hair. She opened the door and looked around. It was dark outside, but the lighted windows from the main house lit the pathway.

She shut the door to the bathhouse and began walking quickly toward the big house. By the time she reached the bottom steps she was almost running. A movement from one of the chairs on the back porch startled her.

"Allie?" someone said as he stood up.

"Oh, Justin—you have to stop doing that!" She grabbed her chest. "My heart 'bout stops when you scare me like that."

"Scare you? I didn't mean to scare you."

"What are you doing out here anyway? Are you in line to use the bathhouse?"

"No, I just wanted to make sure you…" he paused. "Yeah, it's my turn. Did you use all the hot water?"

"No, Vestal left some on the stove."

"All right, then. I guess I'll see you in the morning."

Allie told him goodnight and turned to walk in the house. Justin stepped off the porch. Allie stepped inside and closed the door, but not before she watched him walk down to the bathhouse. But instead of going inside, Justin disappeared behind the building.

"How was your bath, dear?"

Allie jumped again at the voice and dropped half of her belongings. Vestal, dressed in a very large nightcap and gown, had walked up behind her.

"I didn't mean to frighten you, dear. Are you all right?"

"Yes, ma'am," Allie said as she squatted down to pick up her things, "and my bath was wonderful. I appreciate all the trouble you went to."

"No trouble 't all, dear. Is there anything else I can do for you?"

"No thank you; you've done so much already. I think I'll just head up to bed."

"Goodnight, then. Breakfast will be at seven."

"Goodnight, Vestal. See you in the morning."

Allie started up the two flights of stairs to her room. On the second floor she met Uncle John stepping out of the parlor. She hugged him goodnight and made her way to the third floor. She felt much safer inside the house. What made her feel so uneasy down at the bathhouse? And where did Justin go after she spoke to him?

Back in her bedroom, Allie put away her toiletries and carefully folded the brocade bedspread back to the end of the bed. She crawled into bed and settled into the sumptuous mattress before pulling the sheet up under her chin. She usually threw the cover off sometime during the night anyway, but a nice breeze came in through the open window on the wall to the right and went out one of the open French doors facing the bed.

Allie lay there for a while staring at the open door to the balcony. Then she quickly got up to shut and latch the balcony door.

Now she could sleep.

Allie woke to the sound of voices in the hall. She stretched fully and rolled over, not wanting to get out of that glorious bed. But she remembered her meeting at the church to practice with Catherine and definitely didn't want to miss Vestal's breakfast. She dressed in a dark green poplin skirt and a cream-colored blouse, saving her white dress for the ceremony later.

Vestal disappointed no one in her spread for breakfast. Allie was sure Vestal and Aunt Sister must have come from the same stock. The sideboard was loaded with pancakes and maple syrup, scrambled and fried eggs, slices of bacon, ham, and sausage, and huge biscuits alongside a crock of creamy butter, and jars of peach preserves and honey.

"Vestal, you've outdone yourself," Justin said as he piled a second layer of food on his plate. "I just might have to stay here forever."

Vestal beamed at Justin.

Allie smiled, remembering how Justin had won over Aunt Sister with his compliments on her cooking. Vestal's heart had been conquered years before as well.

After breakfast, Julia put Matthew and Justin in charge of setting up tables, chairs, and benches on the porch and lawn behind the house. Jenny showed up with her brood and set about decorating with white ribbon, greenery, and lace-trimmed tablecloths. Allie helped Vestal clear the breakfast table and wash the dishes before she had to leave for the church to practice. Julia and Vestal began the preparations for the food that would be served later on that afternoon.

Julia told Jenny to stop what she was doing and take Allie to the church in the buggy. They walked to the barn where Jenny had left her horse and buggy. Jenny had just taken the reins in hand when her youngest son Luke came running toward them.

"Mama! Maggie picked up a bee, and it stung her!"

"Oh, my goodness! Luke, why aren't you back there helping her?"

"Joshua's trying to get the stinger off, Mama—he told me to run get you."

Jenny handed Allie the reins and apologized as she climbed out of the buggy. She started toward the house and told Allie over her shoulder. "You know where the church is, don't you?"

"Yes, go on! I know exactly where it is. I'll meet Catherine there."

Allie turned and looked at the horse. "You'd better be nice."

She pulled the reins to the left and made a clicking noise like Uncle Junior made with Sassy. The horse started walking as Allie turned the buggy back down the road that ran alongside the big house.

She could hear little Maggie hollering—the kids had been playing in the garden on the far side of the house. It looked like everyone had dropped what they were doing and ran to check on the little girl.

Allie was relieved that the horse was doing what it was supposed to do—follow the road and pull the buggy. She remembered seeing the church steeple above the rooftop off to the right when they first came into town. She figured it was less than a mile away.

Allie felt so good about being able to do something for Justin's family. And driving this horse and buggy on her own—she was surprised at the realization that this was the first time she had done that by herself. She had always been with someone, either family or friends. Even during the clandestine times she met Miguel, she always walked to meet him, although he almost always came to town on horseback. Her asking to use the buckboard or buggy would have raised too much suspicion.

This responsibility today, even as little as it was, gave her a new sense of independence. Allie knew it was going to be a wonderful celebration, and she was happy to be a part of it.

Allie spotted the steeple and turned the horse and buggy down a road that ran adjacent to the church. She pulled up to the front, grabbed the sheet music, climbed out of the buggy, and tied the reins to a hitching post.

The view around the church was incredible. Trees on gently rolling hills bordered fields of varied hues of green and yellow. When facing the church, it looked as if it were the only structure in the entire countryside. Allie realized that someone had put a lot of thought into where to build it.

The church was simple and lovely, built of white clapboard with tall windows on each side, which helped keep it cool in the summer. The steeple topped a small bell tower on the front of the church. Lantana bushes with dainty clusters of yellow and orange flowers grew on both sides of the steps leading up to the double doors in front. Lantana grew wild around Dalton, too, and she suddenly yearned to be home with her family.

Allie walked up the steps and opened the door, hoping that she still had a few minutes to practice before Catherine arrived. Two small rooms flanked each side of the foyer, and another set of double doors opened to the sanctuary. Allie walked down the center aisle to the front of the church. The ceiling followed the shape of the steep roofline. Every pane in the tall windows framed a work of nature's art of the views surrounding the church. Pews provided the seating, along with several chairs near the front where a simple pulpit stood on a raised platform. The upright piano, covered with a canvas cloth, was to the left of the pulpit. It was turned catty-cornered in order to see both the congregation and the pulpit. A single door near the piano opened directly to the outside.

Allie removed the covering and draped it over the front pew. She pulled out the piano stool and arranged herself and her music. She wanted to run through *Amazing Grace* before Catherine arrived, so she began playing it first. The music echoed in the tall, empty room, but the piano had a wonderful tone to it.

Allie almost knew the song by heart from the years of playing it at her own church, so she soon set that aside and began playing *Jesu, Joy of Man's Desiring*. The two more difficult selections needed more practice for her to feel comfortable playing them this afternoon.

Allie didn't hear the door open behind her, but she saw the change in the light across her sheet music. She was on the last line of Pachelbel's *Canon in D*—she was sure Catherine wouldn't mind her finishing it. It was beginning to sound like Julia played it last night. Allie was quite pleased with her finish, and turned around to greet Catherine, who had begun to clap.

"Encore! Encore!"

Allie's smile froze when she realized it was Jimmy that had come up behind her.

"Hello... Allie, isn't it?"

"Hello," Allie said, noticing his eyes were blue, too, like Justin's. But there was something frightening about them. His hair was tangled, and he smelled as if he hadn't bathed in some time.

"You play beautifully."

"Thank you."

"I heard you playing last night, too—it sounded like everyone had a grand old time in the parlor."

"Why didn't you come inside and join us?"

"And spoil everyone's fun?" Jimmy said sarcastically. "I don't belong there."

"Did you see Catherine outside?" Allie wanted him to know she was not going to be here at the church by herself.

"No, should I?"

"She'll be here any minute."

"Good ol' Catherine. I'm always in her prayers, she tells me. I haven't a clue what she tells God about me. I imagine she tattles on me regularly."

"You don't know that. Catherine seems genuinely concerned about you. They all are."

"If you know this family so well, why is it that we've never met you until now? You really don't know anything about us, do you?"

Allie didn't know how to answer that. The only thing she really knew about the Taylors was that Julia and Justin had been captured by some Indians years before, and that her church had been praying for them. Jimmy was right, she didn't know much about the Taylor family, but Allie refused to acknowledge that fact.

53

"I know they're good people, and they want what's best for you," she replied defensively.

"And what about you, Allie," Jimmy said as looked her up and down, "are you a good person?"

"You don't know anything about me either," Allie said, hoping Catherine would step through the door soon.

"I know you better than you think."

Allie felt the conversation shift malevolently. She glanced at the door.

"I know you are hiding things…"

Allie's eyes grew wide. How would he know about her past?

Jimmy laughed at her expression, "So you *do* have something to hide! We all do, Allie." His tone became sinister. "But I'm talking about a birthmark you're hiding."

"What?!"

Jimmy reached over and touched the side of her thigh. "Right here."

Allie slapped his hand away and stood. "Don't touch me," she spat at him, horrified that he had actually touched where her birthmark was. *How did he know about that?* She clinched her fists to keep them from shaking.

"Have you let Justin touch you?" Jimmy sneered. "He's the one who told me about your birthmark."

"You're lying!" Allie reeled at the statement she had just heard.

"Why don't you ask him yourself?"

"Hello! Allie!?" Catherine called out from the back of the sanctuary. "Jimmy, what are you doing here?"

"See you around, Allie." Jimmy turned toward the door and said mockingly over his shoulder, "and keep praying for me, dear Catherine."

Jimmy left through the door behind the piano, not waiting for Catherine to come up to the front.

Allie sat down, visibly shaken.

"Allie, what's the matter?" Catherine asked when she saw Allie's face. "What did Jimmy tell you?"

Allie put her hand to her mouth and shook her head, not able to answer immediately. She couldn't think clearly. How did Jimmy know about her birthmark? And why did he say that Justin had told him? There's no way Justin would know about that, except for…

"—the bathhouse last night," she said aloud. She remembered watching Justin walk around the bathhouse instead of into it. But almost as soon as the thought entered her mind, she knew Justin would never do what Jimmy had implied. She remembered hearing something while she was drying off last night that had frightened her for a moment, but then there were no windows in the wall beside the bathtub. There must've been a hole or a crack to peek through. She felt sick to her stomach.

"What?" Catherine asked. "What about the bathhouse?"

"If I tell you, would you please not tell anyone?"

"Tell me what? I don't know if I can make that promise," Catherine said as she pulled up a nearby chair to face Allie.

"I don't want to cast a pall over this celebration for your parents."

"Allie, what did Jimmy say to you?" Catherine persisted.

"He talked about me hiding something. At first I thought he was talking about the reason I left Dalton last year, but he was actually talking about my birthmark." Allie paused. "Catherine, it's not where anyone can see it except when I'm undressed. He even touched me exactly where it is." Allie put her hand on the side of her thigh and looked at Catherine's face.

"How would Jimmy know about that?"

"Last night…"

"'*The bathhouse*,' you said," Catherine cringed. "That buzzard. Oh, Allie, I am so sorry."

"But he first told me that Justin had told him about my birthmark, insinuating that Justin and I knew each other intimately."

"But you don't think Justin…"

"No, no," Allie interrupted, "I knew immediately that Jimmy was lying about that. Justin has been nothing but a gentleman around me these past couple of days. I trust him implicitly and even more so since Uncle John thinks so highly of him. And besides, Justin and Jimmy aren't even speaking to each other."

Catherine sighed and shook her head. "This is intolerable of Jimmy. And I'm sorry, Allie, but we can't keep quiet about this."

"But I don't want to ruin your parents' celebration."

"I know, but let me think of something," Catherine said. "If we don't do something to change Jimmy's behavior now, he's going to end up in jail or dead. And it's inexcusable for him to do this to any woman."

"What have I done to offend him? Why me?"

"It's not you, Allie. I think he's trying to hurt Justin, and this isn't the first time. You're the object of Justin's attention right now and Jimmy can't stand it."

"But Jimmy met me just briefly last night. Why does he assume there's more to Justin and me than there actually is?"

"Jimmy's extremely smart, but it could've been something as simple as you and Justin sitting beside each other last night. Whatever the reason, though, we're going to do something about what Jimmy has done to you."

"Please don't, Catherine..."

"Don't worry—I won't say anything to Julia or Matthew, but I will talk to Matt and Marcus..."

"But not Justin, please."

"I think you're right about that, although Justin would be furious with us if he found out about it somehow," Catherine said. "It scares me to think what he'd do to Jimmy. That's why Justin left home—Jimmy's behavior kept getting worse and worse, especially toward him, but he wouldn't retaliate because of his mother. Julia doesn't know half the shenanigans Jimmy's pulled. Everyone's trying to protect her, all the while she's trying to protect Jimmy. A mother's love, I guess. It was just easier for Justin to leave instead of having to put up with his brother's anger and try to hide it from his mother. But Jimmy's gone too far this time."

"What do you think Matt and Marcus will do?"

"I don't know, but I trust them to do the right thing," Catherine said as she squeezed Allie's hand, "so I want you to put it out your head for now, and just know that Jimmy will not bother you again. And the anniversary party will go on as planned."

"Good." Allie was visibly relieved.

"Are you ready to practice with me now?"

"Yes."

"Then play me an introduction."

After their rehearsal, Allie followed Catherine's buggy to her house, which was about a half mile east of town and the same distance or so from the elder Taylors' home. Built with the same red brick as their parents' home, this house was smaller—only two stories. Catherine introduced Allie to an older woman named Juanita and asked Allie to help her pack up several prepared dishes to take over to the big house. Then Catherine took Matt into a bedroom to tell him what Jimmy had done to Allie—from the unconscionable act at the bathhouse to the unnerving visit at the church.

Matt came out of the room visibly upset, and apologized to Allie.

"I know he's my half brother, but this is the last straw. He's leaving this family and this town until he can straighten up his life. God knows we've tried to help him, but I don't think he wants to change. I hate what he's doing to our family—especially my parents and Justin, and it's time we did something about it."

"But we'll keep on praying for him," Catherine added, echoing Jimmy's words.

"It's going to take more than prayer for him to change his ways," Matt said. "I'm going to head over to the mercantile to talk to Marcus about this, and then we'll go find Jimmy. I'll meet you at Mom and Dad's later."

Allie felt uneasy about being part of the 'last straw,' which would drive Jimmy away from his family, but she didn't want to have to face him again, either. She busied herself helping Catherine round up the boys and pack their Sunday best clothes to change into after lunch. Catherine told Allie she didn't dare dress them now for the ceremony, or the boys would have their outfits soiled in no time.

Between the two women and Juanita, they loaded the two buggies with kids and food, and Catherine led the way to the 'big Taylor house,' as their eldest son Tres called it. The two oldest boys chose to ride with Allie in her buggy, and Allie even let eight-year-old Tres take the reins.

"We live in the little Taylor house," he explained, "but Daddy says some day we'll live in the big one with MeeMaw and PaPaw."

Allie smiled at him, remembering Uncle John saying that Matthew Taylor's legacy would go to his firstborn, and eventually Matt's legacy would go to Tres. She thought about Uncle John's decision to make Justin his beneficiary, which would give him a place to call his own some day. Jenny and Marcus were doing well with their mercantile store. What would Faith do? Where would she go? And Jimmy. It looked like he may never get the chance to build something meaningful with his family. And that was partly her fault now.

"What's the matter Allie?" Tres asked. "You look sad."

"Me sad? Of course not! I was just worried about you driving this buggy!" she teased.

"But I'm doing good!" Tres insisted.

"Yes, you are, young man. You can drive my buggy any time."

In the couple of hours Allie was gone, the big Taylor house had undergone an amazing transformation. The front porch rails were wrapped in greenery and white ribbons. They took the buggies around to the back of the house to unload the children and food, and Justin walked up to help.

Catherine hollered at the boys to not touch anything as they scampered away to find their cousins. Jenny and Faith were busy arranging branches of greenery and white ribbons along the back porch posts; the cloth-covered tables scattered around the porch and yard were already decorated.

"It's so beautiful!" Allie exclaimed, excited about the day's events.

Faith smiled at Allie. Justin helped Allie carry the dishes into the kitchen and came back outside.

"I'm sorry I didn't get to take you to the church, but I'm glad I was able to get started on this," Jenny said. "It's taking us longer than I figured. Did you have any problems?"

"Problems? What kind of problems?" Allie said, just a little too high-pitched.

"Finding the church? Finding the piano? Playing the piano?"

"Oh, no," Allie swallowed, "not at all. Catherine and I had a good rehearsal."

She couldn't lie worth a darn. And Justin looked at her like he knew it.

"I need a break," Justin said to Jenny. "You and Momma are running me ragged around here. I want to take Allie down to the river—we won't be gone long."

Justin didn't give Jenny a chance to respond before he grabbed Allie's hand and pulled her along behind him. He didn't slow down until after they had passed the barn, then he let go of her hand as they continued walking.

"I think I'd rather be working in a field than getting ready for a party any day. I hope everybody can stay awake during the ceremony this afternoon—we're all going to be dog-tired by then."

Allie laughed. "That's women for you. They want their occasions to be as pretty as they are special."

"I think my father and Uncle John are hiding out somewhere—I haven't seen them for the past hour. They just might be down at the river, too."

They walked along a well-worn trail through a grassy field dotted with cattle before they reached the line of huge trees giving evidence to a steady source of water nearby. The Taylors built their home on the high side of the river, and Allie and Justin came atop a fairly steep bank before they could see the river about thirty feet below them. The river ran clear, shallow in some places and deep in others, but all revealed a rocky bottom. The other bank, just a little higher than the river level, looked more like a dry riverbed made of gravel and native plants spread across a hundred yards or so before it started to gain elevation.

"The river changes its course through here every time a big rain comes," Justin said. "It just shifts the gravel over and carves another path. Sometimes it splits and creates a little island."

"It's beautiful. I imagine you spent a lot of time here."

"We did—come on, I'll show you."

Justin grabbed Allie's hand as he led the way down some makeshift steps dug out of the embankment. It was easy to use small saplings as handholds on the way down. They stopped on a huge flat rock that sat about eight feet above the water. The river ran deeper along here.

"I can see all the way to the bottom. I hate muddy rivers where you can't see what's beneath the water," Allie said, looking down at the perfect jumping off spot. A thought occurred to her. "This is your swimming hole, isn't it?"

"Yep. And I took most of my baths here, too," Justin said as he grinned. "It was a lot more fun than the ol' bathhouse."

Allie flinched at his reference to the bathhouse, but his eyes showed no ulterior motive in bringing that up.

"But does this hole dry up when the river changes course?"

"No, it's spring-fed. There's a natural spring feeding into the river back through those trees over there. Even when the river splits, this current joins it eventually. The area around the spring is the best place to be. We used to camp out down there all the time, especially the first year after we returned. It took us a while to get used to living in such a big house, and Mom understood. We used to stay down here days at a time. We called it our hiding place."

Allie realized he was talking about Jimmy.

"You miss him, don't you," Allie said.

Justin picked up a rock and skipped it across the river.

"Yeah."

"I'm so sorry about Jimmy," Allie said.

"Why are you sorry? He's the one that should be sorry."

Allie nodded. "I guess I'm sorry for the relationship you lost."

"You don't have to worry about that. It's not your problem," Justin said. "And speaking of problems, what happened at church?"

59

Allie looked at Justin's profile. *Who was this man? A mind reader?*

"What do you mean?" Allie pretended to know nothing.

"Something ruffled your feathers back there when Jenny asked if you had any problems at the church. Did you get lost or something?"

"Yes." *No, that won't work since the steeple is visible all over the valley.* "No, I just had a little problem with the horse," Allie lied again.

"Are you talking about Jenny's horse? That old bag of bones is so tame little Maggie could drive her. I noticed you even let Tres take the reins coming back to the house."

"You know how inept I am with horses. I just didn't want Jenny to feel bad about not taking me." Allie was getting entirely too good at duplicity.

Justin looked at her face. "If you're that uncomfortable with horses, I'd be glad to teach you some things."

He believed her. Allie told him she would appreciate his help sometime, but for now they had better get back to the house to help finish the preparations.

Vestal put out the remaining slices of ham and biscuits left over from breakfast for a quick noon meal. Too much remained to be done before the party, so few actually took the time to sit down at the dining table. The ceremony at the church began at four o'clock, and everyone would head back to the Taylors' home for dinner and socializing afterwards.

Allie learned that most of the folks in the community would attend the Taylor's anniversary celebration, as well as some guests from as far away as Waco. She and Uncle John came the farthest distance, though. He had planned his trip around this event to bring Allie back to Dalton, although Allie didn't realize it at first.

Many of the local women would help out by bringing covered dishes. That didn't slow Vestal down one bit, though. She intended to outdo them all.

Allie helped dress Catherine and Jenny's younger children. The older boys did just fine, although they needed a little help with their bow ties. Catherine pulled Allie aside and told her that Matt and Marcus had taken care of the problem—that she wouldn't have to worry about Jimmy coming around.

"Won't Julia wonder why Jimmy isn't here today?" Allie asked.

"Jimmy's made it a habit to come and go when he feels like it. For some time now he's felt no obligation to let his mother know where he's going or when he's coming back. And he feels no part of this union between Julia and Matthew—least of all to celebrate it. I doubt he would've come in the first place."

Allie felt relieved. That was a huge burden to pack around.

Time was short, though. She quickly freshened up a bit before running to her bedroom to change into the white dress. She opened wide the bedroom and balcony doors to try to cool off while she attempted to put her hair up in a bun. She was running out of time, and her hair was not cooperating.

Allie saw Faith step out of her room, dressed and ready with her hair neatly arranged in a simple upsweep.

"Faith, you look beautiful. How did you put your hair up like that? Is there any way you could help me with mine?"

Faith nodded and came into Allie's bedroom.

"How did you learn to do your hair like that?" Allie asked.

"Momma showed me."

Allie realized those were the first words she had heard Faith speak. Faith led Allie back to the dresser bench and sat her down. She undid the tangled mass and began gently brushing Allie's hair.

"That feels wonderful," Allie said, closing her eyes. "I could go to sleep sitting straight up right now."

"Momma used to brush my hair every night," Faith said, "and tell me stories."

"What kind of stories?"

"Stories about our family... or the ways animals act... or the Bible."

"Do you know much about the Bible?"

Faith nodded her head.

"What's your favorite scripture?" Allie asked.

"I have many. I love the stories about Jesus because he gave his life for me, but my favorite story in the Bible is about Ruth."

Allie met her eyes in the mirror. "Why?"

"It's about a young woman who leaves her people to go home with her mother-in-law to a strange place where she didn't know anyone. But she loved Naomi like a mother and told her, 'For whither thou goest, I will go; and where thou lodgest, I will lodge: thy people shall be my people, and thy God, my God.'"

"That *is* a wonderful story," Allie said, and knew without a doubt it was Faith's story as well.

In a matter of minutes, Faith had arranged Allie's hair neatly and securely atop her head.

"You definitely have a gift, Faith," Allie said. "I don't think my hair has ever looked this elegant."

They stood together, looking in the mirror.

"Jimmy likes my hair this way," Faith said, turning her head from side to side. "He said it makes me look grown up."

Allie felt a pang of guilt shoot through her, knowing that Faith would not see Jimmy for some time.

Faith and Jimmy both had to have been around Allie's age of eighteen or maybe a little younger, which actually was grown-up and of marrying age. But Faith still sounded like a little child, so innocent and inexperienced about life. Had Julia been overly protective of her, too?

"Do you get along with Jimmy?" Allie asked her.

"I'm the only one that understands him, and he understands me. He doesn't know how to let go of his bitterness, though. He cradles it and strokes it until it makes him so angry, he does stupid things. It's getting harder for the others to keep loving him, but I still do. And I always will."

Allie couldn't look her in the eye after that.

Chapter 5

*A*llie stood at the window nearest the piano and watched Mr. and Mrs. Matthew Taylor pull up to the church in a buggy covered in greenery and white ribbons—Jenny's handiwork again. Justin and Matt helped their mother down and shook their father's hand. Allie was about to turn her attention to the piano when she noticed a very attractive woman walk up to Justin and hug him. He looked stiff and uncomfortable. That was a good sign, but it still made Allie grit her teeth.

Just who does she think she is? Allie thought to herself. She craned her head out the window to try to see more as they walked toward the front of the church and out of sight. Someone coughed loudly from the back of the church, and Allie realized it was time to sit down and play the first song. The church was full of people, but she tried not to think about that or the fact that some woman had attached herself to Justin, or she would be even more nervous.

As Allie began to play, Matt and Catherine and their sons walked in first and sat on the front row to the left. Jenny and Marcus and their children walked in next and sat on the front row to the right. Justin escorted Faith down the aisle, taking up the remaining space on the front row to the left. Uncle John followed, walking around the front of the pews to sit in the second row on the piano side of the room.

After a minute or so, Julia and Matthew stepped through the double doors, and everyone in the church stood and faced them. Allie played a little slower and louder as they walked down the aisle, and tried to ignore Jenny dabbing her eyes. Allie didn't need her own tears to blur the notes in front of her. From the corner of her eye she could see that the Taylors had reached the front of the church, so she seamlessly moved to the last several measures of the music and ended it. She clasped her shaking fingers and placed them in her lap before glancing at Julia, who had turned to greet her with a beautiful smile. Allie smiled back and took a deep breath to calm down.

Pastor Jenkins began speaking as Matthew and Julia turned to face each other, hands entwined.

"Dear family and friends of Matthew and Julia Taylor, we are gathered here today to celebrate a wonderful marriage that has lasted thirty years. We all know their story and the difficulties they faced, which could easily have torn any marriage asunder, but Matthew and Julia's love and faith have withstood these fiery tests and have come through even stronger. We praise God for the witness of this union today, and hope that it is an example to us all of the faith and hope and love that has endured."

Allie thought Julia looked like an angel in white, wearing the same wedding dress she wore thirty years before, according to Catherine and Jenny, who also wore the dress at their respective weddings. Allie could only see Julia's profile looking up at Matthew, but his face showed such love and tenderness toward his wife that Allie was convinced it was a reflection of Julia's expression as well.

Catherine stepped up beside the piano as Allie played an introduction to *Amazing Grace*. Catherine's clear soprano voice filled the church.

"Amazing grace, how sweet the sound...
that saved a wretch like me;
I once was lost, but now I'm found;
'twas blind, but now I see..."

Catherine could not look at her parents as she sang, but chose to look toward one of the windows on the opposite side of the church to avoid giving in to the emotional atmosphere of the room. Most of the congregation were beyond that, openly sniffing and shedding tears at the memory of the love story of these two people who obviously meant so much to everyone present. Catherine finished the hymn and started to walk to her seat. Julia stepped out and grabbed her in a hug, and Catherine's performance demeanor crumbled. She wept in her mother's arms, and that was enough to get Allie going, too, as she slipped in the pew beside Uncle John. He put his arm around her and handed her his kerchief.

Pastor Jenkins continued. "Thank you, Catherine, for such a lovely reminder of what has become our community's anthem. Matthew and Julia, I won't have to say your vows for you to repeat after me. They have been written on your hearts these past thirty years. You may now share them with each other in front of God and these witnesses."

"I, Julia, take thee *again*, Matthew, to be my lawfully wedded husband, to continue to have and to hold from this day forward, for better or for worse, for richer, for poorer, in sickness and in health 'til death do us part." Her voice broke as she added, "Thank you for bringing me home, Matthew. Thank you for not giving up on me."

A tear rolled down Julia's cheek as Matthew kissed her hand before beginning his vows.

"I, Matthew Taylor, take thee again, Julia Taylor, to be my lawfully wedded wife, to continue to have and to hold from this day forward, for better or for worse, for richer, for poorer, in sickness and in health 'til death do us part. And I would've continued to search for you the rest of my life, if that's what it took. God was merciful and gracious to allow me to find you and bring you home, and I'll be grateful to Him forever."

Pastor Jenkins said, "Matthew and Julia, do you together promise in the presence of God and your family and friends to continue to love, cherish, and respect each other in marriage so long as you both shall live?"

"We do."

"Then by the authority vested in me, I pronounce your continued future as husband and wife. Matthew, you may kiss your wife."

Matthew took his wife in his arms, leaned his head down and gently kissed Julia on the lips. His head came up, and he looked her in the face, grinning, then kissed her again more forcefully, to the delight of the crowd. Allie walked back to the piano, ready to play the last song Julia had requested.

"And may I introduce to you anew, Mr. and Mrs. Matthew Taylor."

The congregation burst into applause. Allie began playing as Matthew and Julia started back down the aisle, followed by the family. She played until the church emptied, then gathered up the music to take back to the house. She smiled as she looked out the window watching everyone congratulate the Taylors.

They deserve this happiness, she thought.

Allie went to the corner and grabbed the canvas cover to drag it over to the piano when a hand reached out beside her. She gasped and flinched before she realized who it was.

"Here, let me help you with that," said Justin, looking puzzled at her reaction.

"Justin Taylor!" she said with obvious relief.

"Why are you so jumpy?"

"You need to start making some noise when you come up on folks like that!" and added when she saw the look on his face, "I'm sorry. My mind was miles away."

"In Dalton?" Justin asked. "Were you thinking about another wedding coming up?"

"No! Not at all. Here, you get that end and I'll get this one," she said, trying to change the subject. They covered the piano, picked up the music and walked toward the back of the church.

Allie could stand it no longer. She tried to sound as nonchalant as possible. "I noticed a friend come up and hug you outside before the service."

"A friend? Allie, I've greeted quite a few *friends* today."

"A lady friend."

"Oh," he paused. "That's just Florine. She's from Waco."

"Just Florine?"

"Yep, just Florine; nothing else."

"It looks like there's more to it on her end."

"That's her problem. How are you getting back to the house? Can I give you a ride?" Justin asked.

"Are you on a horse or a buggy?" Allie asked.

"Does it matter?" Justin said, looking straight ahead as they walked through the double doors into the foyer.

"I should say so—I'm in a dress, and look at the color of it!" Allie turned to face him, and noticed the slight grin on his face. He was teasing her again.

She could play that game, too. "I think I'll just walk, thank you," Allie turned up her nose a bit as she whirled around to go outside.

Justin grabbed her arm and pulled her back to one side of the foyer, away from the outer doors. "Of course, I have a buggy, milady."

Allie laughed as she fell into his arms. She looked at his face—she dared look into those blue eyes, and before she knew it, Justin kissed her. Then all of a sudden he pulled back from her. If he hadn't held her, she probably would have slid right to the floor.

"Oh, my," was all she could say.

"I'm sorry, Allie," Justin said. "I don't know why I did that."

Allie was confused.

"I take that back," he continued, "I know why I did that." Justin paused and looked away. "I'm not very good at this—haven't had much practice. I don't play games when it comes to feelings, and I would always tell you the truth. I just know that I like you, Allie. I've never met anyone like you."

This time Allie took his face in her hands and gently turned it back to her. "I haven't had much practice, either, Justin Taylor, but I do know that I like you, too… very much."

Justin leaned down to kiss her again when Uncle John hollered from outside.

He ended up kissing her lightly on the forehead, saying, "We'd better get going. Everybody will wonder where we are."

All Allie could do was smile and nod.

Back at the house, Allie was introduced to more people at one time than she could ever remember. She tried her best to remember everyone's names, but finally gave up worrying about it and began to enjoy the evening. Most everyone commented on her piano playing, and invited her to come back and play for the church services the following day. She wasn't about to bump Mrs. Wilkins off her piano stool, though. The only way she would agree to it was if Mrs. Mamie happened to be absent.

The tables groaned under the weight of all the food provided by Vestal and the other women of the community. Allie did intend to try a bit of everything, but her appetite wasn't its usual voracious self. The flurry in the pit of her stomach was back, and she hadn't felt that since her time with Miguel.

Throughout the evening Allie made it a point to catch Justin's eye to let him know she was thinking about him. It pleased her to note that most times, he was already looking at her by the time she glanced his way, even when Florine kept trying to occupy his time.

The thought of Allie arriving back in Dalton became more bearable by the minute. The dread she had felt for weeks was slipping away. Who cared what anybody else thought of her any more? As long as she had her family's and Uncle John's love, and now, Justin's affection, she could handle anything—even running into Miguel and his fiancé.

The Taylor anniversary party began winding down around sunset. Most folks wanted to get home by dark, if not before, and most of the friends from Waco had left earlier in the evening, or had been farmed out to stay with local families. A few would even stay with the Taylors, which meant Faith and Allie would share a room this night, and Justin would bunk with Uncle John.

Allie learned, to her chagrin that Florine and her parents were the Taylors' guests. She had learned from Jenny that Florine Locke's father was a former business partner of Matthew Taylor, and the friendship had continued beyond the business relationship. Jenny told her that the Lockes had visited the Taylor home a number of times over the years, and Justin had taken Florine to the opera house in Waco once, at the request of Mr. Locke. Jenny felt the request had originated with Florine pressuring her father to set it up. Jenny also said Florine was still smitten with Justin, but he never showed any interest on his own.

Allie was relieved to hear that.

Allie had successfully avoided meeting Florine most of the evening, but as the number of people dwindled down to family and the overnight guests, she could avoid it no longer. Allie picked up a stack of dishes and turned and walked right into Florine.

"Here, let me help you with that... Allie, isn't it?" She grabbed a single cup from the top of the pile.

"Yes, hello, and you are...?" Allie smiled and feigned ignorance, knowing exactly who the beautiful, blonde-headed woman was standing before her. She was sure Florine had poked around to check her out, too, before this encounter.

Know thine enemy, Allie thought. *Well, 'enemy' might be too strong a word. Know thine' opponent'.*

Florine introduced herself and asked her a question.

"Pardon me? What did you say?" Allie said, smiling as she sized up her *opponent.*

"Have you known Justin very long?" Florine asked again.

She probably already knows the answer to that. "No, we just met a few days ago." *But it seems like I've known him forever.*

"Justin and I are friends from way back. Our families have known each other for years."

Way back, my foot—and the last two years Justin has been away from Grace and you. You're stretching it, Florine.

"You'll have to tell me some stories about Justin—what's he like? What has he been doing these past couple of years? I'm really curious to know," Allie said.

Florine forced a smile. "Well, this past year he's been very busy

68

running his uncle's cattle ranch in South Texas."

That was common knowledge.

"Everyone knows that," Allie said as she started walking toward the kitchen. "He *is* very handsome, don't you think?" There. She laid it out for Florine to know she was interested in Justin, too.

"We've been seeing each other," Florine spurted out.

Allie stopped and turned around to face a defiant Florine, who set the cup back on the stack of dishes Allie carried.

"Oh? Well, I wish you the best of luck in the future," but at the same time she was thinking, *and I know it's not going to be with Justin Taylor.*

Allie hadn't found a moment alone with Justin ever since the church foyer, but she at least wanted to tell him good night before going to bed. She helped Vestal wash dishes and clean up the kitchen while most of the family continued to visit with old friends. She was glad to have something to do—she didn't have a lot of experience making polite conversation with strangers, but at least she felt like she was contributing. Uncle John had noticed it earlier and tried to pull her back into the gathering outside, but after a few minutes, she slipped away again to help Vestal. Allie felt that was the least she could do. After such a special day, she didn't want the Taylors to have to bother about cleaning up from the celebration, and Vestal was so appreciative. She looked exhausted—the years were certainly catching up with her.

The Taylor children and their families were the last to leave with their guests, and gradually everyone else began to make their way toward the sleeping quarters. It had been a very long and glorious day, and they all basked in a happy fatigue.

Allie decided to forgo the bathhouse that night, choosing instead to use the washbowl in Faith's room. A hot bath sounded wonderful, but she couldn't bring herself to go back down there knowing what had happened the night before. She knew Jimmy would not be a problem, but she still felt exposed and vulnerable in that place.

Allie changed from her party dress, donning the skirt and blouse she had worn earlier. She stepped out into the hall and walked over to the French doors leading out to the balcony overlooking the drive. She sat down in one of the big comfortable chairs to wait for Justin and Uncle John to come up to their room. The night breeze felt so soothing, she almost fell asleep by the time the rest of the third floor occupants came up the stairs. Everyone was there—Faith quietly slipped into her room; Uncle

John bid everyone goodnight, including Mr. and Mrs. Locke, and they entered their respective rooms. Florine held Justin's arm like she couldn't remain standing without it, and he was doing his best to say goodnight, but she kept talking. When they were alone, her voice lowered to a whisper.

"Who is this Allie, Justin?"

"Why do you want to know?"

"You'd better watch out. She has her eye on you."

"She does, does she? How do you know?"

"She told me, even after I told her that we'd been seeing each other."

"Taking you to the opera once and a few family visits don't mean we're seeing each other, Florine. Now if you'll excuse me, I'm tired and would like to go to bed."

"But, Justin…"

"Goodnight, Florine."

With that, Justin detached her hand from his arm and went to his room. Florine's face skewed up as she turned with a huff and entered her room, shutting the door just a little too hard.

Allie didn't intend to eavesdrop on that conversation, but much of the balcony was in shadow, and she had a ringside seat. She was disappointed to have missed telling Justin goodnight, but thought she ought to wait a few more minutes before retiring to make sure no else would be roaming the halls.

Allie decided the coast was clear and stood up just as a door opened in the hall, and Justin stepped out. He walked across the hall to Faith's room and knocked quietly on the door. When Faith opened it, he asked where Allie was. Faith said she wasn't in her room yet, and Justin whirled around to go back downstairs to look for her. Allie quickly stepped through the French doors to stop him, and he motioned for her to come with him.

On the second floor landing, Justin whispered, "Uncle John thinks I'm going to the privy, and he'd probably whup me if he knew I was out looking for you."

Allie snickered. "He *can* be highly protective of me."

"And so am I—you 'bout gave me heart failure when Faith told me you weren't in the room yet—I knew you weren't downstairs because I'd already looked there."

"I was waiting on the balcony to tell you goodnight, but Florine had you cornered."

Justin shook his head. "She won't leave me alone, and I haven't done anything to encourage her. Here—let's go outside, but away from the house since everyone has their windows open."

The moon hung huge and bright in the sky—Allie could see the features of Justin's face clearly. He took hold of her hand as they walked down the road toward the river and eventually found themselves on the big rock above the swimming hole. The river took on an entirely different kind of beauty by moonlight.

Allie found it easy to talk to Justin. She felt safe with him. She had no idea she was seeing a side of Justin that few people had—he opened up to her, and told her things he had told no one. He felt safe with her.

It even felt comfortable during those moments when nothing was said. They had gone beyond the point where Allie felt obligated to fill in the silence with chatter. She turned and looked at the view across the river. Justin stepped up behind her and wrapped his arms around her. The exposed white river rocks reflected the moonlight throughout the whole area.

"It's beautiful here," Allie said as she leaned her head back onto Justin's chest. He nuzzled the side of her face, encouraging Allie to turn her head toward him as he leaned down to kiss her.

"It's beautiful here," Justin said to her face just before he kissed her. Then he turned her in his arms and continued a long, lingering kiss.

Time could just stand still, according to Allie. She didn't want the moment to end, but then she felt Justin's muscles stiffen, and pulled back to see what was wrong. She looked at him questioningly, "Justin...?"

"We'd better get back."

He was looking across the river. She turned to try to see what he saw. There! A movement—no, maybe it was just the breeze moving a branch.

"What is it, Justin?"

"Trouble," he said under his breath.

Chapter 6

*J*ustin pulled Allie up the slope and onto the path to the road.

"Justin, you're scaring me."

"I'm sorry—I don't mean to. We just need to get back to the house before Uncle John starts looking for me."

"Did you see something back there?"

"No, it was nothing—probably a coyote. They like to roam around at night."

They walked back to the house in silence, and this time Justin kept his distance from her. When they walked past the barn, though, he pulled her into the shadow and kissed her again. Allie was surprised, and confused again.

"We'll say our goodnights here. I'll watch you walk on up to the house, and I'll follow you a little later."

"I don't understand."

"I don't want you to be seen going into the house so late with me. If anybody's up, you can say you've been to the bathhouse."

"You know I don't care what anybody would say about us."

"I know, but just do this for me." He kissed her again. "I'll see you in the morning." He nudged her toward the house.

Allie couldn't understand why Justin was acting this way—why should he care about their reputations all of a sudden? That didn't make sense. She didn't think his family would mind, and the Lockes, well, she wasn't concerned in the least what those people thought, especially Florine.

She opened the back door as quietly as possible, but before she stepped inside, she turned to look back at the barn and saw Justin heading back down the road toward the river.

Something *was* down there, she thought. That worried her. She decided she had better wait until he came back to the house, so she stepped outside to sit in one of the porch chairs. Allie wasn't sure how much time had passed—maybe a half hour or so, before she saw Justin walking back up the road to the house. She got up and slipped inside before he got close enough to see her, and then made her way upstairs to Faith's room. She tried to be as quiet as possible, but Faith spoke from the bed.

"Are you all right?" she whispered to Allie.

"Yes, I'm sorry I woke you, Faith," she said as she began slipping out of her clothes to change into her sleeping gown.

"I was still awake—I was getting worried about you."

"Justin and I walked down to the river to talk. We didn't want to disturb anyone."

"Especially Florine," Faith said with a snicker.

Allie smiled in the dark. Did Faith just make a joke?

"I'm glad you like Justin, Allie," she continued. "You two are a good match."

"And how do you know this, Faith?"

"I just know—it feels right when I think of you two together. It felt wrong when I thought of Justin and Florine together. Unequally yoked, isn't it called?"

"I hope you're right, Faith. How did you get so wise?"

"I'm not," she answered. "I just watch people. You can find out a lot by just watching and listening."

Allie climbed into bed. "That's true. My mother used to tell me that I couldn't learn anything until I was willing to shut my mouth and stop talking. Sometimes I forget that."

"Have you seen Jimmy today?" Faith asked.

Allie's heart skipped a beat. "No, should I have?"

"He told me he was going to stay around a while—that he was going to try to do better. I wish you could get to know the real Jimmy. He is strong and hard-working and wants to do something with his life."

"I definitely have not seen that side of him," Allie admitted. "He scares me."

"He's a different person when he stays away from the bottle, but he just can't seem to let go of the past and his bitterness. He thinks the bottle will make him forget, but it just makes him mean."

"I wish I could see the other side of Jimmy," Allie said, not really knowing what else to say.

"It makes me think of David in the Bible and the awful things he did in his life, but God still loved him and used him," Faith said.

"Catherine tells me she prays for him regularly," said Allie. "Hopefully, God will do whatever it takes to turn him around."

"Yes, that's my prayer, too... I hope God will answer it before it's too late."

Allie found Faith's hand and squeezed it. "I'm so glad I'm getting to know you better, Faith."

After a moment, Faith said, "Thank you for being a friend to me. I love my family, but I really don't have any close friends outside of my family."

"You do now, Faith. Sweet dreams."

The next morning Allie awoke with a start. Had she overslept? Faith was out of bed and gone. She leaned back, stretched her arms and smiled, remembering the walk to the river with Justin last night. *Sorry, Florine,* she thought to herself. *That man is taken.*

Allie got up and dressed quickly, unsure of the time. She ran a brush through her hair and braided it, hoping Faith could put it up for her before going to church. The worship service was mid-morning, and she knew it wasn't that late, but she didn't want to embarrass Uncle John by showing up late for breakfast. She headed downstairs. On the second floor, she took the stairs to the left that led down to the kitchen.

"Good morning, Vestal! Can I help you with anything?"

"Well, there's the sleepyhead! We wondered where you were."

"Is it that late?" Allie asked. "I am so sorry!"

"Nah, honey—I know you were tired—you worked like a field hand around here last night. That was a big help to me."

"I was happy to do it," Allie said as she looked toward the dining room, which was unusually quiet. "Where is everybody?"

"Oh, goodness—you haven't heard the news! Somebody broke into Kimball's Mercantile Store."

"Marcus' and Jenny's store?"

"Yes, they think it happened during the party last night while everyone was here because neither one of them heard a thing during the night. You know they live above and behind the store, right? Marcus didn't discover it until this morning, and he rode up and told us during breakfast."

"That's awful," Allie said. "What was taken?"

"That's the odd thing. They did more ransacking than anything. Marcus thinks they just took some food and supplies, so we doubt it was anyone from around here. Everybody knows that if someone has a need, the Taylors or anyone else in this community would give the shirts off their backs to help."

"You said Marcus came during breakfast?" Allie asked. "What time is it? Did I completely miss breakfast?"

"No, child, everyone just scattered after Marcus came by. Most of them went to the Mercantile. I think Julia and Faith are upstairs. I brought a few dishes back in here to keep warm, so just fix yourself a plate and take it into the dining room. A few folks are still in there."

Allie did just that and walked into the dining room to eat with whoever remained. She rounded the corner to see Florine and her parents sitting at the big table.

Oh, mercy. Allie put on what she hoped looked like a genuine smile.

"Good morning, Mr. and Mrs. Locke..., Florine."

"Good morning, Miss Black," Mr. Locke said.

"It's *Blake*, Daddy," Florine corrected.

"Fine, good...," he murmured impatiently. "Mrs. Locke and I have already had our breakfast. We were just keeping Florine company while she had hers—she's a late-riser like you, I see—so why don't you girls keep each other company while Mrs. Locke and I go pack up our things before church?"

"Well, I...," Allie began.

"You are so kind, Miss Block. Florine, we'll see you upstairs in a little while."

The smile slid right off Allie's face as she turned to the buffet and added some marmalade to her plate. She pasted the smile back on before she turned around.

"I usually don't sleep this late," she told Florine as she sat down in front of her. "I like to get up and get my chores done and out of the way."

"I usually get to sleep later than this," Florine said, "because we let the *hired help* do our chores."

"Must be nice not knowing how to do anything," Allie said, still smiling. The little voice of her conscience whispered in her ear about *doing unto others...*

Allie ignored it.

Florine glared. The rest of the meal was quickly eaten in an uncomfortable silence. Allie stood up to excuse herself from the table.

"Have you seen Justin this morning?" Florine asked.

"No."

"I think he went down to the river…again," Florine said, emphasizing the last word.

"What do you mean?" Allie asked, realizing Florine must have watched her and Justin from her window last night.

"A girl could lose her reputation if she's not careful," Florine continued, looking smug with her newfound knowledge.

Allie smiled. "I lost mine some time ago, but if you find it, be sure and let me know. And if you will excuse me, I, too, have things to do."

She walked out, leaving Florine with her mouth agape.

Darn it, Allie, she fussed at herself as she took her plate to the kitchen. That smart remark didn't come out quite like she intended. *You just left Florine with the impression that you have questionable morals.* Then as quickly as the thought came, she brushed it aside. Why should she worry what Florine thought of her?

"Thank you for breakfast, Vestal. Can I help you clean up?"

"No, sweetness! I have everything under control." She gave Allie a big hug and thanked her again for helping last night. "Go on and finish getting ready for church."

"How much time do I have?"

Vestal looked at her regulator clock on the wall and said, "Oh, about an hour or so before they bring the buggies around."

Allie walked outside through the kitchen door and looked toward the barn and the river road. She had enough time to walk down there and find Justin before they left for church. She was curious about him returning to the river last night, and she also needed to tell him what Florine had said. The morning was cool—she wouldn't get all soiled and sweaty.

Allie walked across the back porch and glanced in the window to the dining room. No sign of Florine—just her half-eaten plate still sitting on the table. *For the hired help to take care of,* she recalled with annoyance.

Allie sighed and shook her head. "Florine, you're about as helpful as teats on a boar hog," she said as she turned and headed toward the river road.

Allie loved the morning time. Everything always seemed so fresh and clean. Sounds were clearer—the birds chirped up a storm. Her favorite was the mockingbird, and she could hear one as she walked along. She looked around for the little show-off, always singing from the highest point in the tree or on a roof. There he was—she saw him flutter up in the air and come back down to the same place and continue to sing. Allie figured mockingbirds try to get folks' attention that way—to get them to stop and listen to their beautiful repertoire of songs.

She came to the slope leading down to the swimming hole and made her way gingerly, hanging onto the saplings to keep her footing. No sign of Justin yet. She wondered why he had gone back to the river this morning.

She stood on the big rock for a moment, then decided to walk toward the path that led alongside the river upstream. She recalled the stories Justin said about his brother and him staying down there days at a time during the first year they were back. He said they had a hiding place further upstream. The path in that direction looked dark and overgrown, though, and Allie decided not to chance soiling her dress looking for Justin.

A thought occurred to her that maybe Jimmy could still be using their hiding place. Was that why Justin had come back here last night? The idea unnerved her. She decided she had better get back to the house, Justin or no Justin, and turned around and began to retrace her steps.

A twig snapped behind her, and she froze.

"Come to play?" a familiar voice asked.

Allie turned around. Jimmy stood there, looking as if he hadn't slept for some time.

"You aren't as quiet as your brother."

"I can be. But this time I *wanted* you to hear me."

Calm down, Allie, she thought to herself. "Have you seen Justin? He's supposed to be down here somewhere."

"He hasn't been down here this morning ... hasn't been down here since last night... with you."

"So it was *you* he saw."

"I don't know if he saw me, but he knew I was close by. My brother taught me well," Jimmy said as he smirked, but his blues eyes weren't smiling. They were blood-shot and anguished.

"I have to get back to the house—we'll be leaving for church soon," Allie said.

"That's the good Christian thing to do," Jimmy said sarcastically. "And I want to thank you for having me banned from my home."

"I didn't have you banned. That wasn't my decision. Why did you do what you did?"

He ignored the question. "Justin thinks you're special. I think you're probably just a whore, sneaking down here with my brother after dark."

"What have I done to you to offend you?" Allie asked, on the verge of tears. No one had ever talked like that to her face—maybe behind her back, but never to her face. She began to slowly step backwards.

"Are you going to cry now?" Jimmy said tauntingly as he stepped toward her.

"I've done nothing to you, Jimmy Taylor, and you know it," she said as she turned to run along the path.

She heard an expletive, and Jimmy's voice changed, "Stop, Allie! Don't run!" He came after her.

Allie made it to the stretch of rocks leading up to the swimming hole's big rock, but Jimmy caught up to her and tried to grab her arm.

"Be careful!" he cried.

"Leave me alone!" she demanded as she jerked away from him, losing her balance and falling.

Her forehead struck a protruding rock, and she felt something warm running down the side of her face as Jimmy turned her onto her back. The last thing Allie remembered was Jimmy's face coming toward her as those blue eyes faded into black.

* * *

Matthew Taylor, Justin, and John returned from town where they checked the damage at the mercantile. They found a side door that had been forced open. Someone had haphazardly ransacked the place, so it wasn't immediately obvious what was taken and what was simply strewn about. They began to help Marcus straighten up some areas, but he told them it could wait until after church, that it wouldn't take long to get the store ready to open again by morning. So they had returned to the house.

It was almost time to go to church, so the men went to the barn to hitch up the horses and bring the buggies around to the front of the house. Everyone gathered on the porch to load up.

"Anybody seen Allie this morning?" Justin asked.

Vestal stepped forward, dressed in her Sunday best, which included an enormous ribbon-festooned silk hat complete with feathers.

"Yes, she came down for breakfast, and I told her she had about an hour before we would be leaving. Did someone think to call her down?"

Faith said, "She wasn't upstairs. I just came from there."

"That's odd."

"Well, let's go look again," Justin said. "She has to be around here somewhere."

Justin walked back into the house. Florine followed him; her face looked paler than usual.

"Justin."

He kept walking.

"Justin!" She grabbed his arm.

"Not now, Florine."

"I think I know where she might have gone."

Justin turned to look at her.

Florine swallowed. "I said something at breakfast that might have *accidentally* led her to believe that you were down at the river."

"What!? Why would you say that?"

"I just wanted her to know that I saw you two last night."

"What business is that of yours?" He grabbed her shoulders. "What did you tell her?"

By this time, Uncle John and Justin's parents had walked back into the house.

"Justin? What are you doing?" Julia asked.

"What did you tell her, Florine!?"

"I'm sorry! I didn't think she would act on it—I just told her that you'd gone down to the river again."

Justin pushed her away and ran down the stairs to the back of the house.

"I'm going, too," Faith said.

Uncle John said, "Come on, Matthew," and they followed Justin and Faith.

Justin tried to keep his fear at bay, but something was wrong. He could clearly see the recent imprints of Allie's small shoes here and there along the road, so what Florine said was true. But Allie would not have needlessly worried everyone by tarrying down at the river. He came atop the rise leading down to the swimming hole and ran, half-sliding down the embankment. He stood on top of the big rock, shouting Allie's name. He walked down along the riverbank to the right side of the big rock, but saw no sign of her footsteps.

By this time, Faith, Matthew, and Uncle John came up over the rise and began to work their way down the embankment. Justin climbed back on the big rock and walked along the rocks at the edge of the river. His heart stopped when he saw the blood. He looked all around and saw no footprints leading away from the area, but he saw the signs of something that slid into the river.

Back at the house, the rest of the group stood on the back porch waiting for word. The hair stood on the backs of their necks when they heard what sounded like the cry of a wounded animal from the direction of the river.

"Oh, dear God... Justin!" Julia said as she began to run across the backyard toward the river road. She yelled back to the group. "Somebody go fetch Matt and Marcus!"

By the time Julia made it down to the river, Matthew and Uncle John were physically restraining Justin on the other side of the river. They had all been in the water. Faith sat on the big rock, crying. Several boots and socks were strewn about her.

"Faith! What happened?"

Faith just pointed to the blood on the rocks down below.

Julia paled. "So they think it's Allie?"

Faith nodded, sobbing.

Julia knelt down and held her. "Where is she? Have they found her?"

Faith shook her head, no.

"Then let's go look downriver," Julia said. "If she's fallen in, maybe she's pulled herself out down further."

Faith nodded, and they both stood up and began walking along the bank downriver. Julia looked at Matthew across the river and pointed toward the direction they were going to search. Matthew nodded and talked to Justin and John. Justin sat down and quickly emptied his boots of water and wrung out his socks, while Matthew started back across the river to retrieve his and John's boots and socks. John squatted beside Justin with his hand on his shoulder talking to him as Justin determinedly put his socks and boots back on. He stood up and began walking downriver to search on that side of the river, not waiting for his father and uncle to accompany him.

After about thirty minutes of searching downstream, Julia saw something white snagged on a fallen tree at the river's bend. She started to wade out into the river, but Faith stopped her and called out to the men on the opposite side. Since Justin was on the shallow side of the river, he shed his boots and was able to wade most of the way across to retrieve what appeared to be a piece of cloth.

He untangled it and shouted so both sides could hear, "It's just a man's handkerchief!"

He brought it back to his father and uncle. This time Uncle John went to his knees, recognizing the kerchief that he had given Allie during the Taylors' ceremony the day before.

No one said it aloud or wanted to admit it, but it was evident that Allie was in the river, and there was a good possibility she wasn't alive at this point or they would have found her along the bank somewhere. Most of the river was shallow enough to wade across—waist-deep at most, although there were a few places like the swimming hole that were fairly deep. For the most part, though, a person who was *able* to get out of the river... could.

The search continued throughout the day. Someone back at the house had gone to the church to find Marcus and Matt, and a number of people came to the Taylor place to find out what was wrong and offered to help. When the news came back that Allie might have drowned, Florine became hysterical and was put to bed.

The women packed food and water and had riders take it to the search parties throughout the day. At mid-afternoon Matthew put an exhausted Julia on horseback and sent her and Faith home. With the additional help, the rest of the searchers covered a good eight miles that day, hacking through and blazing trails through the underbrush along some areas of the river in order to search thoroughly. Justin stayed in the river much of the way, wading from one side to the other where he could.

Matthew halted the search at sunset and gathered everyone at the Simm's place where several wagons and buggies from the Taylors' and other neighbors met to pick everyone up.

Earlier in the evening Julia had told the Lockes that it might be best if they took Florine back to Waco. She assured them that they were not placing blame on anyone—that it just looked like a tragic accident, and that she would contact them by mail carrier of any news of Allie. What

Julia didn't say, though, was that she honestly did not know how Justin would react around Florine.

The men were beyond tired when they pulled up to the barn after dark. The Taylor women heard the buggies and horses coming up the drive, and lit lanterns to take out to the barn to meet them and to see if there was any news. The silence and the haggard look on everyone's faces gave them their answer: no sign of Allie. Catherine and Jenny embraced their husbands, and Julia squeezed Matthew's hand before comforting her brother, who broke down in her arms. Allie was the closest thing he had to a daughter, and Julia knew the pain he was experiencing. She had lost two children herself for six years, not knowing if she would ever see them again.

Justin wouldn't stop to acknowledge anyone—he busied himself unhitching the horses and taking them to their pens. Faith followed him and tried to comfort him, but he brushed her away. She wasn't offended; she understood. Accepting comfort meant accepting loss, and he refused to face that. Faith walked over to gather hay and began to put it in each stall for the horses.

They all watched, too tired to speak, too tired to think about the next step.

Julia spoke first. "Catherine, Jenny, take everyone up to the house and feed them. I'll stay out here a little while."

Julia walked over and helped Faith finish putting out hay as Justin began picking up all the tack to hang on the wall of the barn.

"Thank you for helping, sweetheart," she said to Faith, and as she hugged her, she whispered, "I'll take care of Justin. He's going to be all right. We're all going to be all right. It's just going to take some time."

Faith nodded sadly as she watched her brother for a moment before leaving the barn. Julia found a place to sit... and wait. Her heart broke to see her son trying to come to grips with what had happened that day.

Justin knew his mother was there, but he wasn't ready. He grabbed a pitchfork and started gathering up the strewn hay into a more compact pile. Then he grabbed a bucket and went to the pump to begin filling several troughs with water. Julia lost count of the trips he made to the pump and back, hauling more water than the horses actually needed until he could hardly put one foot in front of the other. He had started back to the pump with an empty bucket when he just stopped, dropped the pail, and stood there.

"Momma?" he said in a quiet anguish.

Julia flew to her son and held him tight as he began to weep.

"She was the one, Momma," he sobbed.

"I know, son... I know."

Chapter 7

*A*llie tried to open her eyes. The dull throbbing in her head didn't help, nor did the gnawing pain in her hip and back from staying in one position too long. Her eyes felt swollen, like she'd been crying, but she didn't remember crying. What was going on? Where was she?

She tried to sit up, but couldn't find her hands. She finally realized they were tied behind her back. She clumsily rolled onto her back and sat up, which immediately made her almost retch. She put her head down on her knees and took some deep breaths to try to stop the waves of nausea. They subsided after a while.

Allie saw that she had been lying on a blanket. She was tethered to a tree in the midst of a stand of trees, but had no idea where they stood in relation to the Taylor house. It alarmed her to see blood on her blouse, which made her try harder to remember what had happened. What time was it? She looked at the sun through the trees. It wasn't straight up like around noon, and since she hadn't a clue which way was north or south, she couldn't tell if the sun was on the coming up side or the going down side of day.

She remembered breakfast... and Florine. And the river... and why did she go down to the river? She thought for a moment, trying to clear the fog. Justin!! To find Justin. But where was he?

Allie heard horses coming closer. And why was she afraid all of a sudden?

"Justin?" she called out.

The horses came into view, and then she remembered.

He was leading a saddled horse.

"You! What do you think you are doing?" she said angrily.

"Buying some time," he said as he quickly dismounted and walked toward her. She flinched when he reached for her.

"I won't hurt you," he said, untying her hands, "unless you give me reason to," he lied, thinking the threat would insure good behavior on her part.

"It looks like you already *have* hurt me."

"You fell," he said as he pulled her up to stand on unsteady feet on the blanket, "and I didn't deflower you, if that's what you're thinking."

She could smell the whiskey on his breath. "The thought never entered my head," Allie said truthfully, especially since she wasn't even sure what de-flowering involved. She shut her eyes when everything started spinning, and put her hand over her mouth when another wave of nausea hit. He picked her up and carried her to one of the horses and helped her mount. She took several deep breaths before speaking.

"Why did you think you had to tie me up like a dog?"

"You would've wandered off and got yourself lost," he said as he walked back over to the tree to retrieve the blanket. He quickly rolled it up and brought it back to tie onto the back of Allie's saddle.

"Where are we? Are you going to take me back now?"

"Look. You got me banned from my home; I figure our last little encounter will probably land me in jail or get me killed by my brother or Uncle John. I don't think they'd be too understanding seeing their precious *Allie* with a gash on her head."

"I'll talk to them—they'll understand."

"No, they won't understand. I've given them too many reasons not to," he said as he mounted his own horse. "And don't even think about making a run for it—I can outride you."

Jimmy turned his horse to leave the area.

Allie said under her breath, "Don't flatter yourself—*anybody* can outride me."

"What!?" He looked back to see Allie just sitting there. "Let's go!" he said impatiently.

"Is this a nice horse?" Allie asked.

"What does that have to do with anything!?" Jimmy said irritably.

"I'm not very good on a horse."

Jimmy threw his head back and made an audible growl as he rode back, grabbed her reins and led them away from the area.

"I really wish you wouldn't do this," she tried once more.

"Shut up, Allie."

After riding for several hours, Jimmy stopped alongside a shady creek to give the horses water and a short rest. He knew Allie was having a rough time of it, too, by the look on her face. They started traveling in a northwesterly direction, but eventually turned southwest, avoiding roads and any homesteads where they might be seen. Jimmy figured when he had put enough distance between him and Grace, Texas, he would find a town and put Allie on the next stagecoach heading back toward Waco.

He had done some stupid things in his life, but this was by far the worst. He was staying on the river and coming off a three-day drunk when he saw Allie down there alone. He could hardly remember barging in on the family dinner the first night Allie and Justin were there, and he didn't know why he felt compelled to terrorize Allie. Maybe because she was Justin's—he knew he could get to Justin through her. But he had crossed a line back at the bathhouse and the church, and now this—Justin would kill him if he got a hold of him, brother or not. He could never go back. Maybe he was looking for a way to sever all ties. Well, he'd done one hell of a job of it.

Jimmy handed Allie a leather-covered flask of water and she drank thirstily. He dug around in his saddlebag and pulled out some dried apple slices and hardtack to give to Allie. Only then did he drink, and walked over to the creek to refill the flask.

"Did you get this from the mercantile?" she asked while his back was to her.

Jimmy said nothing at first, then he stood and turned around. "My family's very generous," he said as he looked at her with those blue eyes—Justin's eyes.

"Justin will come for me... you know that."

"Yep. But not for a while."

"He's probably on our trail right now," Allie said confidently.

"He's working another trail I left him."

"He's looking in another direction?"

"Yeah, but he'll eventually figure it out, and by then I'll be long gone. You might want to walk around a bit before we saddle up—it's going to be a long ride."

Allie walked over to the creek and knelt down to wash her face and neck and arms. Her skin already felt sunburned and tender. She took Jimmy's advice and walked around for a little while, feeling stiff from the ride. She came back to the horses, and Jimmy walked over her tracks. Then he came back, helped her mount and handed her the reins.

"It's about time you learn."

She took a deep breath. *Oh, mercy. This is going to be a very long day.*

Allie didn't fall off her horse once that day, even during the times Jimmy loped the horses. The only talking they did during the ride was when Jimmy pointed out what she did wrong, or gave her instructions like "to loosen up on the reins," or "to give the horse its head." He told her that the horse could be directed not only with the movement of the reins, but also by the pressure of one's legs in guiding it. Allie had learned a lot about riding that day—the hard way, and her fear of the horse had evaporated hours before. She realized, too, that her fear of Jimmy was quickly evaporating. He wasn't friendly, but he wasn't threatening, either.

Earlier she had questioned God—why did He allow her to be in this predicament? She certainly didn't ask for it. She recalled her conversation with Faith the night before, talking about God doing *whatever it takes* for Jimmy to turn around. A dreadful thought occurred to her.

Oh, Lord, surely I'm not your 'whatever it takes,' am I? I can't do this! I don't even know Jimmy, much less know how to help him! You're going to have to find someone else to try to turn him around. He hates me—he won't listen to me.

And she immediately put that train of thought behind her.

But almost as quickly, the story of Jonah and the whale came to mind. She smugly decided she would just stay away from large bodies of water. But then it occurred to her that she was traveling with her Ninevah.

Oh, mercy.

At the end of the day, Jimmy followed along a river until he found a cove that would shield their camp from any potential passers-by. Allie's face was blistered, her lips were chapped, and her hair had long since loosed itself from the braid. She would not have recognized herself if she looked in a mirror. And she was so stiff and sore from bouncing around the saddle, she could hardly get off the horse. Allie crumpled in an exhausted heap—too tired to even get the blanket off the back of her saddle to spread on the ground.

By the time Jimmy had led the horses to water and back, Allie was asleep where she lay. Her forehead had a nasty bruise, and the gash looked red and irritated. Earlier he had cleaned the blood off her face the best he could after he carried her away from the river—away from earshot of the Taylor house. He had tied her to the tree in case she came to and wandered off. He didn't know how serious the wound was, but when he rode over to Matt and Catherine's place to *borrow* Catherine's saddle, he broke off several pieces of aloe vera growing behind the house.

After their rescue from the Apaches years before, Julia had brought along an aloe vera plant for medicinal purposes. As it grew and multiplied, she would break off and start new plants until she had given almost everyone in town one and told them how to use it.

Jimmy caught a horse for Allie from the Taylor remuda, which numbered several dozen in the open fields between his parents' and Matt's homes. He figured they wouldn't miss it for a while, nor would they miss the saddle, as Catherine rarely rode horseback since the children came.

He unsaddled the horses, hobbled them for the night so they wouldn't wander off, and dug around his saddlebag until he found one of the aloe vera leaves he had brought. He walked over to Allie and knelt down, took his knife and peeled back part of the skin. A pale green gel oozed, and Jimmy smeared it across the cut. Allie squinted her eyes and whimpered a bit, but even the wound's tenderness wasn't enough to waken her. In the fading light he could see her blistered face, and smeared some gel across her nose, cheeks and forehead. Then he retrieved her blanket, spread it out beside her, and gently rolled her over on it.

Only then did he take care of his own needs.

"What have I gotten myself into?" he said to himself as he rolled out his blanket. "I'm a dead man."

* * *

Monday morning breakfast at the Taylor house was somber. Marcus and Matt had arrived just after sunrise, and every face looked tired and strained as another long day loomed ahead of them. Matthew and John tried to determine the next plan of action and areas to search the river.

"I just can't understand why she would go down to the river by herself," John said to the group. "She's smarter than that."

"She thought I was down there," Justin spoke up, the first words he had said that morning.

"But you were at the store—didn't she know that?"

"Florine told her I was down at the river," Justin explained.

"Now why would she tell Allie that?" John asked angrily.

"Allie and I had walked down there the night before—just to talk," he quickly added when he saw Uncle John's forehead crease. "Florine had seen us and tried to make a bigger deal out of it than it was."

"And I told her she had an hour before we'd be loading up to go to church," Vestal shook her head. "If I just hadn't told her the time..."

"Vestal, that had nothing to do with it," Julia said.

"Yeah, Vestal, it was *Florine's* doing. Where is she, by the way? I'd like to talk to her," Justin said angrily.

"I sent them home yesterday," Julia said, "and let's not dwell on who's to blame right now, please. Let's just work on what we need to do now."

Marcus spoke up. "Well, to be honest, when we heard there was a problem out here with Allie, my first thought was that Jimmy must be in the big middle of it."

"Marcus—" Matt said, "we promised Catherine."

"Well, the reason we promised isn't here anymore, so I think it's all right to say something," said Marcus.

"Say what?" Justin asked. "What about Jimmy?"

"We had to tell him to leave and not come back," Matt said, "or at least until he's straightened up his sorry life."

"Why? Why would you tell your brother that?" Julia asked.

"He's been acting like a heathen, and he's just getting worse, Mother. He kept calling himself *'Indeh.'* He doesn't even want to be associated with us."

A cry of anguish came from Julia.

"What did he do, Marcus?!" Justin asked again, his voice on edge. "Tell me!"

"I'm not sure how to word it without being crude in front of you ladies here, so let me say... he took some liberties when Allie was in the bathhouse the other night—the first night she was here," Marcus said.

"What do you mean?" Justin asked. "Did he touch her?"

"No, that didn't happen until the next morning at the church," Matt added.

"Damn it, Matt—this was going on and you didn't tell me?" Justin said angrily.

"Watch your language, son," Matthew said to Justin before turning to his eldest. "What are you talking about, Matt?"

"Allie made Catherine promise, and eventually us, too, not to tell you or Mom or Justin—she didn't want to put a damper on the ceremony and anniversary party."

"I knew something was wrong, but I just couldn't figure it out," Justin said. "I know he was down at the river night before last, too."

"Did you see him?"

Justin nodded. "I went back to confront him, but by then he was gone. It worried me that he saw Allie and me together, I guess because of the way he acted toward us at dinner the other night."

"He wasn't supposed to be anywhere near here," Marcus said.

Julia spoke up again. "I think this conversation is heading in the wrong direction. You all are beginning to sound like you think Jimmy may have had something to do with Allie's accident." Her voice broke as she said, "He's made some mistakes, and his behavior is shameful at times, but Jimmy would never, ever hurt Allie."

"I don't know, Mother," Matt said. "He's been getting worse and worse."

"And if he's capable of violating a young lady's privacy that way and making advances toward her, what's keeping him from going a step further?" Marcus said.

"It's the drinking!" Faith said loudly.

Everyone stopped and looked at her, surprised to hear her speak up. Normally, no one heard a word out of her.

"It changes him," she said more quietly, but sure of her defense of her brother. "Jimmy wouldn't hurt Allie that way."

"Drinking or not, Jimmy's become a threat in more ways than one. I wouldn't be surprised to find out it was he who broke into my store. I think it's worth making the attempt to find him and get to the bottom of this," said Marcus.

"We can't do anything until we find Allie," John said.

No one spoke for a moment.

"What if we don't find her, John? What if the river never gives her up?" Matthew said, verbalizing something everyone in the room had thought about at one time or other during the exhausting search the day before.

"I don't know. I just know that I can't go back to Dalton without her."

Justin pushed away from the table, and headed toward the stairs.

"Hold on, Justin," Matthew said. "Where do you think you're going?"

"To find Jimmy. He may know more about this than we think."

"Wait—some of us can go with you," Matt said.

"I think I'd have a better chance of finding him by myself," Justin said. "He'd disappear for sure if he thinks we've rounded up a posse to come after him."

Justin took the stairs two at a time. After a few minutes, he came back down—this time with his gun belt on. He went to the back of the pantry to get a box of cartridges. He grabbed his hat and walked out the kitchen door, avoiding everyone in the dining room.

"Father, he doesn't need to go by himself—no telling what he'll do to Jimmy when he finds him," Faith pleaded.

"Let him go," Julia said. "He knows what he's doing." But in her heart she wasn't so sure. She went to the kitchen and gathered up some biscuits and ham and tied them in a dishtowel. She took an empty canteen and slipped out the kitchen door.

Dear God, she prayed silently, *please protect my boys. Please don't let them harm each other. Please let them be reconciled to each other. I don't want to lose either one of them.*

She stopped at the pump and filled the canteen. Justin was saddling a horse by the time Julia walked in the barn.

"It may take longer than you think to find him," Julia said as she handed him the food and water.

"Yeah, I know."

Justin opened his saddlebag and stuffed the food in it and then strapped down the canteen before stepping up into the saddle.

"Thanks, Mother."

She grabbed his hand and squeezed it, "Please be careful. Please keep a cool head with your brother."

He couldn't agree to that. He honestly didn't know what he was going to do when he found Jimmy, so he just said, "I'll be back as soon as I can."

He rode out of the barn thinking about what Jimmy had put Allie through the last couple of days. It began to burn hot inside his gut. Finding his brother gave Justin a purpose, a direction—he couldn't stand the thought of going back on that river to look for her body. He didn't want to see Allie that way—he wanted to remember her alive—smiling, teasing, talking with her... kissing her. The thought of her being gone hit him in the stomach again, almost doubling him over.

He rode down the river road, but instead of stopping and walking down the usual path to the swimming hole, he turned the horse north to follow along the smaller, spring-fed stream. He figured Jimmy had been staying at their old hiding place and wanted to check there first. He rode the horse as far as to the head of the springs, dismounted, and walked down through the trees to the campsite.

Their hiding place. He didn't know why they called it that when everybody in the family knew where it was. But they always kept their distance. His mother told everyone to leave them be—it was his and Jimmy's place—a place where they could feel normal and safe. They used it heavily the first year they were back, and then off and on for a couple more years during the breaks from boarding school.

Old memories flooded in as Justin stepped into the familiar place. The trees around the spring were so thick they made a natural canopy over the area, muting the light in green-gray tones. The sunlight had to work hard to find its way in here. The gurgling spring offered a peaceful backdrop of sound. He understood why Jimmy kept coming here—it rested the soul.

When Justin's eyes became accustomed to the shadows, he could see out-of-place items scattered about: empty whiskey bottles and mason jars, a torn shirt, an old, beat-up pan on a cold campfire, a dirty blanket, the remains of a newspaper, some crumpled pages from a book... all of which marred the beauty of the natural sanctuary.

He picked up one of the book pages and smoothed it out—it showed illustrations of different breeds of horses. Jimmy loved horses—he used to say he would raise them some day. Justin knew no one who could ride better than Jimmy—including himself.

He had been here recently.

Justin walked back to his horse and led him around the springs to get to a clearing. The river curved around to meet the flow from the springs at the swimming hole, which made the clearing surrounded by water on three sides. Years before, he and Jimmy made a makeshift pen by piling and weaving brush between the trees to create a fence on the fourth side, using a rope across the only remaining opening. They used to leave their horses in this area, which had an abundance of grass and water. They didn't have to worry about the horses crossing the river due to the difficulty of maneuvering down the rocky terrain to the river and the far side. The horses preferred the grassy area. Justin smiled, remembering the good times they had down here—away from everyone.

But most of the fence had fallen down now, and the pleasant memories faded away as thoughts of recent events shoved them out of his mind.

What happened to you, Jimmy? Why can't you forget the past and get on with your future? Why are you hell-bent on destroying yourself?

Justin found some recent tracks. He mounted his horse and started following them. After about thirty minutes or so, he came across something odd. He saw that the tracks came back upon themselves from the opposite direction and veered off to his left, but then he came across another set of tracks—two horses this time heading back in the original direction.

What was Jimmy doing? Was somebody with him? No, one of the sets of tracks wasn't as deep as the other's—it had to have been without a rider.

Justin followed the tracks a little ways where they came to a stop in a stand of trees. He could see Jimmy's footprints all over the area—even leading to a tree that must have had something sitting on the ground beneath it, as a number of plants' stems were broken. It hadn't been too recent, though, because most of the grass stood upright now. Enough of the blades had been damaged, though, for Justin to see that something substantial had been on that spot. The two sets of tracks took off a different direction away from the area—northwest, but the second set was deeper this time. The second horse carried something, and Justin figured that whatever it was had been under that tree.

What are you up to, little brother?

* * *

"Wake up," the voice said in the dark.

Allie couldn't. She tried to shake her head.

"Allie!" the voice called her by name this time. "Get up—we can't stay here."

"Leave me here," she heard her voice croak, still not able to open her eyes. No, wait, her eyes were open. It was dark.

"It's still dark," she said wearily.

"Come on—go splash water on your face."

Jimmy. It was still Jimmy.

"Will you let me go home today if I do?" she bargained sleepily, trying to move her achy limbs.

"No."

"Then I won't splash water on my face," she said, as if she just showed him a thing or two.

If she could have seen Jimmy's face, she would have seen a slight smile break his otherwise stoic features.

She tried to get on all fours. "I don't think I can ride today. I don't think I can do anything today. Everything hurts."

Jimmy came up behind her and lifted her to a standing position.

"It'll get better the more you move around."

"Something will surely fall off if I move," she groaned.

"You have five minutes while I saddle the horses, so do what you need to do."

Allie limped away for a few minutes, then came back to stand beside her horse. She couldn't even think about lifting her leg to step into the stirrup.

"That's my horse, Allie."

"A horse is a horse. In the dark they all look the same."

"And you always mount a horse from the other side."

"I know that." She walked around to the other horse—her horse this time, and on the correct side, but she still just stood there, leaning her head against the side of the saddle. Jimmy walked up behind her.

"All right, bronc buster, up and over." Jimmy lifted her foot up to the stirrup and pushed her up on the saddle.

Allie made a noise that sounded like a muffled coyote.

"Stay close," he said, "we'll take it slow until we can see better."

A faint pink was beginning to show in the eastern sky. Jimmy knew Allie was hurting, but he didn't have a choice. He decided he would take the first road he crossed and head to the nearest town. Most towns had a stage stop, but unless a small town happened to sit on a main line, it may not see a stage coming through but once a week, if that much. He could drop her off there and keep going. She would get home eventually.

If somebody was already looking for him, and that would most likely be Justin, he figured he had a day ahead of him. He hoped Justin would turn around and go home when he got Allie back. She was slowing him down, but as a greenhorn, he had to acknowledge her for trying. He noticed she was bound and determined to stay on that horse yesterday.

Jimmy stopped again at mid-morning to give the horses a break and for Allie to stretch her legs. This time she immediately headed to the creek—she felt so sticky and dirty. She leaned down to the water to dip her hands in it.

A scream pierced the air.

Chapter 8

J immy kept the horses from bolting before he pulled his pistol and ran over to Allie sitting by the creek with her hands on her face.

"What?! What is it?" he yelled.

"My face!" she cried. "It's rotting off!"

"Damn it, Allie! I thought you'd gotten on a water moccasin!" Jimmy said, visibly relieved.

"But what's wrong with my face?"

"It's just something I put on your cut and your sunburn last night. It'll help it heal faster."

She leaned over to look in the water again and frowned. "It's supposed to help?"

"Yeah."

"Why are you trying to help me now? I thought you hated me."

"I don't hate you, Allie," Jimmy said, as he stood up, uncomfortable with the conversation. "We need to get going. You might as well leave the ointment on your face until this evening. It'll help keep it from burning more."

Allie knew she looked ridiculous with her painted face, but she *had* noticed the pain had subsided since yesterday. Who was she trying to impress anyway? Certainly not Jimmy. She stood up and walked over to her horse and tried to get on it by herself, but still couldn't lift her sore leg high enough to get her foot in the stirrup.

Jimmy came over and lifted her up again.

"I'm sorry I'm not better at this." *What is wrong with me? Why am I apologizing to my captor?* she chastised herself silently.

95

"You'll be able to do it before long. Here, wear my hat—it'll help protect your face."

There he was being nice to her again. Not sure about what to say next, Allie said, "Justin told me he'd teach me about horses and riding, but it looks like you're beating him to it."

"Just one more reason for him to beat the hell out of me," Jimmy said as he effortlessly mounted his horse. "Let's go."

Allie found herself watching Jimmy as they rode along. He seemed to be the antithesis of Justin with his black hair, brooding looks, angry disposition, no direction in his life, and broken relationships. They had two things in common, though—they had the same mother, and they both had her beautiful blue eyes.

All those years of praying for Justin seemed to have paid off—he came through the long ordeal of captivity intact, even stronger for it. Allie's church didn't even know about Julia's other son to pray for him. She wasn't even sure the church would pray for a half-breed; no—that wasn't entirely right. There were some wonderful, caring Christians in her church that would have. But there were others, too, that would be concerned and caring only if the problem remained far off. It would be a different story if the problem was right in their midst. She decided right then if she did nothing else during this ordeal, she could at least pray for Jimmy—that God would soften his heart and heal the hurts in his life.

Allie also wondered what Jimmy's father had been like. When they stopped again in the middle of the day to rest and eat—this time soda crackers and jerky, Allie chanced asking Jimmy about his early life.

"What was your father's name?" Allie asked.

Jimmy scowled at her. "Why do you want to know?"

"He obviously meant a great deal to you."

That caught him off guard, and he didn't speak for a while. Since Jimmy had come to live in Matthew Taylor's home and community, he couldn't remember anyone asking about his birth father by name—it had become just another unmentionable word. He couldn't remember the last time he had spoken his father's name aloud.

"Nantan Lupan."

He looked at Allie then. "Or *Grey Wolf*, in your words. Justin said one of those names also meant *spokesman*."

"What was he like?"

Jimmy was quiet for a moment, thinking. "Justin told me he was a strong man... that he was respected by the other members of our group and other bands of Apaches. They looked to him as their leader when they needed one."

"Do you remember him?" Allie pressed further.

"The only memory I have of him when he was alive is riding behind him on his horse. I can't see his face, but Justin once told me that I looked like him."

"Did your father teach you to ride a horse?"

"He was just beginning to before he was killed," Jimmy said bitterly. "But he had taught Justin how to ride and hunt and fight, and Justin ended up teaching me later. He told me that my father was gone much of the time, though—running raids, stealing horses. Julia was glad he was gone so much."

Allie noticed his reference to his mother by her first name. "Why did Nantan Lupan take Julia and Justin?"

"Why do you care?" he asked, agitated.

"I just want to understand why he felt he had to take them, when he had to have known that they belonged to another man." Allie said, knowing she was treading dangerous waters here.

"I don't know why—I guess any white man or woman was his enemy," Jimmy said, irritably. He honestly hadn't given that much thought. He tended to focus his anger on the fact that he saw his father killed.

"Did your mother ever try to escape?"

"Once, not long after she was taken, but she never tried again after that."

"Why?"

"It happened before I was born, but Justin told me that my father tracked her and Justin down," he said, and then paused. "He crushed her weaker hand with the butt of his rifle to punish her. And he told her that he would kill Justin if she ever tried to run away again. I don't think Julia was afraid of dying, but she would never risk losing Justin."

"Or you or Faith."

"How do you know *that*?"

"She wouldn't come back home without you."

Jimmy just looked at her.

"Think about it, Jimmy. Matthew could've refused to let you and Faith come back with Julia and Justin, but he didn't."

"He was responsible for killing my father."

"Your father *stole* Matthew's wife and son! Wasn't that just cause to fight for his family? What would you have done in Matthew's place? Given up searching for her?"

Jimmy turned abruptly toward his horse. "We need to go."

A realization occurred to her. "The sins of the father..." Allie said to herself.

"What?" He turned around to face her.

"Jimmy," Allie said gently, "don't you realize that you've done the same thing your father did?"

He walked over and grabbed her arm, and jerked her toward the horses. "This is different—I'm not looking for a wife," Jimmy said, his voice low and threatening. "No more talk—just get on your horse."

Allie had said too much. And for the first time, she did get on her horse by herself.

* * *

Jimmy's trail had been easy for Justin to follow, but he wondered why his brother wasn't taking established paths and roads, which would have made travel much easier for him and his horses. Not too far from leaving the stand of trees, Jimmy had turned the horses sharply to the southwest.

Where are you going, Jimmy? And what are you hiding?

Justin wondered why things weren't more simple and peaceful in their lives. Their time with the Apaches wasn't easy, but it was what they knew—they didn't know any other way. Well, that wasn't entirely true. His mother had made it a point to keep telling Justin about his *real* father and brother and sister, and their life in the white man's world. For a while after their capture by Nantan Lupan, Justin could remember his family, but after some years passed, his memories became only what his mother kept telling him. He couldn't remember his father's face, nor his older brother's or sister's faces. He couldn't remember their home. What his mother told him began to be just stories—not what he really knew anymore.

After returning home, Justin had heard several stories of young boys that had been captured by the Indians for lesser amounts of time than he had been in captivity. After they were rescued and returned to their former lives, they found they couldn't adjust and ran away, back to their lives with the Indians. He felt he understood why they did that—he had adapted to life as an Apache, too. But at the same time, he knew there was another world for him because he had something they didn't have—a mother's faith and her continuous prayers and reminders of his true life and family waiting for his return.

Justin knew his appearance masked the fact that he was actually more Apache on the inside than his brother, and his looks gave him a greater advantage in readjusting to the white man's world. Since the rescue, Jimmy had lived much longer in the white man's world than his short time as an Apache child, but his outward appearance branded him an outcast in most places, and he never completely assimilated into the culture.

Justin rode until the middle of the day and passed a grassy area where Jimmy had obviously spent the night. He noticed no signs of a campfire for coffee, which told him his brother was in a hurry. He spurred his horse onward, not bothering to take a closer look.

Some time later, though, Justin pulled up close to a creek where Jimmy had stopped to water the horses. He looked at the horse tracks and noticed something had spooked them at one point—the prints were deeper and all over each other. He climbed off his horse and squatted down to take a better look.

That's when he saw them.

His breath literally caught in his throat when he saw the small footprints amidst Jimmy's and the horses' tracks.

"Allie?!" he said aloud as the blood drained from his face. *Could it be?* But there was no mistaking her small footprints. He followed them to the edge of the creek and let out a whoop!

She's alive!! Justin threw his head back as he shut his eyes and let the thought sink in. But the shock that had turned into relief and joy was quickly replaced by anger.

"What have you done, Jimmy!!" he screamed with a pent-up rage that had been slowly simmering just beneath the surface of his thoughts.

Something primitive emerged in his expression. "You are no longer my brother, of the *Indeh*—you are now *apache*—my enemy."

He calmly let his horse drink for a moment, then mounted his horse and set his face like flint toward the southwest.

* * *

Allie, you've done it again—you don't know when to quit with that mouth of yours, she thought as she and Jimmy rode along for hours in a palpable silence. And even after that, she had determined she would speak only when spoken to.

That decision lasted about twenty minutes.

Jimmy and Allie had been riding hard off and on since their last stop, not even stopping to eat a piece of jerky along the way. Allie was exhausted, and wondered why he was in such a greater hurry than before. She called out to him.

"Can we stop for a little bit, Jimmy?"

"No." He slowed down for her to ride up beside him.

"Why not?"

"It's dangerous."

"Dangerous from what? The only danger I see around here is you," Allie snapped back without thinking, and then regretted it immediately. "I didn't mean that," she said, hoping he wouldn't get angry again.

Jimmy actually grinned. "Yes, you did."

Allie couldn't believe the change in his expression when he smiled. "My goodness, Jimmy. You ought to do that more often."

The mask went back on as he said, "I've seen Indian sign—and it shouldn't be in this area."

"Well, then let's go back," Allie said, her eyes wide with concern. "Or let *me* go back, and you can just go on."

"You couldn't find your way to the backside of your own horse."

"I'm looking at the backside of a horse right now," Allie said, glaring at Jimmy.

He actually laughed at that one. Allie wasn't amused, though.

They rode along in silence for a few minutes.

"Jimmy, how long is this going to continue?" Allie said more softly, close to tears. "I don't think I can do this much longer."

Something in her voice made him pull up. "You'll be going home soon enough," he said to her, and she believed him. "There's a place about an hour's ride ahead of us—we need to get there before dark. Can you hold on until then?"

Allie nodded wearily, grateful for his question of concern, although she was sure he wouldn't stop if she said she couldn't make it until then. *Home? Did he say home?*

"It looks like we're going to get a storm, too, so we need to push it."

"Rain? But I don't see any clouds."

"Look back over your right shoulder—they're coming from the northwest."

Looking back, Allie could see a dark line of clouds on the horizon. *Oh, mercy. That's all we need now.*

* * *

Justin had been increasingly gaining on his brother—he figured Allie slowed him down. Justin rode steadily, but he was careful not to push his horse past the point of no return. He would be of no help to Allie at all if he killed his horse in pursuit of her. He would find them soon, he was sure.

It ate him up inside thinking about what she must be going through. She was no spoiled, pampered Florine, but Allie wasn't used to riding all day long—hell, she wasn't used to riding at all, much less being exposed to the elements.

The anger in his gut kept churning.

Justin had stopped questioning why Jimmy had done this. Now it was down to a matter of getting Allie back, and making Jimmy pay for what he had done. He didn't exactly know what that meant—he wouldn't let himself think any further than that.

It was hot—too hot. Justin pulled up on a rise and looked around, giving his horse a breather. He figured he would be able to reach them by tonight, or mid-morning at the latest. The doubts came, though, when he saw the clouds on the horizon. Up to this point, he could have followed the trail blindfolded—Jimmy had made no efforts to conceal it, but if the rain was heavy enough to wash away the tracks, it could take days to pick up a new trail. He spurred his horse forward.

* * *

Jimmy and Allie came atop a small hill that looked down onto a cluster of houses and outbuildings. They could hear thunder in the distance, and felt the wind shift.

"What is this place?" Allie asked.

"It's the Schaferling Ranch—Josef and Anna Schaferling."

"How do you know about these people?"

"They're a German family I used to break horses for from time to time. They'll let us stay."

"You're trusting me to not say anything about what you did?"

"You can tell them what you want," Jimmy said. "They know a different side of me than my family's seen. I won't be staying long, but this is as far as you'll go. I figure Justin's hot on our trail by now."

Allie looked behind her. "How do you know that?"

"I know my brother," Jimmy continued. "He's smart, and he reads sign better than anyone. We've blazed a big trail for him to follow. The rain may slow him down a bit, but he'll still find you eventually."

They started the horses down the hill and rode past the barn to pull up in front of the big house.

"Something's not right—it's too quiet," he said. "This is a large family—several generations, and there are always people about."

Jimmy hollered a hello. The window shutters were closed; the place looked deserted. The wind was picking up.

Allie looked around. "I don't see any livestock."

"No one's here," Jimmy said as he dismounted and handed her the reins. "Stay here while I go check the house."

Allie watched as Jimmy knocked, and then stepped through the door. After a few minutes listening to the thunder rumble, she decided to get off the horse. Her grandfather had been killed by lightning strike riding a horse. She tied the reins to a hitching post, and watched the open door for Jimmy's return. She jumped when he came walking from around the side of the house.

"They're not here, but it looks like everything's in order. Maybe they'll be back soon."

A bolt of lightning split the sky as a loud clap of thunder followed.

"I'll put the horses in the barn, and you wait in the house," Jimmy said as he took the reins.

Allie took off Jimmy's hat as she stepped through the door and looked around the big room. It was homey and very clean. She walked across to open the back door and saw several small outbuildings, one of which looked like a summer kitchen where meals were cooked on hot days. She left the door open to create a cross breeze in the room. She noticed the temperature had cooled because of the storm, but it felt good after a long, hot day of riding.

The room had a large fireplace and a long table with a bench on one side that seated ten or twelve easily. Allie could see where some items had been taken off the wall, leaving paler outlines of something—pictures, perhaps? And Jimmy was wrong. Not everything *was* in order. A few dishes sat in the dry sink with food still on them. The woman of this tidy house would not have left them unwashed.

Allie picked up a piece of bread. It was hard, but hadn't spoiled yet. She couldn't help herself—she took a bite of it. She glanced at a mirror as she gnawed on the crust and was shocked to see a streaked face framed with wild hair staring back at her. Her standards had lowered considerably the past couple of days. How could one's circumstances change so quickly?

By the time Jimmy returned, the rain was pouring down.

Allie pointed to the dishes. "They left in a hurry."

"Mrs. Schaferling wouldn't have left those unless she absolutely had to."

"Are you thinking what I'm thinking?" Allie said nervously.

"They're probably just being cautious and went to town. They have a Sunday house there that they use when they go in for market day and church since it's so far to travel in one day," Jimmy said.

"We'll be fine," he added when he saw her expression. But he knew it wasn't market day or anywhere close to Sunday. All of the livestock were gone except for a few pigs he spotted roaming around loose, which were something most Indians wouldn't eat. He didn't know if that meant the livestock had been stolen or if the Schaferlings had taken them to protect them. The cattle were usually pastured on the open range, but he had heard talk about fencing the land around here. That would be enough to get the Comanches and the Apaches in an uproar.

Up until then, he knew many of the German people in the area had experienced peaceful relationships with the different groups of Indians because of a treaty agreed upon years ago. The mistake many white people made was grouping all Indians together—an Indian was an Indian. Period. And everyone assumed they were all cutthroat savages. Many people also assumed the worst about Jimmy and had judged him unfairly, and he began to take on the character they expected him to have.

Allie walked to the back door and stepped out on the porch. The rain ran off the roof into several large barrels sitting at the most opportune places to catch the water. For the first time since she had started on the trail with Jimmy, she realized how filthy she was. She stepped out under the cascading water and held her face up to wash off the remnants of the aloe vera and the dirt and sweat from two days of riding. She pulled up a chair and sat down to take off her shoes and stockings. She noticed a bar of lye soap sitting on the windowsill, so she took off her dirt- and blood-stained blouse, grabbed the soap and began to scrub it. She caught Jimmy watching her through the open door and remembered the bathhouse, but she didn't care any more. She glared at him, daring him to keep looking.

He turned away.

She continued her bath, washing her hair and scrubbing herself and her clothes—most of which were still on her body. She hadn't thought ahead as to how she would dry them. She just had the overwhelming urge to be clean. And if Jimmy was right, she would see Justin soon and didn't want to scare the daylights out of him with the way she looked.

Allie stood and wrung out her hair and clothes as best she could, put her wet blouse back on, and sat back down on the chair to watch the rain. She was too tired to even think, and after a while she began to shiver. The rain still had not let up. She picked up her stockings and shoes and stood to go back inside. When she turned toward the door, she noticed Jimmy had placed an old quilt on the floor just inside the doorway. She picked it up, unfolded it and draped it around her shoulders.

Jimmy had started a fire in the fireplace, and had hung his own shirt on a nearby chair to dry. Allie pulled up another chair to the fire and laid out her stockings. He walked into the room buttoning an old shirt.

"You might check the other rooms for dry clothes you can change into," he nodded toward them with his head, "if you want to dry all your wet clothes by the fire."

Allie checked one of the bedrooms, but found few items of clothing that would fit—the odds and ends left behind looked like they belonged to children. She grabbed a pair of socks, though, and put them on her feet. She went to another bedroom and opened a wardrobe to find it almost empty, but there were a few items of clothing that would do: a man's shirt and an old skirt. She quickly stepped out of her wet clothes and donned the dry ones, which were huge on her. To keep the skirt from falling down around her ankles, she took the edges meant for buttoning and tied them around her waist.

Allie brought her clothes back into the front room and draped them near the fireplace. Jimmy had gathered up several jars and brought them to the table.

"I found some of Mrs. Schaferling's preserves—she makes the best apple butter," Jimmy said, holding out a spoon for Allie. "Come eat."

She walked over and took the spoon, and he handed her a jar he had just opened. Allie dipped her spoon into the soft brown substance and took a whiff of it. Cinnamon and apple filled her nostrils. She put the spoon in her mouth, shut her eyes, and tried to remember anything else that ever tasted as wonderful. She couldn't. She ate several more spoonfuls before she sat down at the table and finished off half the jar before trying the peaches and the plum preserves and eating until she almost made herself sick.

Allie had spoken no words to Jimmy since before she stepped out into the rain running off the porch. It took too much effort to speak, and she was exhausted. She stood up and walked to one of the bedrooms and crawled onto the bed, which had been stripped down to the mattress covered in cotton ticking. She didn't care—it felt so much better than the hard ground.

Jimmy didn't have the heart to tell her that they weren't sleeping in the house that night. He had already decided to stay in the barn so he could keep an eye on the horses. The Schaferlings probably had good reason to leave their home, even though he was sure it was a temporary move—they had invested too much in this place over the years to lose it. Maybe they had also seen hostile Indian sign or heard about raids on other places in the area and decided to take the women and children into town to stay while the men came back and defended their home.

Whatever the reason, Jimmy knew it might be just a matter of time before a raid on this ranch occurred, or it might not happen at all. Either way, he wanted to be prepared to leave at a moment's notice, if need be. He would wait until the rain let up, though, before moving Allie out to the barn. He doubted anyone would be out in this deluge, although he had heard of a daring incident several years before when a handful of Comanches stole a large group of horses and mules from the corral at an army fort during a thunderstorm. The guard had taken shelter from the storm, and the livestock was stolen practically from underneath his nose. Jimmy wasn't going to chance that by staying in the house all night.

The rain—Jimmy closed his eyes and listened to it for a moment. He loved a good rainstorm. It was so ...cleansing? ...settling? ...necessary for growth? But rain had the potential for bad in it, too. Coming at the right time, it could bring in a bumper crop. Coming at the wrong time could wipe it out. Rain could break a drought, but it also had the power to destroy by flooding. How could something so good sometimes be so bad?

But on this evening it was a good thing. He opened his eyes and looked out the back door at the rain still pouring off the roof. He walked out onto the porch, stripped down to nothing, and stepped into the rain.

He needed to feel clean, too, for once.

The rain finally let up after a good hour or so, but it looked like more might be coming, and that meant the creeks and washes would be on the rise. He wasn't sure now what to do about Allie. He had decided to come to the Schaferling Ranch earlier that day after recognizing the possibility of hostiles in the area. He knew she would be well taken care of here. The idea of dropping her off at a stage stop somewhere among strangers wasn't the best plan. The rain would buy him more time, though, from Justin finding them.

Jimmy packed up what little food he could find, and took their clothes out to the barn. He came back and carried a mattress from one of the other bedrooms out to the barn before coming back to get Allie. He figured he was in for an argument.

He walked into the room where Allie slept and stood for a moment over the bed, watching her. Her dark hair lay tangled around her face. The aloe vera had done its work—her face looked more tanned than burned. She still looked beautiful, though, and he envied Justin at that moment. The cut on her forehead was the only evidence of the hell he had put her through the last few days—her peaceful expression contradicted it.

She had every reason to hate him, and although he felt her anger at times, he never felt hatred or disgust coming from her. She even talked to him like an equal rather than in a condescending tone or down to him as if he were stupid. Her words had penetrated his armor—they made him think, and he thought he had stopped doing that some time ago.

"Allie?"

No response. No argument. No problem.

Jimmy wrapped the quilt around her, picked her up and carried her out to the barn, placing her gently on the mattress in a pile of hay near the horse stall.

Allie never knew she'd left the house.

* * *

Justin had gone as far as the trail would lead him, even during the thunderstorm, until there were no tracks to see. He knew not to keep going blindly because getting off the trail even minutely in the beginning could mean missing them by miles if he gradually angled away from where he last had their trail. And there was a lot of country to get lost in—

especially west of here, which didn't have the line of forts protecting citizens in the settled areas of Texas. Jimmy had continued to travel southwest, only veering left or right when the terrain demanded it. Justin wondered if his brother was heading to Mexico, but he didn't think Jimmy knew anyone down there. He couldn't even speak the language.

Justin finally sought shelter under a shallow overhang along an outcropping of limestone. There was even room for his horse, although the wind was blowing so hard at times, most every square foot under the natural shelter was eventually dampened by the rain.

He hunched over facing the rock, and ate his last couple of biscuits. He thought he would have found Jimmy by now, that is, until he saw Allie's tracks. Jimmy had a reason to be running, and Justin hadn't learned that soon enough.

The rain had washed away any hope of finding them soon. He knew he would find them eventually, but it was going to take a lot more time to pick up the trail again. He wished there was some way to get word back to Grace to let everyone know Allie was alive, but he was already a couple of days out, which meant losing four days to go back and return. He couldn't leave the trail to grow that cold—that would increase the odds of losing them for months or even longer. It took his father six years to find him and his mother, and he wasn't about to repeat that situation. Allie might have an opportunity to escape if Jimmy went near any settlements, but out in the wilderness they would have to fight to survive not only hostile bands, but the elements, too.

Justin kept going over in his mind why Jimmy did this, and could not understand his motive. He knew Jimmy had done some stupid, hurtful things in the past, but those paled in comparison with this. And why was there blood on the riverbank? Which one bled—Jimmy or Allie? It had to have been Allie; Jimmy could not have forced her to go with him if he was hurt, and Allie would have come back to the house to get help for him. What made him think he had to take her? Was he drunk, and just didn't know how to get out of a situation? Did he do something unforgivable to Allie that risked losing his life or freedom? He could not believe Jimmy would do that, but he also could not explain why Jimmy had taken Allie, either.

He shook his head as if to clear his thoughts.

Justin looked around the overhang, convinced he was not the first person to have used it as shelter. He picked up a rock about the size of the palm of his hand and turned it over to find a well-worn groove down the middle of it. Most folks would have no clue what they held, assuming it was just another rock. But Justin recognized the sandstone abrading tool— he had used one himself in making shafts for arrows. Justin grabbed a stick and ran it across the rock and back to sand and straighten it.

He used the stick to dig around in the dirt. It didn't take long for him to find the remnants of an old fire and pieces of dark flint on the ground. He even found some embedded chert in the limestone walls. He picked up an oval-shaped rock and started chipping away at the hard gray area in the limestone, knocking a substantial chunk out of it.

Might as well pass the time constructively, he thought to himself as he sat down and chipped pieces off the stone. In no time at all, some of those pieces began to take the shape of arrowheads.

It felt good to focus his anger on something.

* * *

Allie and Justin stood on the rock above the swimming hole. She could see the river running swiftly below them, but she felt safe in Justin's arms. As long as she kept looking into his blue eyes, everything would be fine. But something caught Justin's eye, and he lifted his head and looked beyond Allie. The look in his eyes frightened her, and as she turned to see for herself, he pushed her away just as someone hit him with full force, knocking him into the river. She cried out...

"Allie! Wake up!" a voice said. "It's just a bad dream."

Not again! Not the nightmare again, she thought.

Someone shook her shoulder.

She opened her eyes. *Rafters. Where am I?* She sat up and looked around. She was in the barn. Jimmy opened the top half of a door to the corral. It must have been close to sunrise, but the sky was cloudy, giving everything a gray overcast to it.

"What are we doing out here?" she mumbled.

"We needed to stay close to the horses."

"I don't remember coming out here," she said as she looked down and around her.

"I carried you out here," he said as he handed her the clothes he brought from the house. "Change your clothes—we need to get moving."

"I thought this was the end of the line for me," Allie said as she stood up. "Can't we wait for the Schaferlings to come back?"

"I don't know when that'll happen, and I can't leave you here by yourself."

"But..."

"I have no means to defend us here if I have to, Allie—I only have one pistol, and the Schaferlings have taken all their weapons. Our best chance would be to get you to the nearest town."

Allie looked scared again. "It sounds like you're expecting an attack."

"No, it's just best to be prepared for the worst," he said as he stepped into the horse stall.

"Apaches or Comanches?" Allie still stood there, clothes in hand.

"Change while you're talking—I won't look," he said as he started to saddle Allie's horse. "And Apaches don't call themselves *apache*—it means *fighting men* or *enemy*. They prefer to call themselves *Indeh* or *Tinde*—it means *the people.*"

"Can you still speak the language?" Allie asked as she changed back into her blouse.

"Not much—I remember a few words. Justin and I used to keep speaking it when we were by ourselves. It was forbidden to speak at school or at home, though. I used to get whipped for that."

Allie cringed thinking about that as she slipped on her pantaloons under the oversized skirt. "But what will you do after you take me to town?"

"I'll find a job on a ranch somewhere—I'm good with horses." He turned to saddle his horse.

"That's what Justin told me," Allie said, pulling up her skirt and untying the borrowed skirt to let it drop to the ground. "He sounded very proud of you."

"He doesn't feel that way now; I've made sure of that."

"He's missed you, Jimmy. He feels like he's lost you." She sat down and pulled on her stockings and shoes.

Jimmy didn't know how to respond to that. "Aren't you dressed yet?" He asked as he tightened the cinch.

Allie suddenly felt an urgency to make things right. "Jimmy, why don't we just go home?"

"I have no home."

"You would if you would just forgive them."

"Why should I forgive them? They killed my father."

"Why do you blame everyone for that? Don't you think he would've killed Justin's father if he'd had the opportunity? This anger's destroying *you*, Jimmy, and your bitterness is trying to destroy the only people who really love you. You need your family—they're on your side—you just haven't figured that out. You need to forgive them for *your* sake if you want to have any kind of meaningful life at all."

"I don't need to hear your sermon, Allie. What would *you* know about forgiveness?"

"I forgive *you*, Jimmy," she said quietly.

Those words were almost his undoing. He could not look at her, much less respond to that. He reached inside for his anger, the feeling he knew best, but it wouldn't come this time. She had done nothing to him, and yet he chose to hurt her. Why would she forgive him after all he had put her through? He didn't understand it.

"Just let it go," she said.

All he could say was, "I don't think I can. I don't even know how."

"I can show you how."

At that moment, one of the horses raised his head and pricked his ears forward. The other one nickered.

"Get on your horse, Allie," Jimmy said quietly.

"What is it?" she whispered back.

"There's someone or something outside."

The tone of his voice told her this was no time for more questions. She got on her horse. Jimmy walked his horse over to the barn door and opened it a crack. He didn't see anything, but the horses' behavior told him otherwise.

"We're going to head back the way we came—I'm sure we'll meet up with Justin soon. He'll know what to do. If I tell you to run, though, you run without looking back."

Allie nodded; her heart was trying to beat out of her chest.

"Do you remember the trail we came in from?"

Allie nodded.

"Then let's go—me first until we're out of the barn. If someone gives chase, then you'll lead and I'll follow."

He got on his horse and started to push the barn door open, but hesitated.

"Allie..." he said, facing the door, "I'm really sorry for everything—"

"I know, Jimmy," she interrupted as she reached out and put her hand on his arm.

He nodded and pushed the door open, scanning the tree line and around the buildings as they stepped out of the barn.

"Well, do you think you can stay on your horse?" He whispered tauntingly, without taking his eyes off his surroundings. They continued to walk their horses away from the buildings.

Allie was terrified, but she gave him a half-smile, "You just watch me, Mr. Big Britches," she whispered back with more bravado than she actually felt. "I bet that was your Indian name—*Too Big for Britches.*"

"If it's a raid, I'm not sure where they'll be coming from—we may have to change directions, but we'll eventually work our way back to the trail we came in on," Jimmy said as he looked behind him. His expression told her before he said the words, "I see them—they're back behind the big house."

"Oh, dear Lord," was all Allie could say.

"Take the lead and run, Allie! Give it everything you've got—I'll be right behind you!"

Allie kicked her horse and let her have her head, leaning forward and holding on to the saddle horn for dear life. She could hear some whooping—they had seen them.

"Run her, Allie!!"

She thought she was running like the wind, but she could hear Jimmy right behind her. And then she heard several gunshots and a cry of pain. She chanced turning around and saw Jimmy drop his pistol and double over on his horse. She started to pull up, but Jimmy looked up and screamed at her.

"Don't stop, Allie!! I'm right behind you," he yelled.

She kicked her horse and kept running. Allie made it to the top of the hill and chanced looking around again, hearing Jimmy's horse coming up fast.

It was without a rider.

She pulled up and turned around. "Oh, dear God!" she cried. "Jimmy!!" she screamed.

She could see Jimmy lying on the ground about thirty yards back—this time with an arrow in his shoulder, trying to get up. At least five warriors were bearing down on him.

"Father God! You can't have brought me this far to see him murdered!!" she cried. "In the name of Jesus, please spare his life," she shouted as she kicked her horse to run back to Jimmy.

He saw her coming and tried to wave her off. "Get the hell outta here!" he yelled. An arrow pierced his thigh, knocking him down again.

Allie reached him just before the riders did and jumped off her horse. She threw herself between Jimmy and the braves, screaming, "Don't kill him!! Please don't kill him!!"

One of the warriors grabbed her by the hair and jerked her head back as he raised his knife.

"He is Indeh!! He is Tinde!!" she cried as a knife flashed down toward her.

Chapter 9

The knife halted at Allie's forehead. The other warriors stopped yelling and stared at her. One spoke to her in a language she didn't understand, so she pointed to Jimmy and repeated, "He is Indeh. He is Tinde."

She didn't know if they understood her or not, but something got their attention. The Indian holding her by the hair dragged her away from Jimmy and let her go, and the others turned him over to see his face. He was semi-conscious, and groaned at the movement. He was bleeding from his side, and arrows still protruded from his shoulder and thigh. One of them rubbed his hand across Jimmy's cheeks and made a comment.

Allie felt sick to her stomach with the fear that Jimmy could be dying, and a horrible death may be in store for her, but she chanced speaking again, saying, "He is the son of Nantan Lupan," and then repeated it more slowly, "Nan-tan Lu-pan."

One of the braves repeated the name, so she knew he at least understood those two words. They argued among themselves, some of it heated. Allie knew some Spanish and tried to listen for any words that sounded familiar, but it was halted gibberish to her. She could hear more yelling down at the house and barn, and saw a number of horses circling the area—how many Indians were there?

After saying a few words, one of the braves jumped on his horse and rode after Jimmy's horse. Another one removed Jimmy's gun belt and held his arms while a second brave held his legs. An older warrior grabbed hold of the arrow and forced the point through Jimmy's shoulder and out the other side, causing Jimmy to scream and writhe in pain. The older man broke off the tip and pulled the rest of the arrow back out of his shoulder. Allie recoiled at the sight. The screaming stopped when Jimmy fainted. The brave then cut Jimmy's pants around the arrow shaft sticking out of his thigh. Allie could see the bulge of the arrowhead, so it wasn't too deeply embedded. The old warrior slit the skin along the bulge, releasing the arrowhead and shaft, wiped the blood on Jimmy's pants, and handed it to one of the other braves, probably to be used again. A dark stain spread quickly across Jimmy's pant's leg.

Allie found herself retching, but there was nothing in her stomach to throw up. One of the men mounted his horse, and the other three carried Jimmy and laid him across his lap. He started his horse back toward the ranch headquarters. The warrior who had almost taken Allie's scalp turned around and motioned for her to mount her horse.

Allie followed the braves to the back of the house where they carried Jimmy to the porch. All but the old warrior scattered to join the others in ransacking the house and other buildings. Allie dismounted and rushed to Jimmy, whose shoulder and thigh wounds were bleeding profusely. She looked around for something to help stop the flow of blood and saw nothing that would be of use, so she started to pull up her skirt to use it as a bandage when the older warrior pushed her away. She watched as he cut off Jimmy's shirt and began dipping water out of one of the barrels to wash his oozing wounds. She could hear the others breaking things in the house, but no one seemed concerned about treating her as a captive, so Allie ran around the house and out to the barn to retrieve the borrowed clothes they had left there earlier. Had it only been minutes before? It seemed like a lifetime.

The barn door was still open, and she ran inside to get the skirt and shirt. She swung around the corner post inside the pen where the mattress was and ran head on into a brave. He was as surprised as she was, and when she tried to step around him to get the clothes lying on the mattress, he grabbed her arms and pushed her down. With a horror, she realized he wasn't one of the braves who had spared her and Jimmy's life, and found herself in the same dangerous situation as before.

You stupid, stupid girl! She thought as she pushed herself up on her elbows. She saw the intent in his eyes and began scooting backwards. Several other young braves came up behind him and began yelling and taunting and pushing him toward her. Allie realized, though, that she wasn't afraid this time as much as she was mad. When he leaned down over her, she kicked him as hard as she could in the *tenderloins,* as her.

brother used to refer to them. The brave fell on her in agony as the other two laughed. She attempted to push him off when someone suddenly lifted and threw him over to the side by the stall.

The barn went quiet, other than the grunts of the young man she had kicked the dickens out of. Allie looked up into the face of the brave that had almost lifted her scalp earlier. She grabbed the clothes in an attempt to show him what she was doing, and he grabbed her by the arm and jerked her to her feet and pushed her toward the door. As she ran out of the barn, she could hear him angrily berating the other young braves. The man who had almost killed her earlier just now defended her. She didn't understand these people at all.

By the time she made it back to Jimmy, the old warrior had made a poultice of something he had poured from a small leather bag attached to his belt. She began ripping the skirt into strips of cloth as he spread the substance on five different wounds—the front and back of the shoulder, the thigh, and the front and back of Jimmy's side where the bullet had passed clean through. The old warrior motioned for Allie to cover the wounds, and he walked away.

Allie had never bandaged anything other then a few minor cuts and blisters. But common sense told her that she needed to add some pressure to help stop the bleeding, which was still oozing through the poultice, and to cover the wounds to keep them clean. She started on the leg wound first since she could move it to wrap the strips around it. She folded a larger wad of cloth and pressed it to the wound while she did her best to wrap strips around it to hold it in place. Jimmy moaned when she pressed on the wound.

Allie grimaced, feeling a sharp jab in her gut, knowing she was hurting him.

"Damn, that hurts!" he said through gritted teeth. His forehead was furrowed; his eyes were clinched shut.

"I'm sorry, Jimmy!" Allie said, "but I have to bind these, and I... I've only gotten started." She almost told him she didn't know what in the heck she was doing. "Do you think you can sit up?" She hated asking him that, knowing any movement would cause excruciating pain.

Jimmy exhaled, like he had been holding his breath, and finally opened his eyes. He looked around to get his bearings.

"Come on, Jimmy—I don't know how much time I have to do this." Allie reached for his right arm and put it over her shoulder. Jimmy let out a cry of pain as she helped pull him up to a sitting position, and leaned him against the porch post. His breath came in ragged gasps. Allie knew he was hurting, but she could tell he was mad, too.

"Why didn't you keep running when I told you to!" he said, still clinching his teeth.

"I couldn't watch them kill you!" Allie said defensively, as she tore more strips of cloth from the skirt. She was grateful that it was as big as it was.

"So you came back so you could get yourself killed, too. That makes no sense at all!" Jimmy groaned again when she pressed another wad of material covering his side wounds.

"Hold this in place while I wrap these around you," she said as she tied the ends together and began wrapping his abdomen. "Lean forward."

He leaned forward and groaned again, shutting his eyes.

"And haven't you noticed, Jimmy—that we're not dead?!"

"Yet," he said.

She started the same procedure for Jimmy's shoulder wounds. "Besides, they would've caught me anyway—you know I can't ride worth a darn."

"You were doing all right when I saw you." He didn't sound so mad now.

"Thank God for saddle horns," she brushed off his compliment as she took a couple of wider strips of cloth and tied the ends together, "and for saving us—I believe He's the reason we're not dead."

"Yet," Jimmy repeated himself.

She picked up the borrowed shirt and gingerly guided it over Jimmy's left arm with minimal movement to the wounded shoulder to pull on the first sleeve, draped the shirt across his back, and was able to get the other sleeve on his right arm without causing too much pain. She couldn't help letting out a sigh of relief.

"Why do you think they went to the trouble to doctor your wounds?" Allie asked him.

Jimmy looked down as Allie began buttoning his shirt. "They doctored me?"

"Yes, the old warrior made some kind of nasty-looking paste and put it on your wounds before I bandaged them."

"He did? I thought that was my guts falling out. That was medicine?"

"Yep. Now we need to put your arm in this sling so you don't move your shoulder too much."

"Do you know what you're doing?" Jimmy asked.

116

"Nope," she admitted, "but my brother hurt his shoulder once falling from a tree, and the doctor made him put his arm in a sling so he couldn't move it. In your case, I don't want it to start bleeding again."

"I don't know why we're still alive, Allie, unless they want to torture us later."

"Jimmy, I told them you were an Indian."

"But they don't go by the word *Indian*."

"Well, I told them the words you told me—*Indeh* and *Tinde*. I told them you were the son of Nantan Lupan."

"And they understood you?"

"They didn't kill us, did they? They must've understood something."

"Well, I'll be damned," Jimmy said, rubbing his chin with his good hand.

"I think *blessed* is a better word to use," Allie said. "Do you think they'll leave us alone now and let us stay here?"

"I doubt it... they'll probably parade us around to a bigger group bragging that they *rescued* us," Jimmy said as he looked around. "We need to leave Justin a sign."

"How do you know Justin will know we were here?"

"He won't leave a stone unturned looking for you, Allie—he'll find this place eventually."

"What do you mean by *a sign?*" Allie asked.

Jimmy pulled his knife from his scabbard on his belt. "Here, scratch a message in the wood. Make it fast."

"What do I write?"

"Taken by Indians—no, say Indeh for short—and don't use all the letters."

Allie started scratching—**TKN** – "I can't do it fast enough! And I think they're coming!"

"Here—give it to me," Jimmy said, and he quickly scratched—**BY N'DE.**

Allie looked around and saw the soap on the windowsill. She grabbed it and made a smear in the lower right hand window pane. She quickly scratched out the letters with her fingernail:

J᠊ᷤ HURT. A

and turned around and began washing the blood stains off her hands as several of the braves came around the house leading their horses. They had found some items to steal—one of them had bundled up some stuff using the old quilt Allie had slept under last night.

Jimmy slipped his knife back in the scabbard under his shirt and pulled what was left of his tattered bloody shirt over the scratches on the porch. More warriors appeared on horseback—Allie counted sixteen in all. Jimmy just sat there glaring at them.

One of them pointed to his own eye and said something to the others and pointed to Jimmy.

"I guess they've just now noticed my mother's eyes."

"They're beautiful eyes, Jimmy." Allie said, noting the fierce look he gave her. It made her realize the statement seemed ridiculously out of place at that moment. She slipped the bar of soap in her pocket and wiped her hands on her skirt.

"Allie, pay attention on the trail," Jimmy said quietly, watching the Indians getting ready to leave.

"What do you mean?" she asked.

"Pay attention to landmarks—rivers, hills, the direction we're going based on the sun, if you can see it. Watch how the landscape changes—from flat to hilly, or the change in trees and vegetation. Do you understand?"

Allie nodded, but she didn't understand. What did that have to do with their predicament?

The old warrior motioned for Allie to go to her horse as he walked toward Jimmy. She leaned over to help Jimmy up, but the old man pushed her out of the way, and looked at the bandaging. He grunted what sounded like an approval and pointed to her horse.

She hesitated.

"Go on Allie—I'd rather you not see this," Jimmy said.

Gray clouds covered the sky, and the early morning coolness still lingered, but Jimmy's forehead was already beaded in sweat.

She did as he asked, but picked up the remnants of the skirt before turning around to walk to her horse. Allie cringed when she heard Jimmy holding back the cries of pain as they picked him up, none too gently, and put him on his horse.

Allie mounted her horse and watched as the braves tied Jimmy's boots to his stirrups to keep him on his horse. Then she walked her horse up beside him. His face was several shades paler than a few moments ago. He leaned forward, holding onto the saddle horn. The gnawing jabs in the pit of her stomach were back, seeing how much pain he was in.

Jimmy turned his head and saw the fear and concern for him on her face.

"I'll be all right," he said for her sake.

"Jimmy…"

"Thank God for saddle horns," he gasped, trying to make a joke.

She giggled, and immediately felt horrified that she had actually laughed in their situation. She lifted her right hand. It shook uncontrollably. Then she looked at Jimmy, and the tears came with the realization that they had come so close to dying that morning.

"Don't let them see you cry, Allie," Jimmy said. "We're going to get through this." But he doubted those words as soon as the horses started forward.

"Why did you ask me to watch the trail, Jimmy?" she asked as she quickly wiped away the tears.

Jimmy couldn't look at her when he answered. "Because I may not be around to get you back home, Allie," he said, raggedly.

"Don't say that!" Allie said, as the tears continued to fall. She didn't care if they saw her crying. She couldn't even think about being alone with these men.

"You're going to have to be strong, Allie—stronger than you've ever been."

"Justin will find us, won't he?" Allie asked, but Jimmy couldn't answer by then—the roaring in his ears had blocked out everything except the monumental effort he was making to stay upright on his horse.

Allie didn't know what else to do at that moment except pray: *Dear Father, don't let him die. Please don't let him die. His body needs healing, but his heart needs healing, too. Please give him a chance to make things right with his family, and especially with Justin. Please help me to be strong for him and to pay attention like he said. Lord, help me bring him home.*

But when she prayed this time, she kept her eyes open and watched the trail.

After an hour or so, the raiding party pulled up to cross a swollen creek. Allie had been watching Jimmy struggle to keep himself upright, and decided to do something to help him. She walked her horse up to stand beside Jimmy's, lifted her leg and skirt over the saddle horn, and using her stirrup, she stepped across to sit behind Jimmy to help support him. She battled to hold her horse and Jimmy both as they started across the creek when another brave came up and grabbed her horse's reins for her. She thanked him out of habit, and then remembered he didn't understand her words.

Allie could barely see over Jimmy's shoulder, and her nose found itself against Jimmy's long hair much of the time. She couldn't help but notice the clean smell and realized he must have washed in the rain the night before, too.

That's a good thing, Jimmy, to start caring about yourself.

The sun stayed hidden all day, but Allie noted that they had traveled away from the Schaferling Ranch in the opposite direction she and Jimmy had ridden in from the day before. It was a blessing that the sky had remained overcast so Jimmy wouldn't have to deal with the hot sun as well as his injuries. They had been traveling through a lot of trees—fairly good-sized trees. Allie wished she knew more about trees, but the only thing she could determine was that these were bigger than mesquite trees and smaller than the huge oak trees around Waco and Grace. She also noticed that the riders seemed to be avoiding open areas. The creek they had crossed earlier looked more like it was normally a dry wash instead of a creek—she thought it was probably the runoff from the rain heading down to a river somewhere nearby.

Allie's back ached from letting Jimmy lean against her. She found it a chore trying to stay in place behind the saddle, too, and her stomach growled with hunger. But the braves showed no sign of stopping, other than to allow Allie to give Jimmy's horse a rest by switching them to her horse after a couple of hours. When they stopped at another swollen creek, all but four of the raiding party left them—maybe because she and Jimmy were moving too slowly, Allie guessed. After watching the braves talk to each other and point certain directions, she figured they would meet up with them eventually. Or maybe they were still raiding in the area. She hoped any other people around were prepared to defend themselves, or at least were forewarned like the Schaferling family had been.

Allie tried to give Jimmy water every so often, and she only took a swallow or two herself, not knowing when and if they would get to stop or how long they had to make it last. It was hard enough to get Jimmy off the horse when they switched horses earlier, and Allie hoped the next stop would be for the night. Jimmy needed to rest and be still.

At one point when the group started up a steep rise, Allie almost slid off the back of the horse. If it weren't for Jimmy holding her arms around his waist with his good arm, she would have.

"Don't let me go, Allie," he had labored to say afterwards.

He was delirious, she thought, but couldn't help but correct him. "It was *you* who held on and kept *me* from falling."

He shook his head, no, and repeated himself, "Don't let me go."

And she realized he wasn't talking about staying on the horse.

"I won't, little brother," she said as tears welled up in her eyes, and she lifted up another prayer for him.

Allie noticed that they had begun to travel more to the west as the day progressed—even heading north at times. They eventually came to a swollen river. It was too swift and deep to cross safely, so they rode alongside it until they found a place to set up camp for the night. Several braves untied Jimmy's feet and took him off his horse. Allie rushed to get a blanket spread under one of the trees before they put him down. The brave that had been leading Jimmy's horse dropped the reins beside her horse, and walked on.

Allie checked Jimmy's wounds—they had bled some, but not substantially. She went back to the horses to get the water flask and a jar of preserves out of the saddlebag and brought them back to Jimmy. His eyes were shut, so she sat there for a few minutes, not sure what to do. He finally opened his eyes.

"The horses..." Jimmy said weakly, "you need to tend to the horses first."

"Oh—the horses!" Allie said, "Of course."

She sat there nodding her head for a moment, and then said meekly, "What exactly do I do with the horses?"

"Don't you know what to do with the horses?"

Allie shook her head, no, and smiled apologetically. "What do I do first?"

"Well, they're wandering off right now, so you'd better go get them and bring them back over here so I can tell you what to do," Jimmy said wearily.

"Oh! Darn!" Allie jumped up and hurried after the horses. During the short time she had caught them and brought them back, Jimmy's eyes were closed again.

"Jimmy?"

No response.

She turned around and watched what the other braves did with their horses. They had already taken off their horse blankets or buffalo hides or whatever it was they had been sitting on. She noticed a couple of the saddles were just crude wooden frames that looked like they had a saddle horn in the front and a tall, flat, and wider piece in the rear. The other two horses had strips of something—maybe leather—tied around the horse's middle with a looped knob on top—like a saddle horn without the rest of the saddle.

Allie walked the horses over to a fallen tree not too far from Jimmy and tied their reins to separate limbs. She figured out how the saddles came off the horses and remembered to pay attention to each step, knowing she would eventually have to put them back on the horses. She carried the saddlebags and another blanket over by Jimmy, then each of the saddles, and kept watching what the others were doing, unsure of what to do next. By then several braves had led their horses to water.

"We can do that, can't we, girls... or boys... or whatever you are." She hadn't bothered to look until then. "Looks like we have a girl *and* a boy." Allie walked her horses over to where the others were watering theirs and let them drink.

"All right, we're watering our horses," she said quietly to herself.

She stood there a bit longer and watched what the braves did next. She could see them putting something on the horses' front feet that made them look like they were tied together, probably to keep them from wandering off. But she hadn't a clue how to do that, and besides, she was scared to even touch their feet.

She walked the horses back over near Jimmy, thinking that maybe she could just stand there and hold them for a while until they ate enough grass, and then she could tie them back up to the tree limbs again for the night. But the horses kept trying to go different directions.

"You need to get the hobbles off the saddles," Jimmy said weakly, trying to get up on his good side, "and hobble them."

"Wait and let me help you," Allie said as she tied the horses' reins back up to the tree limbs and rushed over to Jimmy to help him sit up against the tree. "How are you feeling?"

"You don't want to know," he said with some effort. "I see you got the saddles off all right."

"I hope I can remember how to put them back on," she said as she looked for the hobbles on the saddles. She hadn't even noticed them tied to the saddles—she thought they were just another part of the rigging. "So these are the hobbles," she said as she lifted them up. She hesitated. "Jimmy, I don't think I can do this—what if the horse steps on me or kicks me?"

"You can do it—they're used to being hobbled," he said. "I'll tell you exactly what to do—you'll do just fine."

He talked her through it, and she did just fine. She untied the reins to her horse and was about to drop them when Jimmy said, "Now you need to take the bridles off so they can graze."

Allie hesitated again.

"Start with *your* horse again—she's as gentle as a lamb," Jimmy said patiently. "Just open your left hand and place it lightly between the horse's eyes and mouth to hold her head if she tries to pick it up."

Allie did as Jimmy said.

"All right, now reach up and get a hold of the leather straps behind the ears—it's called the headstall—and pull it just over her ears and let it go. As it falls down, she'll open her mouth and let the bit drop out, and the bridle should drop onto your left hand. Simple as that."

Allie was surprised to see that the bridle came off exactly how Jimmy told her. She smiled with relief and then jumped as the horse snorted and shook her head—seemingly happy that the bridle was off. The horse immediately put her head down and began grabbing tufts of grass. Allie realized for the first time that she didn't know if her horse even had a name.

"Does she have a name?" she asked Jimmy.

"We've always called her *Dunnie,* because of her color."

"Dunnie. All right, now what about your horse?" Allie asked as she walked over to him.

"What about my horse?" Jimmy said guardedly.

"Does he have a name?" Allie asked.

"Go ahead and take the bridle off first," Jimmy said.

Allie did, although she had to hold his head firmly when he tried to pick it up as she pulled the headstall over his ears and let it go. The bridle dropped in her left hand, same as before.

"Now what is this sweet boy's name," she said, scratching his mane as Jimmy's horse started grazing.

"Demon."

Allie took a quick step back from the horse. Jimmy snickered, in spite of his pain, then paid dearly for it. Allie didn't notice.

"What a horrid name for a horse!" Allie said, alarmed. "Why would you call him that?"

"Because he acts like one half the time," Jimmy said with difficulty. "I have to keep a firm rein on him or he'll unseat me."

"He was just fine today," Allie said.

"He had two people riding him most of today." Jimmy shut his eyes and put his head back against the tree.

"Goodness, Jimmy—you need to eat something and rest, and I'm just chattering on like we're at a Sunday picnic," Allie said apologetically as she dug around in the saddlebag for a spoon and opened the jar of preserves. "What is wrong with me? Here, eat some of this."

Jimmy just looked at it like it was nothing. "Just give me a couple of bites and let me just shut my eyes for a little bit."

He should be starving, Allie thought. She felt his forehead—it was hot. That wasn't good. She grabbed a rag from the torn up skirt and wet it with the water from the flask. She bathed his face and neck, and helped him lie down again.

Allie sat there, not sure about what she should do next other than keep the wet rags on his forehead. She was exhausted, too, but was afraid to go to sleep for fear something might happen to Jimmy. It was still light, but there wasn't much movement around the camp. Where did the others go? She scooted back and leaned up against the tree, and before she knew it, her eyes closed.

It seemed like only moments had passed when something fell on Allie's feet, and she opened her eyes with a start. She looked down.

It was a rabbit.

A dead rabbit.

Chapter 10

*A*llie almost cried out until she saw the brave standing before her. He pointed at the rabbit and motioned to his mouth and pointed to Jimmy.

"You want me to DO something with this dead animal?" Allie asked him.

He just turned and walked away.

She looked at the rabbit and grimaced, but also realized with a twinge of guilt that the Indian had just given them a gift, and she had responded with irritation. She stood up and walked quickly to catch up to him.

"Pardon me," she said to his back, not knowing what to say. He kept walking. She ran around in front of him, and this time he stopped.

"Thank you," she said, and tried to quickly think of some hand signals to show what she meant. She put up two fingers like bunny ears hopping up and down in front of her chest. She pointed back at Jimmy and motioned to her mouth.

"Thank you," she said again and leaned her head down a bit.

He didn't say a word, but Allie felt like she made him understand. She walked back to the dead rabbit. She had never handled food that had eyes looking back at her. She had helped Aunt Sister pluck chickens, but had never had to deal with a chicken face looking at her—Aunt Sister was the one that wrung the heads off. Allie couldn't be around when any killing of meat was going on. And by the time Allie handled any beef or pork, she made sure it was far removed from ever looking like it was once alive, otherwise she couldn't even think about eating it.

She looked at Jimmy. He slept fitfully. She looked at the other braves and saw the old warrior. Allie decided to walk across the camp to try to communicate to the old man somehow that Jimmy was running a fever, but along the way, she noticed two of the braves in various stages of skinning several rabbits. She stopped to watch them. They had hung each rabbit by a single hind leg from a tree limb and had cut off the head to let them bleed out. Then they cut the front feet off first, and then cut around the joints of each of the hind legs and down to remove the tail, and pulled the skin down over the rabbit. At this point, they gutted the rabbit, cutting from the tail area to the middle of the lowest rib.

Allie had seen enough. She walked over to the old warrior and tried to tell him about Jimmy's fever by pointing back toward Jimmy and placing her hand on her forehead. He reached into his belongings for something and returned with her to Jimmy, where he felt his head and chest. He pointed at the saddlebag and cupped his hands together. She rummaged through Jimmy's saddlebag, and pulled out a tin cup and a small, beat-up coffee pot. The old man nodded his head, pulled out another leather pouch and poured in her hand what appeared to be shavings of some kind of bark.

"I boil this like coffee?" Allie asked.

"Café," the Indian nodded.

Allie's eyebrows raised in surprise. He had spoken a word that sounded like English.

"Do you speak English?" she asked.

He shook his head, no, and said, "Español—café," he said again, and added, "medicina."

He started to stand up, and Allie put her hand on his arm.

"Thank you—gracias," she said, and asked, "Como se llamo?"

He looked at her and said, "Me llamo *Castro*."

Allie understood him. "Gracias, Castro. Me llama Allie."

He nodded, and turned and walked away.

She rolled up her sleeves while she looked at the rabbit and decided she could let it bleed out while she built a fire and started heating the water. She touched the soft fur, and a tear rolled down her cheek.

"I'm sorry, rabbit," she said wearily, as she picked up the rabbit by its feet. "I don't want to do this, but I have to, for Jimmy's sake."

A while later, Allie had a smoky fire going, thanks to *borrowing* a burning stick from the Indians' fire. The bigger pieces of wood she found lying about were too damp from the recent rain, but Allie ended up breaking a bunch of smaller branches off the fallen tree that seemed dry enough to get the fire started. When the water started boiling in the coffee pot, she dropped in the bark shavings and set the pot off to the side of the fire to let it steep.

Skinning the rabbit didn't take as long as she thought it would, and after shedding more tears and gagging a number of times while gutting it, she swore she would never eat it nor any other rabbit... *ever.* The one thing she did differently than the braves, though, is that she washed it off before she attempted to cook it.

She hadn't a clue how to cook a rabbit properly, although she remembered her mother boiling a rabbit one day for the dog to eat, but it stunk up the house so bad Allie stayed outside all day. But here she didn't have a pot to boil it in, so she figured it should be hung above the fire without being directly in the fire. She impaled it on a stick and stacked some bigger pieces of wood on two sides of the campfire to make it high enough to set the spit just above the fire. The logs on the sides kept falling, though, so she added a back wall to the campfire to make it more secure. Then she piled several more logs on top of the ends of the spit so it wouldn't roll off.

Then she walked down to the water and took out her soap and scrubbed her hands and arms and face before going back to wake up Jimmy to drink his medicine concoction. She couldn't stand the feel or smell of rabbit on her.

The sun had set some time before, and Allie could just barely see the way back to her campfire. She was exhausted, and didn't want to wait for the rabbit to cook before going to sleep, but she knew she had to get some food into Jimmy, if possible. She turned the spit over again and wondered how long it would take to get done. Then she grabbed another piece of the old skirt to pick up the coffee pot and poured about a half a cup of the brew. She walked over to Jimmy and knelt down beside him.

"Jimmy?" she said. "Jimmy, wake up!"

She felt his face—it was still hot. She set the cup down and picked up his head and placed it in her lap. She could see his features by the firelight. Was this the same man that had frightened her so before? He looked so much younger now.

"Jimmy! You have to drink this." She propped up his head.

He half opened his eyes, and she put the cup to his lips. He gagged on the first swallow—it must have been bitter, but he got the rest of it down eventually. He laid his head back down on her lap and was asleep again.

She moved her legs to a more comfortable position and reached over and grabbed her blanket and draped it over Jimmy, who seemed to be alternating between shivering and sweating.

Allie ate half a jar of peach preserves while listening to the sounds of the night. The frogs croaked at the top of their lungs—happy to have all that extra water, she guessed. She could hear the crickets and other kinds of insects all around. She never realized how loud the night could be. The human part of the camp was quiet, though, as the braves had long since eaten and gone to sleep. She felt so alone, but a part of her knew she really wasn't. She bowed her head and prayed silently.

Lord, I just thought I'd had some bad days before this. Thank you for getting me through the worst day of my life. Thank you for your protection and wisdom. I'm going to need your help tomorrow and the next day, Father, and for however long it takes. And I hope you'll lead Justin to us soon. Please help Jimmy get well. I can't do this by myself.

Allie looked down at Jimmy. "Don't you dare leave me," she whispered threateningly.

She sat there and stared at the fire... and that darn rabbit.

Something touched her shoulder. Allie opened her eyes. She was lying on her side, wrapped around Jimmy's head. It was early morning.

"Allie?" a muffled voice said.

She sat up wearily, untangling herself from Jimmy's head.

"Sorry," she said, rubbing her eyes, too tired to even be mortified. She carefully helped him to a sitting position, then remembered the fever and felt Jimmy's head. It felt cool to the touch.

"Your fever's broke!"

"I had fever?"

She nodded, yes, and said, "Last night, and the old warrior gave me some kind of bark shavings to boil and make a tea for you—it must've helped."

"I have a nasty taste in my mouth, but I don't remember drinking anything."

"I was cooking you some rabbit... oh, darn it!" Allie looked at the campfire and the petrified corpse perched above the ashes.

"You cooked... a rabbit?" Jimmy asked slowly. "Where did you get a rabbit?"

"One of the braves brought it to me to cook for you. I think he assumed I knew how to do it."

"Did you?"

"Heavens, no—I had to go watch how they did it."

"That's one hell of a campfire, too—with a back and sides, I see."

"It does look sort of like a cook stove, doesn't it," Allie said, admiring her work, "although it looks like part of it burned."

"How long did it take you to build that thing?"

"I don't know—I think everybody was asleep by the time I got that rabbit cooking," Allie said as she crawled over to the campfire and grabbed the stick holding the rabbit. "Well, I think it's done," she smiled apologetically.

"That's an understatement," Jimmy said under his breath.

Allie brought it back and pulled Jimmy's knife out of his saddlebag. Jimmy lifted up his shirt to see his empty scabbard.

"Hey—"

"Sorry—I used it to leave Justin a sign, and don't worry, I washed it after I skinned the rabbit."

"You skinned the rabbit... all by yourself?"

"Of course," Allie said as if it were something she did regularly, "and now I'm going to cut some off so you can tell me how it tastes."

"I'm... sorry... it's a bit... tough," Allie said as she struggled to saw off a few mangled pieces.

Jimmy tried it and told her it was very similar to jerky, but he was thinking the leather on his saddle might taste better, and would probably be more tender.

She cut up several more pieces for him and said, "I'll pack the rest of this up for later."

"You're not going to try it?" he asked.

"It's all yours," she said.

Jimmy tried not to think about that statement and concentrated on chewing and swallowing his last bite, hoping it would stay down.

"After what I went through skinning and gutting this poor little nasty thing," she said assuredly, "rabbit will never pass through these lips."

* * *

Four days had passed since the night of the fierce thunderstorm, and Justin still hadn't picked up Jimmy and Allie's trail. He had gradually crisscrossed the country, beginning with a narrow swing and eventually going wider with the chance they might change directions. It hadn't rained anymore, but he knew the trail was getting cold since he hadn't found any more sign. If he didn't find something soon, the chance of Allie being lost for weeks and months was a very real possibility.

Justin had also seen signs of a raiding party, and that added another fear to his list of concerns for Allie. Kidnappings and murders by Indians used to be very common, but every year brought more people to settle in Texas and push the Indians farther west, so violent attacks occurred less and less. Many of the Indians were already settled on reservations in Oklahoma, Texas, and New Mexico, but Justin had heard of rogue bands that still roamed freely and refused to accept the white man's civilized ways. Most of them had settled in Mexico and raided across the Rio Grande.

But where Justin had seen signs of a raiding party in this part of Texas was a bold move since a number of forts had been built along a line from Fort Duncan near Eagle Pass through Central Texas up to Fort Worth, west of Dallas. Soldiers patrolled this line regularly, and Indians took big risks if they raided it.

The lack of food was another problem Justin had to contend with— he didn't want to waste precious ammunition on that, but in the days after the thunderstorm, he had shot several rabbits and a turkey for food. He decided if the search for Allie extended into weeks, he needed to start depending on more primitive weaponry for food sources. Justin had kept the abrading tool he found in the cave. Along the trail, he came across some salt cedars and cut a small bundle of straight branches for arrow shafts. He began to spend a little time each evening in front of his campfire to scrape, sand, dry, and straighten the wood. He also came across a lightning-split osage orange tree, and cut a good size limb off the deadwood side. He planned to make a bow to use for bringing down birds and small game. He had saved some of the turkey feathers to use on the arrows.

Green wood usually took weeks and months to dry and cure to properly make bows and arrows, but Justin didn't have that kind of time. He knew the dead wood would speed up the process considerably, but he still took a chance on it breaking.

Justin had seen whitetail deer often on the trail, but wasn't ready to kill one. When the bow was ready to be strung, he would bring down a deer and use its sinew to string it. Simmering the skinned hide in water made a type of hide glue that he would use to prepare the bowstring. It had been years since he had made a bow and arrows, but he hadn't forgotten how. It felt good to be working creatively with his hands again, and work made a good companion to his anger.

At the end of the day, Justin saw smoke on the other side of a hill. Coming atop the rise, he could see a ranch headquarters—the smoke drifted up from one of the houses' chimneys. He rode in and stopped in front of the main house. He opened his mouth to holler when a voice spoke from behind him.

"Hold it right there. Put your hands out in front of you and identify yourself," a man said in a thick accent.

Justin did as he asked and slowly turned to look down the barrel of a shotgun. "I'm Justin Taylor from Dalton, but I'm originally from around Waco," he said.

"Well, land o' Goshen, son," the man said, "I saw that bundle tied across your back and thought you was a Mescalero. Get off your horse and come to the house."

Justin dismounted and extended his hand to the older man. Several other men stepped outside from the house. Another one came from the barn.

"I'm Josef Schaferling—welcome to my home," he said. He introduced Justin to the other men: three sons and a son-in-law. "Come on inside and rest your bones—we'd be glad to share a bite with you, and you're staying the night, too. It's not safe to be roaming about these days by yourself."

The idea of eating a good meal after a week on the trail sounded very appealing to Justin.

"Much obliged, sir. Where can I take care of my horse?" Justin asked.

"The barn—Otto and Max will show you, and you need not worry, we've been watching our horses 'round the clock."

After taking his horse to the barn, Justin and Otto left Max there and walked back to the big house. Justin hung his hat on a peg right inside the door and was invited to sit down at a big table with the four men. Josef handed him a bowl of some sort of thick stew, and Justin dug into it hungrily.

"I'm sorry my Anna is not here—she is a very good cook, but it's been too dangerous for our womenfolk and children to be here right now. It's been many years since we've had any trouble with the Indians, but we'd heard a band has been raiding on some neighboring places—they even killed a friend of ours for his horses. We decided last week that we'd better move our families and livestock closer to town, and they hit us while we were gone. They tore up the place pretty good. We're just thankful they didn't burn it down."

"We figured the only reason that didn't happen was because they didn't want to attract undue attention to their presence here," Otto added.

"The soldiers will find them if they continue to raid in this area," Karl said confidently. "And we'll be ready for them if they come back."

"How big do you think this group is?" Justin asked.

"By all the tracks we saw, there was at least a dozen, maybe even fifteen or twenty," Otto said.

"And we're pretty sure they had taken some captives, too," Josef said. "We found the tracks of shod horses."

Justin looked up with alarm.

"And even blood and signs of a struggle," Karl added.

"What!?" Justin's heart sank.

"When we came back, the houses and barn had been ransacked, but my Anna and our girls had taken the things we value most, bless their hearts. But the first thing we found out of place was a mattress in the barn. It had been cut up, but we didn't think the Indians would bother dragging it out there just to cut it up," Josef said.

"So we figured someone had used our barn to sleep in," Karl said.

"Tell me about the blood," Justin said.

Josef nodded his head. "Well, as we looked around and started cleaning up, we found a bloody shirt on the back porch, and some letters scratched in the wood."

"Can I see them?" Justin stood.

"Yes—get the lamp, Edwin, and let's give 'er a look."

Josef stood, and they all walked out onto the porch. Edwin squatted down and placed the lamp near the scratches. Justin knelt down and ran his fingers over the letters: **TKN BY N'DE**

"It's obvious someone was saying they were taken, but we don't know what this N'DE is," Edwin said.

"Apaches," Justin said. "Indeh is what they call themselves."

"Well, why would a captive use that word? I've never heard of it."

Justin knew with a sinking dread that it had to have been Jimmy, but he had to be sure. "The shirt," he said, "was it a man's or a woman's?"

"It was a man's shirt," said Otto, "no doubt about it."

"Can I see it?"

Josef shook his head. "We burned it—I figured whoever was wearing it probably didn't have a chance anyway—it looked like he'd been shot by a bullet *and* an arrow. It was a mess. There was quite a bit of blood on the porch."

Justin stood and turned away.

"Who are you looking for, son?" Josef asked, placing his hand on Justin's shoulder.

Justin looked at him with questioning eyes—*how'd he know?*

"You look like you just lost your best friend," the old man said.

"My brother," Justin admitted. "My brother and... a friend ." He wasn't sure how to describe his relationship to Allie. "A girl."

They all looked somber, thinking the worst.

"Tut mir leid," Josef shook his head. "I'm sorry, son. What are their names?"

"Jimmy and Allie."

"And you said your name was *Taylor?*" Otto said.

Justin nodded.

"Papa, it must have been *our* Jimmy."

"Oh, dear Lord above, that can't be." Josef said as he backed up to the porch chair and sat down.

"You know my brother?" Justin asked.

Edwin spoke up. "Yes, he comes by to break horses for us several times a year. He's the best we've ever seen with a horse."

Justin nodded. "That's Jimmy."

Josef was visibly upset. "He came to us for help, and we weren't here to help him."

"Papa, we had no way of knowing that," said Karl.

"Now it makes sense—" Otto said. "We found another message on the window here."

"It's good Mutter wasn't here because she would've scrubbed that window by now," Edwin said. "It says *J's hurt A.*"

"What?" Justin thought with alarm. Was Allie saying that Jimmy had hurt her? Justin read the scrawl for himself on the pane.

J's HURT. A

The period changed the whole meaning. Jimmy was injured, Allie was saying. There was no doubt now that they had been here. Why were they even still alive?

"I have to find her," Justin said, feeling the urgency of the situation and wanting to leave immediately. They followed him back in the house.

"It wouldn't do you any good to leave tonight—you look exhausted, and you wouldn't be gaining anything by traveling in the dark," said Otto.

"You won't be any closer to them tonight than you would be in the morning," Josef said. "Stay and rest, Mr. Taylor. That would do you more good than anything right now."

"Call me Justin," he said without volition, trying to think through the situation.

"I'll even go with you," said Otto. "Jimmy meant a lot to us, and we want to help."

Justin looked at them. Were they talking about the same person?

"All right," he conceded, "but let me relieve Max and sleep in the barn and watch the horses for you—that's the least I could do for your hospitality."

When they tried to argue with him, Justin insisted, saying that was the only way he would stay the night.

"Fair enough," said Josef.

Then Justin thought of something else. "Could I ask a huge favor of you when any of you head back to town?"

"Anything," Josef said.

"Could I leave a note for you to wire to my family—I'm sure they're sick with worry right now, and it's been a week since I've seen them," Justin said. "I know it may be a while before you go to town, but it would still be sooner than I could get back to them."

"Of course," Josef said. "Karl, find something for Justin to write his note."

Karl brought him a scrap of paper, a quill pen, and ink. Justin scrawled a quick message and handed it to Karl. He turned back to the elderly gentleman.

"Thank you, Mr. Schaferling," Justin said as he shook his hand. "I really appreciate your help."

"You are welcome, son," Josef said.

Otto took the lantern from Edwin to walk Justin out to the barn. Justin grabbed his hat and turned to shake the younger men's hands.

"You didn't eat but one bowl of my stew," Josef said. "Here, take the rest of this flat bread." He handed it to Justin.

"Thank you for being a friend to my brother," he told them.

"It was our pleasure, Justin," Josef said, knowing he wouldn't be seeing him in the morning.

He was right.
Justin was up and gone before the others had risen.

Chapter 11

*E*very time the braves stopped over the next several days, Allie tried to convince them to leave her and Jimmy behind, but to no avail. The travel took its toll on Jimmy—he wasn't able to rest and recuperate from his injuries. The leg and side wounds had closed up roughly and looked as if they were slowly healing, but the shoulder wound continued to look inflamed and open. Jimmy was so weak by the end of each day he could barely stand.

Allie could not remember ever being so tired. The Apaches' stamina amazed her—riding day after day—like they lived on horseback. They regularly went long stretches of time without eating, too—content to wait until they had made camp to find food. Some evenings they brought in plenty of game, other times very little or none. By day two, Allie was chewing on the tough pieces of rabbit she had sworn never to eat.

Their smaller group traveled at a slower pace each day, camping in a different place each night, but seemed to stay in the same general area. The larger raiding party finally met up with them on day five of Allie and Jimmy's capture. She was horrified to see fresh scalps on several of the braves' shields. It reminded her anew that she did not understand these people—the Indeh, and that it was only by the hand of Providence that her own hair was not dangling from a warrior's belt by then. The warriors had also stolen a number of horses, which were driven along with the band. Allie realized that they had been tarrying in the area waiting for the larger band to finish raiding. From then on they traveled steadily to the northwest.

At the end of the sixth day, a brave dumped a gutted deer at Allie's feet, expecting her to skin it and cook it for them. After he walked away, she just stood there and sobbed. Jimmy tried his best to help her, knowing he was breaking a cardinal rule with the Apaches—a man did not do the work of a woman. The best he could do, though, was to use his good arm to help her get it tied up by its head and off the ground. He was so weak with that little bit of effort, though, he had to immediately sit down. But he was able to give Allie verbal instructions on how to skin it, and she accomplished the task. It took her so long, though, that the same brave that brought it to her lost patience and came over to retrieve the carcass. He cut off part of a hindquarter, leaving it where it lay. Then he took the deer down and carried it off for him and the others to cut up and cook for themselves. Allie could hear him fussing and the others laughing at him... or probably her, she decided. She didn't care, though.

Allie then went through what had become a nightly ritual for them—to gather up wood and make a fire each time they stopped for the night. She was getting better and faster at it, and had substituted rocks to surround the fire rather than logs. Jimmy had also told her how to tie three long sticks together near the top, and spread them out like a pyramid to make a freestanding frame to stand over the fire. She could hang larger pieces of meat from the center or could prop skewered meat on the branch nubs along the sides.

Jimmy was still in pain—especially his shoulder, but it was gradually lessening. But what continued to increase was the guilt he felt for putting Allie in this dangerous and difficult situation. He noticed that she seemed to be confident at times—or to have the faith, as she put it, that they would be rescued. But they talked less and less, spending much of their strength trying to make it through each day, and what talking they did usually involved instructions that were closely related to mere survival.

Allie tried to keep up with the days, but they were beginning to run together. Was it Sunday or Monday now? Had it only been a week since they left Grace? She kept telling herself that Justin would find them, but she wondered what was keeping him so long. Maybe Jimmy hadn't left clear enough tracks for him to find. Could the rain have washed away every bit of their trail? And what if Justin never made it to the Schaferling Ranch? Then she would put those thoughts out of her mind so discouragement wouldn't drag her down further. God had given her a peace about their future, but sometimes doubts crept in around the edges of her mind.

Allie realized that Jimmy wasn't sure of his own future, nor did he care much about it, but surely God didn't intend for *her* to disappear forever from her family. She did care about her life and future. She questioned again why God allowed this to happen to her. But then she remembered Julia, and that God had allowed Julia to experience that very thing. Allie wondered how she survived even six months, much less six years with the Apaches. That seemed like an eternity, and Allie decided that Julia was much stronger than she.

When the opportunity presented itself, Allie tried to communicate more with Castro. It was apparent since the day he doctored Jimmy's wounds that he was the shaman of this group. He showed Allie how to mix the poultice to keep doctoring Jimmy's shoulder when she changed his dressing. He pointed out which type of tree bark was good to boil to make the draught he had given her earlier for bringing down Jimmy's fever, which continued to return for several days. Castro had even picked up the discarded deer hide and showed Allie how to rub a mixture of deer brains and fat into the hide, then wet it and roll it up.

Allie tried not to show her revulsion during that process, which she assumed was preparing the skin for tanning. She thanked him in Spanish for what she figured was another tedious task she would be expected to do before too long. After Castro tied it onto her horse, Allie sarcastically told Jimmy that if he got separated from her, he could easily find her by following the cloud of flies that would surely envelop her on the trail.

That actually brought a smile to Jimmy's face, and she couldn't help but grin back for the first time in days. Then she did something crazy. She threw her head back and laughed. It actually startled several of the braves' horses nearby, and they put a little more distance between her and them.

"What are you doing?" Jimmy asked, thinking she had lost her mind.

"That felt so good," Allie said, still smiling. "I've made up my mind. We're going to get through this if it kills us," she said, then laughed again. "Maybe that wasn't the best choice of words."

She had definitely lost her mind, thought Jimmy. If they survived this, he would be taking a crazy woman home to his brother.

"Allie, you're beginning to scare me now," he said.

"No, Jimmy," she said, "I just remembered that God says He won't put on us more than we can handle, and I've been feeling pretty sorry for myself lately. But if what God says is true, then I must be a lot stronger than I think I am. I just haven't realized it."

"You are one of the strongest women I've ever met," Jimmy said. "You saved my life—more than once. And I don't know how you held me up in the saddle that first day, either."

"I'm not that strong—I just couldn't stand the thought of you dying before you really got to live," Allie said, with tears filling her eyes.

Jimmy couldn't respond to that. She was right—he felt like he had been in limbo his whole life. How does a person get that way?

"Look at me," she said, wiping a tear off her cheek, "I *must* be crazy— laughing and crying in the same conversation. But Aunt Sister told me something that I really hadn't understood until now," she continued. "She said that every one of us makes choices every day of our lives. We can choose to be happy, in spite of our circumstances, or we can choose to be miserable and defeated, like I've been feeling lately. We can choose to stay ignorant, or we can try to learn from every situation we find ourselves in. We can choose to laugh rather than cry—my choice a while ago. We can choose to keep trying instead of giving up—my choice from this point on."

Jimmy nodded, thinking about what she said. Then he told her, "I'm going to get you home, Allie."

"And I'm determined to get you home, too," Allie said back.

And for the first time, he thought that maybe she could.

* * *

Justin rose before daylight so he could slip out before Otto Schaferling came to join him in the search for Allie and his brother. This was *his* problem, and he didn't want to put anyone else in danger. And as good as their intentions were, he knew Mr. Schaferling couldn't spare losing a son at a time like this. Besides, with the size of the raiding party he was going after, two men weren't going to be much better than one. The odds were stacked against him in rescuing Allie and his brother, but he still had to try. And after everything Jimmy had done, Justin wasn't even sure he wanted to include Jimmy in any kind of rescue attempt. His concern was only for Allie.

The raiding party had made tracks on wet ground, so even days after the raid on the Schaferling ranch, their trail was still visible—dried as if cast in mud. He had no problems following them. About midday, he came across more tracks of a group of shod horses—maybe a dozen or so coming across the raiding party's tracks. An army patrol must have picked up their trail. He followed the mangled tracks for several hours, and something didn't set quite right with him, but he could not figure out what it was.

Justin heard the riders coming before he saw them, and he rode his horse into a thicket to hide. He recognized the army patrol, and they looked as if they had been in a fight. He hollered a hello before he stepped out into view—they looked upset and skittish, and he didn't want to get shot before they figured out he wasn't an Apache.

The patrol pulled up and hollered back. Justin rode out to meet them and learned that they had been ambushed recently by the very raiding party they had been tracking. They had lost some men and some horses, and were going back for reinforcements.

"Did you see any captives with them?" Justin asked the sergeant in charge, "A woman in particular?"

"No—we didn't see any with this bunch of savages—and especially not a woman. I don't think she'd have a chance in hell surviving this group. We're going to get them, though. Their tracks are easy to follow— we were just too small in number and unprepared. We may even wire for help from Fort McKavett up north of here. You really shouldn't be traveling alone."

Justin thanked them for the information, and watched until they were out of sight before he backtracked to a creek the tracks had come alongside earlier. He crossed it and followed along the opposite direction than the raiding party and army patrol had traveled.

There! It hadn't been obvious, but the Indians had split into two groups at that point, and the creek hid their tracks. The army patrol had gone after the larger raiding party. The tracks of this smaller group included Jimmy and Allie's shod horses. They must have been slowing them down, or maybe the warriors had scouts out that knew an army patrol was in the area, and they led them away from the smaller group. But why? To ambush the patrol? To protect Jimmy and Allie? That didn't make sense. The former was probably their intent. Jimmy and Allie would have been a hindrance to them in an attack, or could have given the army patrol a reason to keep pursuing them.

But on the other hand, he knew it was common for Indians to hide their captives. That was one reason it took so long for his father to find him and his mother—their captors moved them regularly.

He followed the smaller group's trail to where they had camped alongside a river the first night. He walked around the area and found the remains of a campfire and of several rabbits. Everything looked typical, except... what was that?

Justin stared at the oddest-looking campfire. It had sides—tall sides and a back to it. Who in the heck would build this monstrosity? Then the corner of his mouth turned up in bittersweet recognition. It had to have been Allie—she was no woman of the outdoors. He dug around the campfire, finding nothing, and turned his attention to search around the tree nearby. He found what he was looking for there on the side, out of view. A small *A* was carved in the bark.

"I'm coming, Allie," Justin said determinedly. "Hold on."

* * *

For several days, Jimmy and Allie noticed that they consistently traveled in a more northwesterly direction—heading farther out into no-man's-land where forts were very few and far between. The landscape had more hills in some places, and the trees and vegetation grew sparser and lower to the ground. They also saw less and less water.

On day ten or thereabouts of their captivity, they rode into an Indian camp near a wide, shallow river. By the way they were greeted, it was obvious that the raiding party was now among their families. Allie could see twenty-five or thirty tipis and a handful of branch-covered structures that Jimmy said were wickiups that spread out along the river's edge.

Everyone celebrated the warriors' plunder, and Jimmy was right; he and Allie were paraded around and shown off in front of the Indian community. Allie wasn't sure where she fit into the celebration, but as for Jimmy, he seemed to be put on display as the long-lost captive Apache that the warriors had rescued from the white man.

Jimmy and Allie dismounted their horses and were surrounded by well-wishers. An old woman with a moon-shaped scar on her right cheek made a big fuss over Jimmy, hugging him and wailing, and he and Allie were eventually handed over to her. As she led them to her tipi, Jimmy told Allie that they had probably been given over to the tribe's meanest torturer.

141

The hide covering on the lower part of the old woman's tipi had been pulled up to let the breeze waft through. Curious children gathered around the open walls to look at the newcomers. The old squaw shooshed them away and turned to motion for Allie and Jimmy to sit down. She pulled at Jimmy's shirt where old bloodstains still remained from his shoulder wound, and indicated that she wanted him to take it off. He leaned back, trying to avoid her.

"She wants to check your shoulder, Jimmy," Allie said.

So Jimmy reluctantly took off his shirt. The old woman fussed and clucked over Jimmy's wound. They had no idea what she said, but she seemed agitated. She cleaned it and reapplied another poultice, and had Jimmy extend his arm and try to lift it, which affected his shoulder. He howled and grimaced with the pain. She made him do it several times anyway.

"I told you," Jimmy grunted, "she's trying to kill me."

"Your arm's probably a little atrophied," Allie said. "I didn't think about that."

"And what does *that* mean?"

"If you don't use something, it gets to where it's useless," Allie said thoughtfully. "She's a smart woman."

The old squaw looked at Jimmy's side wound and clucked like she was satisfied with that one, and then saw the ragged tear and the old bloodstains on his pants leg. She started pulling at his pants, like she wanted him to take them off, too.

"Now hold on, Grandma," Jimmy said, suddenly embarrassed in front of Allie. "You're not taking my pants."

The old woman stopped and looked at him. "Gah-ma," she said, pointing to herself, nodding. "Gah-ma." She had tears in her eyes again.

"Does she think she's already adopted me or something?" Jimmy said. "They sure don't waste any time around here."

Allie put her hand to her mouth. "No, Jimmy!" she said, feeling goose bumps rising on her arms. "She's saying she's your grandmother!"

Jimmy stared at her in disbelief.

"Nantan Lupan's mother?" Allie asked.

The old woman smiled and nodded her head, yes.

Jimmy didn't know what to do or say. He finally put his head down, overwhelmed. When he looked up at her, she smiled and reached out to him, and he couldn't help but pull the old woman into his arms and weep.

And Allie cried right along with them.

Jimmy sat there and watched his grandmother go about her evening routine. Castro had brought some fresh meat to the old woman, and she began preparing a meal with it. Castro told them in Spanish that her name was Nah-kay, and that she was the last of her family—no mas familia—that is, until Jimmy came back. Jimmy was frustrated that he couldn't communicate with her. Thirteen years had passed since his *rescue* from the Apaches, and he had lost much of the language due to lack of use.

Justin was five years old when he had been taken by the Apaches, and ironically, Jimmy was five years old when the white men took him. The effect on Justin of six years with the Apaches was profound, but he had eventually adjusted and re-entered his birth family's world. The adjustment should have been easier for Jimmy since he was so young, but a lack of acceptance of him by many in the white community created a constant wound that would not heal. He didn't know what or who he was, and now the lack of communication with his grandmother reaffirmed his feeling that he failed to belong in either world.

One thing Jimmy did learn about Nah-kay was that she was a good cook. He didn't know what she put in the meat to season it, but he wolfed it down and held out his bowl for more. Nah-kay seemed pleased with his show of appetite.

Allie couldn't help but notice and said, "I think I'll offer to cook some rabbit for us tomorrow."

Jimmy about choked on his bite, and tried to be nonchalant when he said, "I'm sure she's very protective of her cooking fire."

Allie laughed at his attempt to be diplomatic. "I'm just kidding. It's a wonder my cooking didn't kill you back there on the trail."

Afterwards, Allie was so tired, but she wanted to scrub ten days of trail grime off her clothes and body before bedding down. Allie hoped she could make Nah-kay understand. Allie had used her bar of soap sparingly on the trail, prizing it now as her most valuable possession. She pulled it out of her pocket and pantomimed washing her arms and face and clothes, and Nah-kay nodded in understanding. She led Allie down a path away from the rest of the camp to a secluded area with several large flat rocks in the midst of the water. Allie thanked her, and Nah-kay left.

Allie walked over to an area partially hidden by reeds, and she stripped down to her underclothes, leaving the rest of her clothes on the bank. She and modesty had parted ways some days before, and getting clean was uppermost in her mind. She waded out a little ways to thigh-deep water and went down on her knees so she could wash her hair.

The water felt wonderful—she hadn't immersed herself in water since the bathhouse back at the Taylor house. After washing her hair, she waded back to the flat rocks in the shallow water and sat down to scrub her body. She decided to wait to wash her outer clothes until the morning when she could wear them in the sun until they dried since she didn't have anything else to change into in the meantime.

After she finished, she waded over to where she had left her clothing, but to her surprise, everything but her shoes was gone. In their place, though, lay a gray suede leather dress adorned with intricate beading.

Nah-kay, Allie said to herself. She ran her hand over the velvety soft leather, marveling at the handiwork of it. She quickly looked around and then stepped out of her wet underclothes and pulled the leather dress over her head. She had never worn anything that felt so luxurious. She put her shoes on and made her way back to Nah-kay's home.

Allie smiled when she saw Nah-kay, and ran her hand over the suede and beading as she thanked her. Nah-kay looked very pleased, and motioned for her to sit down. Allie obeyed. Nah-kay began combing her tangled masses, and it took every ounce of strength to stay awake while the old woman gently tamed the dark tresses.

Allie wondered what Nah-kay was using to brush her hair; it wasn't a brush, but something hard and rough-textured, which worked just fine. After two weeks of brutal travel, living with dirt, sweat, smoke, and animal carcasses, Nah-kay made Allie feel like a pampered princess.

When Nah-kay finished combing out Allie's hair, she said something and pointed to a pile of buffalo robes, indicating that would be where Allie slept. Allie looked around and saw a woven blanket to one side, and she motioned to Nah-kay that she would take that one. The old woman shook her head, picked up the blanket and walked out of the tent. She began to lower the hide covering around the tipi.

Allie stepped out to help, and Nah-kay motioned her away, so Allie walked a ways from the tipi to look at the panoramic array of colors in the sunset. The sky never seemed this big before. She thought about the events over the past two weeks, especially Jimmy rediscovering his grandmother today. Allie basked in a sudden awareness that God was doing something big in Jimmy's life—that His hand had been on this whole ordeal from the start. She knew now that it was no coincidence that she ended up on this wild and dangerous ride with Jimmy, although she would never have chosen this path herself. It was no coincidence that this particular raiding party had attacked and captured them. They *had* recognized Nantan Lupan's name—he was once one of them!

Allie still wasn't sure what the outcome would be for her and Jimmy, but she was willing to continue to trust God, knowing that He knew what was best for their lives. And Allie realized, too, even as hard as it had been, that she'd had the privilege of witnessing all this. She shut her eyes and slowly raised her face to heaven, and the tears came again, but this time in praise and submission.

Jimmy limped back to his grandmother's tipi and noticed the beautiful Indian girl looking to the west. He was taken aback when he realized it was Allie, and he couldn't help but watch her for a moment.

Jimmy knew something was happening in his life, but he didn't understand it, nor could he explain it. He had no doubt that Allie was the key, somehow. It pained him to see her quiet tears again, but then he couldn't understand why she was smiling, too. She must have made another choice, he decided. And it made him that much more determined to get her back home, safe and sound.

Allie turned around and caught Jimmy's eye, and walked back to the tipi.

"Your grandmother is spoiling me terribly," she said, looking down. "Look at this beautiful dress she gave me to wear until I can wash my clothes. I've never felt anything like it."

"It's beautiful," Jimmy said, looking at Allie's face.

Allie looked up. "You remind me so much of your brother."

Nah-kay had pulled all of the hides down around the tipi except for a few gaps to let a breeze drift through. She walked up to Allie and Jimmy and took each of their hands and placed them in each other's, and said something before pushing them toward the tipi entrance. Then she turned and walked away.

"Where is she going?" Allie asked, pulling her hand away.

"I think she's giving us some privacy," said Jimmy.

"Why would she do that?"

"I think she thinks we're married."

Allie's eyes widened. "Well, you just go get her and tell her otherwise."

"And break her heart?"

Allie socked Jimmy in the arm—his sore shoulder arm. He yelped and doubled over.

145

"I was just teasing," he gasped.

"I am so sorry, Jimmy!" Allie said taking his good arm. "I can't believe I just did that. Here, come on inside and sit down—I'll go get Nah-kay and bring her back, and we'll try to get her to understand."

"Wait a minute, Allie," Jimmy said as he stiffly sat down. "It might be safer for you to let them think you're my woman. Otherwise, you could be handed off to the next brave who comes up with the largest number of ponies."

Allie hadn't thought about that. She hadn't felt threatened by the Apaches since the morning they had been taken, but she realized now that it was because of Jimmy's blood relation with this band. Without Jimmy, she would still be considered the enemy and vulnerable to their whims and potentially brutal form of judgment.

Jimmy watched her weighing the words he had spoken.

"Would it be so terrible?" he asked her.

"Would what be so terrible?"

"If you were my woman," Jimmy said. "Could someone like you ever have feelings for someone like me?"

Allie's face softened as she realized what he was saying. "In a heartbeat, Jimmy, but under different circumstances," she said. "And I met your brother first."

Jimmy looked away. "That figures."

"Let me tell you something, Jimmy Taylor," Allie said sternly, "kidnapping isn't the best way to start a relationship with a girl, nor is scaring them half out of their wits a good way to impress her."

He just nodded his head. He couldn't argue against that. She was right.

"Can you tell me honestly, though, if the circumstances were different—would it bother you to be seen with me?" he asked.

"A year ago I had a relationship with a wonderful man whose skin was darker than yours. It didn't bother me, but it bothered just about everyone else in town. I think my parents would have accepted him eventually, but they couldn't get past worrying about me getting hurt, so they sent me away for my sake. What I'm trying to say, Jimmy, is that there are girls and people out there who *can* see beyond your skin color to who you are inside. Look at the Schaferling family—they accepted you, didn't they?"

Jimmy nodded again.

"It's not going to be easy, but it's worth pursuing. I believe God has someone out there for you, and what you need to work on is *you*. What a treasure you are going to be to some woman some day, if you'll just recognize that," Allie said, as she reached over and turned Jimmy's face toward hers. "So in answer to your question: no, it would not bother me in the least to be seen with you."

Allie hugged him, and Jimmy felt the warmth of another flicker of hope for his future.

"And we've slept side by side all this time on the trail together, so it won't bother me a bit to sleep in the same tipi with you," Allie said. "Just don't hog the hides."

As she lay down on the softest bed she had ever felt, she smiled when she thought about what the women in the Dalton Ladies Home Club would think about her now—sleeping in a tipi beside a handsome Apache brave.

And Jimmy was thinking that he couldn't remember it ever being this uncomfortable lying beside Allie on the trail, so he dragged a buffalo hide off to one side to sleep on.

"Too hot?" Allie asked naively.

"Yeah," Jimmy said. *You're exactly right,* he thought as he pulled off his shirt and wadded it up for a pillow.

Chapter 12

*N*ah-kay indulged Jimmy and Allie by letting them sleep past sunrise. Allie sat up and stretched—it felt so good to sleep on something other than the hard ground. She found Nah-kay outside scraping on the deer hide she had found with Allie's saddle. Allie felt a twinge of guilt, knowing she had ignored the hide on the trail, mainly because she didn't know what she was supposed to do with it. Castro had showed her how to wet it and fold and roll it back up, but she had no idea when she was supposed to start scraping it, or with what. She crawled out of the tipi and walked over to Nah-kay.

"I'm sorry, Nah-kay," Allie said, smiling apologetically and pointing to the hide, now stretched tautly on a frame.

The old woman smiled and patted the ground beside her. Allie sat down and watched as Nah-kay showed her how to use a scraping tool to scrape off any remaining meat or fat from the hide. She handed Allie another scraper and watched her attempt to scrape it. The fat and other tissue came off easily—Allie guessed the repulsive mixture Castro had put on it had some kind of softening effect. Nah-kay showed her on the edge of the hide how easy it was to scrape too deeply, even to the point of making a hole, and she shook head, no. She took Allie's hand and had her feel the width of the hide in the areas she had already scraped, helping her gauge the thickness in order to be consistent across the hide.

Nah-kay was a good teacher. Allie understood what she said with her movements and gestures. She wondered if Nah-kay had taught Julia these same lessons.

Jimmy rolled over and sat up. His grandmother had already raised some of the sides of the tipi, and the morning air felt good on his face. He could see Allie sitting beside Nah-kay, and it looked like the most natural thing for her to be scraping a hide. Allie's face was tanned dark from the days traveling in the sun. Her dark brown hair contrasted his grandmother's silver hair. The old was teaching the young. Where had he heard that before?

Allie looked like she already belonged here, although he knew she didn't. Why was that? He was the one with Indeh blood—not her, and yet she seemed to be more comfortable in this environment than he. Was it another choice she had made? To learn what she could even in the most difficult of situations? He had been in many difficult situations, too, but instead of making him stronger, he seemed to have lost pieces of himself and became more and more withdrawn from the world. Were there choices in those situations? Why had he not seen them? Did God help her see this?

After Matthew Taylor brought them back to Grace, Jimmy's mother made him go to church until he was old enough to take off on his own, but he always felt like that was their God—not his. The words he heard meant nothing to him—he had no room for them in his mind or heart. They couldn't exist alongside the anger he felt.

The anger—he hadn't nursed it for days now. His wounds and his concern for Allie's well-being had crowded the anger out of his mind. He should have been angry at the Apaches for almost killing him and Allie, but he hadn't picked up that particular demon for some reason. Why was that? If it had been a white man that had almost killed him, the anger would have continued to burn in him like fire. But the anger he had felt most of his life had never been in defense of the Indeh.

Why should this situation be any different in riling his anger? It shouldn't have, and he knew it. He had chosen to spew hatred toward his family over much less offense than this, and they had never even come close to hurting him like the Apaches had done. Was he now accepting of the Indeh because they had spared his life and accepted him as their own? Why then, couldn't he accept his own family?

What was wrong with him? Allie was right—his family members were some of the few people who actually loved and accepted him, and yet they received the brunt of his blame and anger toward the world.

And as much as he hated to admit it, Allie was also right about his birth father. Nantan Lupan had broken not only a legal law, but more importantly—a higher moral law by taking what wasn't his against their will. Julia's husband had every right to find and protect his family. And he had no doubt that Nantan Lupan would have killed Matthew Taylor if he had the chance. Was that just?

But on the other hand, this group of Indeh accepted him as their own now because of the blood that ran through his veins. He had no doubts about his grandmother's love and acceptance of him, and the others for that matter, even though his mother was white. But he had lost most of the language and still felt like an outsider. He'd also had enough of the white man's ways to feel comfortable in that physical environment. The past two weeks of living on the back of a horse told him that the Indeh way of life was much harder than he ever imagined, much less remembered.

For several years, he toyed with the idea of going back to the people that he most looked like, but he was sure now that he couldn't raid and pillage as a way of life. He'd also had enough of his mother's teaching to know that was wrong. The cultures clashed, and he was caught in the middle of it. But now something was different in the midst of this, and it seemed to change everything.

Allie? Yes, but Jimmy knew it was more than that. She saw a future for him that he couldn't see, but he was beginning to. And she, more than anyone else, had the right to be angry and to hate those around her at this moment—especially Jimmy. But she chose not to. He never realized he had the power to choose. The anger always chose him, and he accepted it.

"Hey, sleepy head!" Allie said, seeing Jimmy sitting up.

He looked around for his shirt and couldn't find it before stepping out of the tipi barefooted. Allie had to look away and concentrate on her scraping—she had seen Jimmy without his shirt before, but until then she hadn't noticed how pleasing he was to the eye. A blush crept up Allie's cheeks.

"Clothes keep disappearing around here—anybody seen my shirt?"

"I think Nah-kay has already done half a day's work before we woke up—your *clean* shirt is drying over there next to my clean clothes," Allie said. "Your grandmother puts me to shame."

Jimmy came over to watch Allie work. She became even more self-conscious of his being half-dressed beside her. She covered her discomfort by talking.

"This is what I woke up to Nah-kay doing—scraping the hide that *I'd* been carrying around this past week. How she got all this other work done, and then had time to stretch this hide before we woke up—I don't know how she does it."

"I could stand to learn some things from her," Jimmy said.

Nah-kay had moved over to her cooking fire and began patting what looked like corn meal cakes. She said something to Jimmy and raised her arm up and down.

"You'd better work the stiffness out of your arm before she comes over here and does it for you," Allie said, grinning.

"I was hoping she'd forget about that," Jimmy said as he squatted down beside Allie and gingerly raised his arm. "We need to talk about getting you home."

Allie stopped scraping. "I figured you'd let me know when you were ready," Allie said. "I don't think you're ready yet, though."

She watched him struggle to raise his arm.

"Give me a couple more days, and in the meantime maybe I can get my pistol back and—"

"You're not going to shoot your way out of here, are you?" Allie said, alarmed.

"No, but I can't take you all that way back home without some sort of weapon to defend ourselves—you know, from snakes or outlaws or such. And I'm not fast enough to catch our food," he said, "at least not in the condition I'm in."

Allie smiled at his humor. "Keep lifting," Allie ordered as she started scraping again.

"You're starting to act like her now," Jimmy said.

"I wish we could take her back with us, Jimmy," Allie said. "She has no other family."

"The others seem to have a lot of respect for her, and they're providing for her just fine," Jimmy said.

"I think Castro is sweet on her," Allie said.

Jimmy smiled. "That old dog—he's a smart one, too. But I don't know if Nah-kay would want to come with us."

"Well, let's try to find out before we leave, all right?" Allie asked.

Jimmy nodded, yes, watching his grandmother.

"Jimmy," she paused, "do you think Justin's still looking for us?"

"I'm sure of it," he said. "Tracks left in damp ground will last for days. We'll probably meet up with him on the trail going back."

Allie nodded and continued scraping.

"He'd never let you go, Allie." Jimmy assured her. *He'd be a fool to,* he thought silently.

151

That evening, Castro joined them for a meal. With her limited Spanish and even more gesturing, Allie tried to think of simple phrases and questions to ask Nah-kay through Castro. Between hand signs and a few words, she was able to communicate her and Jimmy's gratefulness for the food – comida, and clean clothes – ropa, and comfortable bed - cama. She asked Castro to ask Nah-kay if she remembered Julia, Jimmy's madre - mother.

Nah-kay didn't even look at Castro for the interpretation. She heard the name *Julia*. She looked at Jimmy across from her and reached over and gently brushed her fingers across his blue eyes, nodding.

"Jew-ya," she said sadly, and said something else to Castro.

When Castro spoke, Allie recognized something about mother's ojos - eyes, and hija - daughter, and amor - love.

"I think she loved your mother like a daughter," Allie told Jimmy.

Nah-kay gently tugged on Allie's leather dress, which she was still wearing from the night before. "Jew-ya."

Allie was wearing Julia's dress! She took a deep breath to keep her emotions in check before she started to speak to Jimmy.

"I know what she said, Allie," Jimmy said, watching his grandmother's face. "Ask Castro to ask her if she would like to see my mother again."

Allie struggled to find the right words: "Vamos, no, that's not right... de visita a la Julia."

Castro looked angry. What was he thinking?

"Nah-kay's familia—Julia, Justin y Jimmy... uh... visitar, comprende?" Allie asked. "Amigos, familia... amor."

Castro looked doubtful, but he said something to Nah-kay. She raised her eyebrows almost wistfully, then shook her head, no, and said something. Castro related it back in Spanish. The only words Allie made out had to do with being afraid and *muerte*.

"She's afraid for her life, I think," Allie said. "Muerte means death."

"Don't be afraid, Nah-kay," Jimmy said, taking her hand, frustrated that he couldn't speak her language. "No muerte, only love and life awaits you with my family."

Allie could not believe her ears—Jimmy had said, *my family,* and in the same sentence with *love* and *life*.

"Can you tell him to tell her that?" Jimmy said, wondering why Allie was hesitating.

"Yes, of course," Allie said, regaining her composure. "El amor y la vida... en mi familia, I mean, Jimmy y Julia's familia. I'm sorry I'm not better at this, Jimmy."

"I should be the one that's sorry—I should be able to speak to my grandmother in her own language—my language, too," Jimmy said while Castro talked to Nah-kay, "and I've lost it."

"You could learn it again," Allie suggested.

Nah-kay listened to Castro and shook her head, no, again.

"No!" Castro said abruptly, and stood up to leave.

"That word didn't need interpreting," said Jimmy.

Allie quickly got up and said, "Buenas noches, Castro, y gracias."

Castro grunted and walked away.

"Have we offended him?" Allie said. "Do you think they will let us go?"

"I don't know," Jimmy said, watching him walk away into the night. "We may have ruined our chances of leaving anytime soon by involving Castro in trying to talk to Nah-kay. We may have to try to sneak away, but that will be hard to do."

"Do you know where the horses are?" Allie asked.

"Yeah," he said.

Nah-kay started preparing for bed, and this time, her obvious intent was to stay with Jimmy and Allie in the tipi.

"Looks like the honeymoon's over, sweetheart," Jimmy said dryly, and then cowered from the expected sock in the arm.

Allie giggled. "You need to let that show more often."

"What?" he said as he straightened up, checking himself to see if something was unbuttoned.

"Your sense of humor," she said "It's very attractive."

He planned to remember that.

The next day, Jimmy half expected to have guards outside the tipi after the conversation with Castro and Nah-kay, but everything seemed to be the same as before. Jimmy said he would go check on the horses, and Allie didn't see him again for hours.

That afternoon, Allie changed back into her own clothes, and tried to return the dress to Nah-kay, but the old woman seemed to insist that she keep it. Allie hugged her, and Nah-kay responded, seemingly pleased that she had accepted her gift.

Allie had finished scraping the hide the day before, and today Nah-kay showed her how to mix some water and ashes to soak the hide in. She pulled out some of the hairs to demonstrate that the mixture would help remove the hair from the hide.

Castro brought Nah-kay some fresh deer meat, and Allie helped her cut it up and ready it for cooking. She watched how Nah-kay seasoned it and prepared some as a stew, and the rest she had Allie cut into thin strips that they smoked and dried over the fire. Then she showed Allie how to use a mallet and grinding stone to pound and shred some previously made jerky into small pieces. They mixed the meat with ground berries and some kind of fat to hold it together, and then placed it in greased leather pouches for storage.

Nah-kay motioned for Allie to taste the finished product, and to her surprise, she discovered it had a wonderful flavor. Nah-kay laughed at the expression on Allie's face.

During the night, a thunderstorm rolled over the camp. A loud clap of thunder awakened Allie—she sat up, and from the lightning flashes she could see Nah-kay and Jimmy pulling and tying down the hides covering the tipi. The wind already blew fiercely. Allie worried about Jimmy's shoulder and jumped up to help, but Jimmy shouted for her to stay inside. He and his grandmother came back inside just as the downpour struck.

"Will this tent hold?" Allie asked above the howling wind.

"I sure hope so!" said Jimmy as he hunkered down beside her. "It's staked into the ground pretty tight." He paused for a moment, then asked, "What is that!?"

Allie listened—it was a loud humming, and it came from the direction of Nah-kay.

"Maybe she hums when she's scared!" Allie said loudly. "It sounds familiar."

Jimmy listened a minute. "She's humming my mother's favorite song."

"You're right! It's *Amazing Grace*!" Allie said. "She must have learned it from your mother."

The wind died down after a bit, but the rain continued to fall. Jimmy propped open a flap on the protected side. The lightning continued to flash, and Allie jumped each time the thunder boomed.

"We'll be all right," Jimmy said reassuringly. "Nah-kay has obviously survived many storms in this sturdy tent."

"I wonder if Justin's out in the middle of this," Allie said, and then realized something else. "Oh, Jimmy, it's going to wash away any tracks he

154

might have been following. I don't know if he'll ever be able to find us."

"He's a good tracker," Jimmy said, but he knew the chances of Justin picking up the trail after this storm were slim to none. He couldn't see Allie's face, but he could hear the disappointment in her voice. She knew the truth, but she still wouldn't confront him. He reached over to find her still sitting up. She grabbed his hand and put it to her face to feel her nod in agreement. But he saw her face in the next flash of lightning and recognized a sadness and resignation in the gesture. Then in the darkness, he could feel her lie back down.

Jimmy didn't know how long he lay there after Allie had lain down. His thoughts gave him no peace or rest. He couldn't stand to disappoint Allie anymore, and that was all he had ever done since he met her.

He finally got up and ran out of the tent into the rain. Why couldn't he change for her sake? Or for *his* sake, for god's sake! *For God's sake*—why do people even say that? What does it mean?

Jimmy headed to the river and stood by the bank for a moment. Then he walked into the water. He leaned his head back and let the rain fall on his face. He didn't know the words to say, but he knew God was there. He lifted up his arms in invitation.

"I know you are there," Jimmy said aloud, "I see you in Allie... and I want you in me." He was silent for a moment and then said earnestly, "I want to live! My burden's too big for me to carry anymore. Take the bad and make it good. Take the hate and make it love. Take the sadness and make it joy. I know I can't do it, but I believe you can. And I need your help to get Allie home. Please don't let me hurt her again."

Some might say it was the rain that made him feel clean, but something else washed over him that night, and it went all through him—body, mind, and spirit.

Jimmy didn't realize that Allie had followed him outside—his thrashing around had kept her awake, too, and it scared her to see him run out of the tipi that way. When he stepped into the river, it took everything she had to keep from screaming out at him, recalling the nightmares she'd had about the water. But the river current wasn't deep or swift enough to wash him away... yet. His bare back was to her, and in the lightning of the storm she could see him standing out there with his hands and face raised.

The lightning still scared her, though, and she waited until she could stand it no longer.

"Jimmy!!" she called out.

Jimmy turned around and saw her standing on the riverbank. He waded back to her, stepped out of the river, and grabbed her by the arms. The rain ran down their faces.

"Allie, I'm so sorry I hurt you. I don't know why you don't hate me right now—I've given you every reason to, but I need to ask you to forgive me," he cried.

"I already told you, Jimmy, that I forgive you," she said, recognizing that something significant had happened.

"I guess I needed to hear myself ask you," he said. "It's been haunting me."

He still held her at arms' length when something hit him at a dead run, grabbed him and knocked him away from Allie. She fell back as she saw someone pull Jimmy into the river. A man—another brave? Why would anyone attack Jimmy now, knowing he was the son of one of their former leaders?

Allie screamed Jimmy's name.

The two men struggled to stand in the water, and in the flashes of lightning, Allie saw a streak of light-colored hair. She didn't recognize the face, though—the face frightened her. He pummeled Jimmy as Jimmy held up his good arm to ward off the blows.

But he wouldn't fight back. Why wouldn't he defend himself?

Justin! Allie realized with a shock. Justin had found them, and he must have thought Jimmy was hurting her.

"Justin, no!!" she screamed as she leaped into the river.

Allie tried to pull Justin off of Jimmy, but he pushed her away. She screamed at him to stop, but he couldn't seem to hear her. She forced herself between them and felt a crunching blow to the side of her head. And after one blinding light, the lightning seemed to have stopped. Or was it that her eyes had closed? She couldn't tell any more. Everything seemed to slow down, and she felt herself slipping under the water, but she couldn't make her arms and legs work to stand up.

"Allie!!" a voice screamed from far away.

Strong hands grabbed her before she slipped away... no, too late... her mind slipped away in spite of the effort.

Chapter 13

"**W**hat did you do to her?" Jimmy yelled. "Did you *hit* her?"

"Help me, Jimmy!" Justin hollered back at him as he picked up Allie and waded toward the riverbank. "Get out and let me hand her to you."

"My shoulder's too weak," Jimmy said. "Let me get her feet, and we'll both step out."

"And don't bleed all over her," Justin said as he saw Jimmy's bloodied face in the flashes of lightning.

"Whose fault is that, brother?!" Jimmy argued back.

Nah-kay and a group of Apaches stood on the riverbank, drawn out of their tipis by all the commotion going on outside. In the heat of the moment the brothers neglected to remember where they were. When several hands reached down to take Allie from Justin's arms, they were immediately brought back to the present. At Nah-kay's orders, they proceeded to walk away with her.

"Allie!!" Justin yelled as he climbed out of the shallow river and lunged toward the braves carrying her.

Several more grabbed Justin and wrestled him to the ground. Justin fought back, and Jimmy quickly jumped to his defense. Justin kept yelling for Allie.

"Stop! He's my brother!" Jimmy cried, to no avail. In the darkness and periodic flashes, it was hard to make anyone understand.

In the midst of the chaos a sickening thud was heard, and Justin suddenly went quiet. The Apaches knew a stranger had come into their midst and harmed one of their own as Jimmy's bleeding wounds gave evidence. They thought Jimmy was trying to continue the fight with their captive—he was yelling and attempting to pull them away from the intruder, so they kept pushing him away. There would be time for that later. They dragged Justin away from the riverbank and bound him, deciding to deal with him at daylight.

Jimmy refused to leave, so two braves stayed with the captive to keep Jimmy from prematurely killing him. They thought he should show some patience and restraint—everyone should be able to watch this. They couldn't understand why he continued to rant about it. They watched him finally sit down nearby, still obviously upset.

* * *

Allie felt something cool on her forehead. She tried to open her eyes—why did they feel so heavy? She turned her head to see Nah-kay stoking a small fire within the tipi. Allie realized she did feel rather cold for some reason.

Then the nightmare began to come back to her in bits and pieces. *Not again,* she thought. But this time Jimmy and Justin were in the river. She must have awoken Nah-kay with her crying. She shut her eyes and smiled, thinking the old woman must have made a fire so Allie wouldn't be cold and afraid anymore. She drifted back to sleep, hoping the nightmare would not return.

* * *

The rain stopped after a while, and the clouds moved on to the southeast, leaving a clear sky and a cool, crisp feel to the air. In the gray light just before dawn, Jimmy sat watching his brother. He hadn't slept the rest of the night for fear that if he did, he might lose Justin for good, and he couldn't risk that. The two braves guarding him nodded off several times, but made no further attempts to hurt his brother.

Justin started coming to. Jimmy moved a little closer. The two Apaches immediately straightened up and were on guard at Jimmy's movement. One of them noticed Justin stirring and said something to the other brave and left. The remaining guard positioned himself between Jimmy and Justin.

"Justin?" Jimmy said.

Justin raised his head slowly, trying to get his bearings.

"Justin, are you all right?"

Justin couldn't speak for a moment; the nasty pain in his head held his utmost attention.

"What happened?" he finally said weakly as he struggled to sit up. His head felt as if it would burst.

"They thought you were trying to kill me," Jimmy said.

"Well, actually, I was," Justin replied, closing his eyes.

"And I know I deserved that," Jimmy said quietly.

Justin looked at his brother. Did he hear remorse in that statement? Then he suddenly remembered. "Where's Allie?!" he demanded to know.

"She's in good hands," Jimmy said, "with my grandmother."

"Nah-kay?" Justin said. "Nah-na's here? In this camp?"

"You remembered her name?" Jimmy said. "You called her Nah-na?"

"You did, too, and she was my grandmother, too," Justin said, and then thought for a moment. "That explains it."

"Explains what?"

"Why you and Allie didn't look like you were being held against your will yesterday. I watched you from a low bluff as you moved around the camp. I was afraid they might have held off killing you both until they brought you back to their camp—I've been riding hell-bent to get here in time. And you two were safe all along."

"They almost killed me at first," Jimmy said. "Two arrows and a bullet—"

"Allie's the only one I'm concerned about," Justin interrupted. "Did they hurt her?"

"No, she's fine, or was fine until you showed up."

Justin glared at him.

Jimmy didn't speak for a spell, trying to find the right words, but when they came, they spilled out of him.

"Justin, I'm not sure how to say this, and I don't blame you for hating me the rest of your life, but I'm sorry for what I put you and the family through. I didn't mean to put Allie in danger—I wasn't thinking clearly and thought I needed to buy some time. I'd already done enough for you to want to kill me by then. I was going to send her back to Grace in a couple of days. Then the raiding party attacked us and shot me out of the saddle as we were running away, and Allie came back and saved my life."

"How could that little girl have saved you from a bunch of braves who were already in the process of killing you?" Justin asked.

"She told them who I was."

159

"That wouldn't mean anything to them."

"She told them I was Indeh—that I was the son of Nantan Lupan."

"How did she know *that?*"

"She had asked me earlier—she asked me about my father; she asked me about the Apaches. I told her what they call themselves—that it wasn't *Apache*. I told her they call themselves Indeh. And she remembered that and took a huge risk coming back to defend me," Jimmy said.

"I can't believe this is the same group we lived with all those years ago," Justin said as he looked around. He looked closely at the young brave guarding him. No recognition. "Are you sure?"

"I think there's only a handful of the original group here, but the older ones remember my father, and they have a great respect for Nah-kay."

"This is too big of a coincidence," Justin said, trying to grasp the idea.

"Allie made me realize that it's not a coincidence, but there's a reason for this happening," Jimmy said. "I'm not sure what it is, though."

But Justin wasn't finished with his own anger. "If you've laid one finger on Allie, Jimmy, I swear I'll..."

"I haven't touched her, Justin!" Jimmy said. "And I didn't see anything but the side of her leg that night in the bathhouse—I promise! And I'm really sorry I did something so stupid. Are you listening to me? Allie's taught me some things about making choices and choosing to live in peace, and she's had every reason to hate me, but she doesn't, Justin."

"What are you talking about?"

"She doesn't hate me—she told me she forgives me."

"For kidnapping her? For putting us through hell thinking she drowned?"

"Well, she doesn't know about that part."

"Jimmy, do you know what you've done? Do you really know what you've done?" Justin asked.

"I was still half-lit when she came down to the river—I had scared her, but I really didn't mean to; then she started running," Jimmy rambled on, "and I told her not to, but she fell, and there was all this blood, and then I got scared and figured you'd assume I was the one that hurt her and would kill me. And then later, when I was thinking straight, I realized I'd already gotten in over my head, but I never meant to hurt her or you..."

"You haven't been thinking clearly for years, Jimmy," Justin said.

"But now I am, and I want to change," Jimmy said. "I want things to be different. And I want to do something with my life."

"I'd kind of like that for myself, too, Jimmy, but with Allie," Justin said. "I just hope I get the chance to do that."

"I'll get us out of this somehow," Jimmy said. "We were going to leave soon—I just needed to give my shoulder a little more time to heal up and..."

But Jimmy was interrupted by a group of braves walking up to them. Castro was leading them.

Castro said something, and motioned for them to get Justin. Jimmy stepped protectively in front of his brother.

"You're not going to harm my brother," Jimmy said threateningly, holding his arm and hand out in a gesture for them to stop.

Justin looked at his brother again—something *was* different about him.

"It's all right, Jimmy," Justin said, turning to the old man. "Castro?"

The old man looked at Justin and said something. Then Justin answered him in words that were completely unintelligible to Jimmy, and the Apaches untied Justin, helped him stand, and stepped back.

Justin grinned at the old man. "Well, if it isn't my old friend."

"You remember him?" Jimmy asked.

But Justin was already embracing Castro.

* * *

Allie could hear words, but she couldn't understand them. Justin! It was Justin's voice, but why wasn't he making any sense? She remembered her nightmare again—this time almost losing both Jimmy and Justin in the water. No, she was in the water, too. Did she save them? She must have woken up before she found out. But why did she still hear Justin's voice? Was she dreaming?

Something touched her cheek. She opened her eyes. Yes, she was still dreaming— half of Justin's face hovered above her. She shut her eyes again.

"Allie? Are you awake?"

Justin's voice spoke again, and she understood him this time. She opened her eyes again and smiled at the half face. His half face was so handsome. She liked this dream. She shut her eyes again.

Allie heard Nah-kay say something.

"No, she hasn't lost her mind, Nah-na," Justin said. "She's just a bit addled." And he repeated something Allie didn't understand.

Justin was talking to Nah-kay, and she understood him.

161

Her eyes flew open. She reached up and touched Justin's face. She felt the stubble of several days' growth. It was real. He was there. A small fire in the middle of the tipi illuminated the side of his face.

"You're really here?" she whispered as tears filled her eyes. "Jimmy kept telling me that you'd find us." She reached for him, and he pulled her close.

She could feel Justin trembling as he spoke into her ear, "I thought I'd lost you—I thought I had moved heaven and earth to find you, and then I almost lost you again. And it was my fault this time."

Allie was content to stay in his arms forever, but then she remembered Jimmy and pulled away from Justin. "Where's Jimmy? Is he all right?" she asked, fearing the answer.

"I'm right here, Allie," Jimmy said, "next to Nah-kay."

She turned with obvious relief; that is, until she looked at him.

"Oh, Jimmy..."

His grandmother was cleaning the dried blood from his face and attempting to dab something on a cut above his swollen eye. He was favoring his wounded shoulder again, too.

"I'm fine, and I deserved every blow," he said. "Justin and I have come to an agreement, though. He's promised to hold off killing me until we get you home."

"What?!" Allie said, eyes flashing. She turned to Justin. He was grinning.

She was just about to light into him when Jimmy said, "I'm just kidding, Allie."

"Careful, brother, she has a mean punch," Justin said.

"You two," Allie said, with obvious relief. She turned to Justin. "Is everything all right between you two?"

"I don't know what you did to him, Allie, but he doesn't appear to be the same angry, obnoxious little brother I remember," Justin said. "He even took up for me out there. I don't know if that's the real Jimmy, though, or the one that knows he's in big trouble. Ask me again if and when we get home."

"But, Justin, he's..." she began to defend him, but Jimmy interrupted her.

"That's fair enough, Allie," he said. "I know I have some proving to do to Justin and my family, and I'm willing to do it."

Castro stuck his head in the opening, and Justin invited him in. He came in and sat down near Nah-kay, telling Justin that they had brought his horse and belongings into camp. He carried a bow and cluster of arrows, and began fussing at Justin as he worked to bend and straighten the arrows.

"I didn't have any way to keep them dry," Justin said as he defended himself haltingly in the language of the Indeh.

Jimmy looked at Justin. "I didn't know you remembered the language."

"I hadn't thought about it, either, until I understood what Castro said to me earlier," Justin said. "It's a little rusty, but my memory's good."

"Are those yours?" Jimmy asked, pointing to the weapons.

"Yeah, I made them on the way," Justin said. "I didn't realize it would take so long to find you, and I needed to come up with a means to get food without using up all my ammunition."

"You made them yourself?" Jimmy asked, as Justin nodded.

"Castro taught me years ago—that's why he's having a fit. They're not up to his standard," Justin said.

"Can you teach me?" Jimmy asked. "I'd like to learn how."

"Sure."

"And I have a lot of questions I'd like to ask Nah-kay," Jimmy said.

"So have I," Justin said, and he turned to the elderly couple and began asking questions, faulting at first, but eventually making himself understood with their help in finding the right words.

The brothers wanted to know why Nantan Lupan had taken Julia and Justin in the first place. Nah-kay told them that Nantan's own wife and son had been killed by white soldiers on a raid of their camp, and he retaliated by taking a white woman and her son in revenge. He hated the soldiers, and made it a point to attack and raid any patrols to cause as much damage as he could. Nah-kay said her son had a temper and that he never got over losing his first wife and child. He calmed down, though, after Jimmy came, and life became more tolerable for Julia and Justin.

Nah-kay said Nantan was wrong, though, to hurt Julia—motioning to her left hand—that his anger had clouded his thinking, and that he didn't realize until later what a hardship he created for her trying to do all the work a woman does with the strength of only one hand. She said Nantan grew to respect Julia, though, because she was a strong woman in spirit and never complained or cried.

Allie asked if Julia had taught her the melody to *Amazing Grace*, and Justin didn't know how to make Nah-kay understand, so Allie hummed the song. The old woman nodded in recognition. Nah-kay said it protected

163

her home. She said that Julia always sang it during a frightening storm or whenever something worried her. Justin told Allie that his mother was terrified of losing him to the Indeh ways of raiding and killing. Nah-kay said that Julia didn't understand that they were defending their land. They were some of the last of their kind still roaming free—most were imprisoned, she said.

Justin tried to correct her by saying they were moved to their own land—he didn't know an Indian word for *reservation*, but Nah-kay shook her head and kept repeating the word for *captives* in describing her people and other clans and tribes.

Castro pointed to some scars on Justin's chest and back and prompted him to share some stories about how he got them—some during training and others from dares by the other boys he grew up with. Allie could sense a strong family bond as Justin reminisced with Nah-kay and Castro. She saw no sign of the savagery she grew up believing about the Indians, although she knew that side existed toward their enemies—she had witnessed it herself. But she also learned that the Indeh had experienced savagery from the white man, too. She thought she had already learned the lesson that there were good and bad in every race from her experience with Miguel, but she realized she had never applied that to the Indian, the Indeh.

Allie watched Jimmy soaking up everything that was said—wanting to learn more about the people who gave him his face and skin. She looked at the contrast again between the two brothers: Justin, the fair-headed, still retained much from his time with the Apaches—the language, the memories, the skills. Jimmy had retained nothing from the Indeh except his appearance. Maybe he would find and use the best of both cultures now rather than fighting and denying the two worlds from which he came

They talked well into mid-morning, and Jimmy began nodding off. He hadn't slept all night, and Justin was exhausted, too. Nah-kay rummaged around and found a leather pouch and passed it around, telling and motioning for them to eat and then to lie down and rest. Jimmy took a handful and chewed it quickly, handing the pouch to Justin before lying down. Castro and Nah-kay left the tipi.

Justin looked in the pouch and said, "Pemmican."

"What?" Allie said.

"We used to eat a lot of it—especially when we were moving around," Justin said.

"I helped Nah-kay make some yesterday," Allie said as she dipped into the pouch. "I didn't think I would, but I liked the taste."

Jimmy began snoring quietly.

"I watched you working yesterday," Justin said. "I almost didn't recognize you—you looked like any other woman in camp."

"—but prettier," he added quickly.

Allie smiled at his attempt to compliment her. "I was wearing your mother's dress. Nah-kay gave it to me."

"You must like it—I see you have it on again."

Allie looked down. "When did that happen?"

"Nah-na must've stripped you out of your wet clothes last night," Justin said, pointing to her skirt and blouse tied onto the side of the hide wall. "She took our soiled shirts, too, before she let us in here."

"How does she do it?" Allie asked. "I've never seen any woman as strong as she or work as hard as she does, and she's an old woman."

"Do you think Jimmy will be ready to ride tomorrow?" Justin asked, changing the subject. "We need to get you home."

"I'm not sure—he may need another day to rest and heal," Allie said, "and you, too, after your long ride. What have you and Jimmy been doing all night?"

"I was tied up," Justin said, rubbing his stiff neck, "and Jimmy was there when I woke up, so I guess he sat there all night with me."

"Tied up? Why did they do that to you—you're Jimmy's brother!?"

"They didn't know I was his brother until Castro came around before sun-up."

"Why didn't you tell them?"

"Somebody knocked me out before I even thought about saying anything other than your name," he said.

"Oh, Justin—I'm so sorry," Allie said. "Are you all right? How do you feel?"

She felt around on his head, and he winced when she found a good-sized knot.

"Tired, but I don't want you out of my sight," Justin said, reaching for her.

"Please rest—I'll stay right here close—I promise," she said as she hugged him, and was suddenly aware that he didn't have a shirt on. The fluttering in her stomach was back. "Now lie down and get some sleep. We're going to need it for the journey soon."

He pulled her down beside him and wrapped his arms around her. In less than a minute, he was asleep. Allie basked in the strength and security of his arms around her, then shut her eyes, feeling a peace she hadn't felt in quite some time.

Chapter 14

*J*immy and Justin slept until mid-afternoon, but Allie awoke several hours earlier and rose to help Nah-kay grind corn and make cakes for their next few meals. Allie thought about how fragile the line was from hand to mouth with the Indeh, but Nah-kay seemed to accept it and not fret about it. Justin had told Allie he remembered as a child often going through times of hunger with the Apaches, and it made him appreciate food all the more. She smiled, remembering the way he fawned over Aunt Sister's and Vestal's cooking.

Nah-kay had already washed and hung the brothers' shirts to dry outside the tipi. To her chagrin she realized that this simple task should have been *her* responsibility. She could stand to learn a few things from Nah-kay about taking care of a man. She needed to, for Justin's sake. She didn't want to be a pampered millstone around his neck—a vision of Florine came to mind, and she shook it out of her head as quickly as it appeared. Allie wanted to be of value to Justin, to learn to work hard alongside him. She wanted him to be proud of her. She determined in her heart to start looking for ways she could meet Justin's needs, and she paid even closer attention to the tasks Nah-kay did that seemed to come so naturally to her.

The next day Castro told Justin that most of the men would leave again in the morning—this time to head north in search of a herd of buffalo that one of their scouts had come across recently. He said it was time to prepare for the colder months, and Castro invited Justin to ride with them. He declined, saying he wanted to make sure his grandmother was taken care of before he left, and Castro understood.

Justin told Allie that among the Indeh, the husband goes to live with the wife's family and begins to provide for them. Nah-kay had no family since losing her son and ultimately Julia and the children. Up to that time, Nantan had continued to live with and provide for his mother since she had no daughter and Nantan's wife had no other family. Justin recalled the feeling of a tearing in his heart when he and his mother and his siblings were taken away from Nah-kay. He didn't know if it was fear or respect that he felt for Nantan, but he had no doubt that what he felt for Nah-kay was love, and it was mutual. She adored her grandsons, and later, Faith when she came to live with them the last couple of years before they were all taken from her.

Ever since then, this group of Indeh, especially Castro, made sure Nah-kay had food since she was alone. Justin thanked Castro for his part in taking care of his grandmother. Upon returning to her tipi, he tried to convince Nah-kay to come home with them. He felt that it was just a matter of time before their group would be rounded up and sent to live on a reservation. He tried to explain that to Nah-kay, but she wouldn't listen.

"You are a stubborn woman," Justin told her.

She smiled and nodded, patting his cheek.

"You know Jimmy and I have to return home, don't you?" he continued.

She nodded sadly, but told him she was grateful to see her grandsons again. She told Justin that she had even asked Jew-ya's God for the chance to see them again, and believed He had granted that request. Nah-kay told him that she could die in peace now.

The next morning, just before sunrise, everyone went out to send the hunters off. Castro caught Justin's eye and nodded his head goodbye. Some of the young boys were going on their first hunt, and everyone seemed to be proud and excited for them. The rest of the women would follow the hunters later with their travois, ready to take care of the buffalo once the men harvested them. Nah-kay had already begun packing up the tools she needed. She said the camp would move soon to follow the herd, but she would wait to take down her tipi until they heard from the hunters.

Nah-kay prepared a stew to feed them breakfast. While Allie made the corn cakes, Nah-kay told her through Justin that the women would face their hardest work field-dressing and preparing the carcasses at the site of the hunt. Then they would have to process all that meat back at the camp. They used every part of the buffalo, and none of the work came easy.

Nah-kay rummaged around and found the brush she had used on Allie's hair. She told Justin to tell Allie that it came from the buffalo, and pointed to her own tongue to say what part it was made from. Allie was impressed with how industrious and creative they were with the little they had. But she also felt relieved they would be leaving soon—she couldn't imagine the work of the women being harder than what she had already experienced and observed.

Nah-kay told them if the herd drifted too far, that the men would do the field-dressing and skinning, cut up the meat, wrap it in the hides, and bring it back to the women for processing. She thought the women took better care of the hides when they skinned the buffalo, so she hoped the herd would be close enough for the women to get there to do the skinning. She seemed to look forward to it and didn't waste any time preparing her own travois to follow the men.

After eating the meal Nah-kay and Allie had prepared, Jimmy and Justin decided to go get their horses, leaving Allie to help Nah-kay clean up. Nah-kay handed Justin a rope halter and a pouch with a little bit of corn and told them to bring her horse back, too, which she would use to haul her travois. She described the horse to Justin, and he told Jimmy to watch for a bay mare with a white face, blue eyes, two stocking feet, and a short tail. Nah-kay said the other horses kept chewing it off.

"I think the bald face and blue eyes are enough information to spot the horse," Jimmy said to Justin as they walked toward the area in which the horses were kept. "How often do you see that?"

Since there were fewer horses in the camp after the hunting party had left, Jimmy and Justin had no problem calling up their own and Allie's horses by shaking the pouch of corn and whistling. Nah-kay's horse was another matter altogether. Jimmy laughed out loud when he spotted her, which was easy. She stood out like a big wart on a pretty face.

"That has to be the ugliest horse I've ever seen," Justin said.

Not only that, but the mare completely ignored them. She wouldn't let them near her.

"Nah-na must not use her very much," said Justin, shaking the pouch at her. The horse wouldn't even look his way. "Maybe she doesn't want to come around our horses."

"Or maybe she's just plain deaf," Jimmy said. "I think she has one foot in the grave already. Here's the halter; let me hold our horses, and you go get her."

"Me?!" Justin started to complain, then remembered Jimmy's healing wounds. "Oh, right," he said. "I'm sure I can sneak up on her."

After Justin trailed the old horse all over the area twice, the old brave in charge of the horses had pity on him and took him a rope. Justin had the horse roped in a matter of minutes after that. He put the rope halter on Nah-kay's horse and removed the borrowed rope. He and Jimmy walked the horses over to the old man, who laughed and greeted them with a toothless grin. Justin handed him the rope and thanked him.

"I think you put on a good show for him," Jimmy said as they started walking back to their grandmother's tipi.

Justin nodded and chuckled, and thought how good it felt to be comfortable around his brother again. But then he remembered the circumstances that brought them here, and the smile faded.

After cleaning the cooking utensils, Allie reluctantly decided to change back into her wrinkled cotton skirt and blouse, which seemed so bland and inadequate out here in comparison to the magnificent leather dress Nah-kay had given her.

She slipped into the tipi to change, and thought about how different her life had been these past several weeks. She wasn't the same person as before, and her worries about returning to Dalton seemed so insignificant now. Her greatest concern was for her parents and Uncle John—what they were going through, not knowing where she had been all this time. She hated that her absence brought them pain, but she hoped they could find it in their hearts to forgive Jimmy. He was a different person now, and she would do her best to convince them of that, but she also knew Jimmy had the biggest role in proving that to everyone—especially his own family. She noticed Justin still wasn't entirely convinced, although he knew Jimmy had changed somehow.

Allie came out of the tipi just as Jimmy and Justin were returning with the horses. She took one look at Nah-kay's horse and tried her best to keep a straight face.

"They should've eaten her a long time ago," Jimmy said to her. "Surely she knows this horse is pretty worthless."

"Jimmy!" Allie scolded him.

Justin's curiosity got the better of him. He asked Nah-kay in her language, "Where did you get this horse?"

Nah-kay said she chose her.

"But there were other horses out there—much better horses. Did they leave the cull for you?" Justin asked. "They should treat you with more respect."

"I could've had any horse, but I wanted her," she said firmly, lifting her chin. "I know she's not good horse flesh, but they were going to kill her."

"Why didn't you *let* them?" Justin asked teasingly.

Nah-kay's voice broke as she answered him, "Because she had my daughter's eyes—she had my grandson's eyes." Her own eyes filled with tears.

Her answer knocked the wind out of Justin. He said nothing, but walked over and wrapped his arms around his grandmother.

"What did she say, Justin?" Jimmy asked. "What's the matter?"

Justin was too emotional to speak, but Allie knew. "It's the eyes, Jimmy. It's the blue eyes she loves about that old horse—because of her family."

"Oh, Nah-na," Jimmy said as he wrapped his arms around both of them. The brothers laughed when the old horse stuck her head right in the middle of them, too.

"So now you're being sociable," Justin said to the old mare.

Nah-kay pulled away to tie her mare to a tether line near the tipi, and the others stood there for a moment before Allie walked over and picked up her saddle, took it to her mare and began saddling it. Justin was surprised to see that she even knew how, and she didn't seem nervous at all. He asked Jimmy if he needed help with his saddling and Jimmy shook his head and waved him off, but on second thought he asked if Justin would tighten the cinch for him when he finished.

Justin reached down to get his saddle and noticed some additional leather items among his things. The arrows Justin had made on the trail were now in a leather quiver, and the shafts were marked with some kind of dye. A leather holder cradled his bow. *Castro.* Justin smiled, moved by the gesture. *He's still teaching me,* he thought. He saddled his horse and strapped the quiver and bow to his back.

Nah-kay brought several pouches of pemmican to put in their saddlebags for the trip home. They had come to the point of goodbye.

"You are amazing, Nah-kay," Allie said as she hugged her. "I am so glad to have met you. Thank you for all you have taught me. I'll be taking a part of you home with me," Allie said, touching her head and then her heart.

Justin translated what words he could for Allie, and said a few of his own, again trying to convince Nah-kay to come with them. Nah-kay told him that the younger women could not make it without her help in harvesting the buffalo. He told her she was probably right.

Nah-kay smiled, and then she fiercely hugged her grandsons again. She did nothing halfway. Allie turned her head, trying to keep from crying. She mounted her horse and waited for the Taylor brothers to finish saying goodbye to their grandmother.

Jimmy told Justin to tell Nah-kay that he would learn the language again—and that he would never forget her. She nodded, and then said something to Allie, and turned to continue working on her travois, although they could see that there was little more that needed done to that contraption. Allie looked at Justin questioningly.

"She said something about thanking your God for the gift," he translated, and then explained,"—of her grandsons coming back to her."

"She's a believer?" Allie asked.

"Enough to believe in asking him for the chance to see us again," Justin said as he stepped into the saddle.

"So this all has been *her* doing, and I just got caught in the middle of it," Allie smiled thoughtfully as she watched the old woman. "She should still be a part of your lives."

"Yeah, but she's set in her ways," Justin said. "I don't know that she could ever adjust to our way of life now."

"Would she have to?" Jimmy asked as he mounted his horse. "Should she be forced to?"

Justin thought for a moment as he watched her work. "Maybe not, but she can't continue working at this pace much longer." He looked at Allie. "You ready?"

Allie smiled and nodded.

"Can you stay on that horse?" he asked, grinning back.

"Your brother asked me the very same thing a while back! But you just watch me," she said. "Jimmy's taught me a few things since you've seen me last."

"She didn't fall off once," Jimmy said.

"Well, that's good to know," Justin said as he turned his horse. "Let's go home."

"Follow the river south, then turn toward those hills," Allie said as she pointed.

"You *did* pay attention like I asked you to," Jimmy said.

Allie nodded, grinning and feeling pretty confident about herself at that moment.

Justin felt a pang of jealousy at their interaction, wishing that he had been the one to teach Allie those things, but he didn't let the feeling take root. He should be glad that Jimmy and Allie seemed to have learned something of the best from each other. His time would come, but he wondered what was the best that he could offer Allie.

They set off trotting and walking their horses at an easy gait alongside the river. They had gone two or three miles and had just turned toward the hills when they heard gunfire behind them.

"What's that?" Justin said as they all pulled up and looked behind them. They had gone too far to be able to see the camp anymore, but the gunfire continued.

"Do you think the hunters are back after only a couple of hours?" Allie asked.

"They wouldn't waste their ammunition firing around the camp like that," Justin said. "Something's wrong."

"Nah-kay!" Jimmy said as he spurred his horse back toward the direction of the camp.

"Wait up, Jimmy!" Justin yelled. "You don't know what you're riding into!"

To his surprise, Jimmy pulled up and waited for him and Allie to catch up. That was definitely out of character for his hotheaded brother.

"We need to get back to Nah-kay!" he said.

"Yes, but let's go carefully—we won't be any good to her if we get shot out of our saddles riding back in there," Justin said as they started forward. "Let's make a wider turn away from the river and come in from the northeast—there's a low bluff that will allow us to see the entire camp."

They rode quickly up to the back of the bluff and almost ran over several cavalry soldiers standing there. Justin didn't recognize any of them from the earlier group he had encountered a week before.

"What are you doing!!" Justin yelled at the man obviously in charge.

The officer turned around to face them. "Who are you?"

"Are your men down there shooting women and children and old men?" Justin yelled again, ignoring the officer's question. "There are no warriors down there!"

"We know, and we're not shooting anyone," the man said. "I'm not a savage, Mr. ... ?"

"Taylor, Justin Taylor," he said. "Who are you, and what are you doing here?"

"I'm Captain Hartman, and I have orders, Mr. Taylor," he explained, "to round up and transport all hostiles to Fort Concho and then on to certain areas the government has set aside for them."

"Why are your men shooting their guns?"

"To show their authority and to expedite the process before the warriors return. And may I ask what you're doing here in this god-forsaken country?"

"Excuse me, sir," a soldier interrupted them.

"What is it, Corporal?"

"We have everyone rounded up and contained except for one old squaw, sir."

"What's the problem? Just pick her up and carry her over to the others."

"But she's holding a big stick and won't let anyone near her, sir."

"Then use force, Corporal—" the captain said impatiently. "Surely you can over-power one old woman."

"But, sir, she's humming a church hymn as loud as she can."

"What!?" the captain exclaimed. "How in the world would she know a church hymn out here?"

"Nah-kay!" Allie said, and spurred her horse down the hill.

"Hold on, now, Miss! You're not allowed to interfere with—"

But by then the Captain found himself yelling at the backs of the three young riders scrambling down the side of the bluff.

Jimmy reached Nah-kay's tipi first, and it almost cost him his life. One of the young soldiers thought a brave was bearing down on him and fired his pistol at him, but the shot went high.

"Hold your fire!" Justin hollered as he put himself between the private and his brother.

The young man was shocked to see white civilians present.

Allie and Jimmy dismounted and ran to Nah-kay, who stood guard in front of her tipi. They faced three soldiers whose drawn guns pointed straight at them.

"What are you doing?" a sergeant asked them. "Who in the hell are you people?"

"This is our grandmother," Justin said as he dismounted, "and she's coming with us."

The sergeant shook his head. "All hostiles in this area are supposed to be taken to Fort Concho."

"This is no hostile," Justin said, although he did think she looked quite intimidating as he rode up. He thought she could probably do some damage with that big stick. "She's our grandmother, and she's coming with us. That's why we're here."

He said something to Nah-kay, and she nodded her head.

At that moment, the captain and his entourage rode up and dismounted.

The sergeant started to explain the situation when the captain held up his hand to stop him and said, "I was just speaking with Mr. Taylor before he and his... *accomplices*, for lack of a better word, left so abruptly."

"My *accomplices* are my brother, Jimmy Taylor, and Allie Blake, sir, and I apologize for my rudeness, but we thought our grandmother's life was in danger," Justin said, attempting to use a little more tact once he realized he would have to negotiate with this man for the release of his grandmother.

"I told you, Mr. Taylor, that I'm not a brutal savage. I do have respect for human life," Captain Hartman reiterated. "We knew the warriors had left—our scouts have been waiting and watching them from a distance. We hope to be able to use their women and children to convince them to come in peacefully. I don't want to see any more bloodshed over this. I've seen enough of that in my lifetime."

"Can't you just let them be?" Jimmy said. "Are they bothering you?"

"Unfortunately, we are at war, Mr. Taylor, and I don't have a choice but to follow through with my orders," said the captain. "But I *can* choose the method we'll take to fulfill our mission."

"I understand, sir, and I appreciate your concern for their welfare," Justin said, "but we're here to take our grandmother home."

"Nah-kay's old and needs our help," Allie added.

Justin told Nah-kay in her language to look more weak and pitiful. At that, she raised her chin in defiance and gave the captain an even angrier glare. Justin rolled his eyes and exhaled.

"Old and helpless as an angry badger, I see," said the captain, almost smiling. "I think she could hold her own against most anything. And pardon me for saying, Mr. Taylor, but you look nothing like your grandmother, although I see that you speak the language. Your brother favors her, though."

"It's a long story, sir," Justin said, "but I give you my word that I'm telling the truth. We're the only family she has left. The reservation won't miss her."

The captain thought for a moment as he looked at the feisty old woman. "I think we'd be saving ourselves a lot of grief to not have to contend with... Nah-kay? Is that what you called her?"

"Yes sir," Justin said. "Are you saying we'll be able to take her with us?"

"No, I can't officially say that, but my men and I are going to finish our work at the other end of the camp, and I hope this part of the camp is cleared out by the time we return. Is that understood?"

"Yes, sir, thank you, sir," Justin said as he offered his hand to the captain.

Jimmy stepped up and shook his hand as well. "Thank you, sir," he said.

The captain looked at Jimmy and said, "Would you be interested in scouting and translating for the army?"

"Sorry, but I don't speak the language," Jimmy answered.

The captain looked at Justin, then to Jimmy and then back to Justin again before throwing up his hand saying, "I know... long story. I wish you well, then," he said, and he turned and walked away with his men.

Justin turned to his grandmother. "Nah-na, you don't have a choice now—you must come with us."

She sat down and put her face in her hands. Allie sat down and put her arm around her.

"They'll be coming back, and if you're here, you will have to go with them as a prisoner," Justin said in her language.

Nah-kay nodded resolutely, and suddenly stood. She told Justin something and began packing the rest of her belongings on the travois she had prepared for the buffalo hunt. Justin looked up at the tipi.

"What'd she say?" Jimmy asked.

"She said she won't leave without her home," Justin said, "but we can't haul this back with us."

"What if we just took the covering and left the poles here?" Allie said as she walked around the tipi. Nah-kay followed and showed her the main seam and how to pull out the wooden fasteners.

"What are we going to use to haul it with?" Jimmy asked. "Our horses can't handle that. And look at that pile of stuff on her... what do you call that thing?" Jimmy pointed to the travois.

Justin told Nah-kay that she would have to leave most of her belongings.

Nah-kay shook her head, no.

"They've probably driven off your horse by now, Nah-na," Justin said, but Nah-kay kept packing up her things.

"You're not going to believe this, Justin," Allie said from the back of the tipi. "Open the front flap and look inside."

Justin walked over to the front of the tipi and laid the flap over. Nah-kay's old horse stood inside with the leather pouch strapped to her mouth.

Justin threw his head back and laughed. "Oh, Nah-kay—you wise, old fox! No wonder you were guarding your home so fiercely!" He opened the flap wider, stepped in and led the mare out. "Let's get her hitched up and get out of here."

"How did she keep her so quiet?" Jimmy asked. "What was she feeding her?"

Justin took off the pouch to find the crumbled remains of something in the bottom of it.

"Ahh—corn cakes," he said.

"So that's why they didn't hear her chewing," Jimmy said as he and Allie pulled the last of the hide covering off the poles. "How did she think of that in all the chaos?"

Nah-kay didn't understand a word they said, but she noticed they were obviously impressed with her cunning, and seemed very pleased with herself.

Chapter 15

*A*fter three days of slow travel heading south and then due east, Justin led the bedraggled group into the first small town they came to. They must have looked quite the sight based on all the stares they received from the townsfolk. Justin, with his unruly blond hair, had the bow and quiver of arrows strapped to his back. Jimmy, with his long, black hair and distinct Indian features was dressed in white man's clothes. Allie looked entirely Indian with her tanned skin, dark hair in a braid, and wearing the suede dress again. Only her shoes and bloomers hinted at her heritage. And Nah-kay sat as regal as a queen atop her old blue-eyed nag pulling a loaded-down travois. She stared straight ahead as if a trip to town was a regular occurrence for her.

Allie might have been amused by the situation if she weren't so exhausted from traveling. Nah-kay's head never turned, but Allie saw her eyes cut this way and that from time to time. She wondered if this was the first time the old woman had ever been in a town.

Justin stopped the group under a big tree near a general store, and he and Jimmy dismounted and tied the horses to several hitching posts. Justin pulled the bow and arrows off his back while Jimmy helped Nah-kay off her horse. The women waited while the brothers emptied their pockets, counting out a few dollars between them, hoping it would be enough buy a few supplies for the rest of the journey home. Then they all walked into the store together.

Allie watched Nah-kay's face as she took in everything in the store. She touched the pretty glass jars and sniffed the tobacco and in-season vegetables. She ran her hand over the bolts of material stacked on a table.

Allie wished she knew what was going on in Nah-kay's mind; it was hard for her to imagine what it must be like to see a place like this for the first time. Even now, though, after Allie experienced only a short time living off the land, it seemed almost otherworldly to step back into a store with supplies so easily at hand—if one had the money to pay for them. It dawned on her that they had been surviving without money the past several weeks. Nothing came easy in the world they left—it was a hard way to live, but Nah-kay seemed to have endured it just fine throughout her lifetime.

Justin picked up some coffee and flour and brought it up to the counter. He asked the proprietor if this town had a telegraph office, but the man said they wouldn't have one until the railroad tracks were laid, and that was only in the talking stages. Justin asked about any stage lines that came through town. The man said the stage from Fort Concho to Waco came through once a week, and that it was due to come through tomorrow afternoon. Jimmy walked up and placed a can of molasses and a salt mill on the counter, and walked away again.

Justin figured that a letter by stagecoach would beat them home by a number of days, so he peeled off the label from the can of molasses and turned it over to write a short note to his parents. He borrowed a dip pen and ink from the storeowner and wrote that he had Jimmy and Allie with him, and that they were fine, and that they would all be home in a week or so. He wasn't sure how to break the news that Nah-kay was coming home with them, so he simply wrote: *and we're bringing Nah-kay back with us. Will explain later.* He knew only his mother would recognize that name, but he figured she could prepare everyone else for the shock and potential disruption in their family.

"Where are you folks headed?" the storeowner asked.

"To my family's home in Grace," Justin said. "It's outside of Waco."

"I've heard of it. Looks like you've been on the road a while," he said.

"Yeah—it's taking longer than I'd planned since we're having to travel with my grandmother's travois. We're ready to get home," Justin said. "Could I buy an envelope from you?"

The man walked over to a desk and picked up an envelope. He handed it to Justin and said, "No charge."

"Thank you, sir," Justin said. "By the way, what is the date?"

"Friday, September 24th."

Justin signed his name and dated the note before he placed it in the envelope and sealed it. He quickly addressed it, wrote URGENT on the front, and gave it to the man for postage.

"Add the two cents to our bill, please," Justin said.

Several women who had been in the store walked up to the counter. One of them lowered her voice before speaking.

"Mr. Samuel, we thought you might want to know that they're touching the merchandise," she said as she looked back at Allie and Nah-kay.

"So... " the storeowner said.

"Don't you have rules about that?" she prodded.

"But you touch the merchandise, Mrs. Petty," he said. "What are you saying?"

"You know," she said, insinuating that he knew.

"I know," Justin interjected, "because the dirty Indian is touching it?"

"I didn't say that," she said.

"But you were thinking it, weren't you," said Justin, seething. "That happens to be my grandmother and my girl, and they're two of the finest women you could ever meet, ma-damn, but you would never know that because you would never lower yourself to be in my grandmother's company."

"Justin!" Jimmy walked up and put a hand on his brother's shoulder. "That's enough," he said calmly. "I'm sure these fine ladies meant nothing of the sort."

The women recoiled at Jimmy's presence; his bruised face and ripped and stained clothing added to their concern.

In the smoothest of voices Jimmy addressed them directly. "Pardon us, ladies, but my brother is exhausted. We've been shot at, taken captive, and beaten by the Apaches, the U.S. Cavalry, and not to mention—each other, so it's been a difficult few weeks for us. Please accept our apologies for upsetting you."

The women were completely disarmed by Jimmy's charm and shocked to hear that voice coming out of someone so obviously... Indian. "We're so sorry, Mr....?"

"Jimmy Taylor, and this is my brother, Justin," he said, "and you have a lovely town."

The ladies nodded, and smiled awkwardly. "We'd best be going," they said. "Goodbye, Mr. Samuel."

"Goodbye, ladies," Mr. Samuel said as they walked out the door. He held up a hand to the brothers and leaned an ear toward the open door.

They could hear the women whisper outside, "Who were those strange people?"

"Well, the dark-headed one didn't seem so bad, did he?"

"Did you see his eyes?" the other said as they walked out of earshot.

Mr. Samuel burst out laughing. "That was smooth, Mr. Taylor."

"And the biggest load of—" Justin started to say when Allie walked up with Nah-kay. She had overheard the conversation and was glad Nah-kay couldn't understand it.

"I'm learning that honey works better than firewater," Jimmy said.

"I don't think that's how the saying goes, Jimmy," Allie said.

"Well, it fits me," he said, grinning. "I've been a slow learner."

"I think the saying has something to do with drawing flies," Justin said, "like that elaborate oration you just performed..."

"Justin!" Allie said as she placed some baking powder and a tin of lard on the counter. "It sounds like you and your brother are switching roles."

"What do you mean?" he asked.

"You used to be the charming one," Allie said, smiling, but she didn't say aloud that he was getting entirely too comfortable with his anger—like Jimmy used to be.

"I could still be," Justin said defensively. He turned to Mr. Samuel. "Do we have enough money to pay for this stuff?" he asked.

"More than enough," he said, pushing some of the coins back to Justin. "Hope you have a safer trip on this last part of your journey home."

They thanked him and said goodbye.

"Justin, I know it's earlier than we usually stop for the night," Allie said, "but would it be all right if we made camp around here somewhere? I don't think I can face another three minutes on horseback, much less three hours."

Justin looked at Jimmy and Nah-kay. They looked exhausted, too.

"I'm sorry I'm not stronger for you," Allie said.

"No, Allie," Justin said. "It's me that should be apologizing to you. I didn't realize I was pushing you all so hard. I just want to get you home."

"I know," Allie said.

Justin embraced her. "I'm sorry, Allie—of course, we can make camp around here. Let me go back and ask Mr. Samuel where there's a good place to camp with water available."

When Justin told Mr. Samuel their plans, he insisted they come home with him. Justin tried to decline, thinking they were imposing, but Mr. Samuel wouldn't hear of it.

"My wife loves company," he said, "and we hardly ever have guests come through."

"Well, I don't think my grandmother would be comfortable staying in a house, but if we could use your barn, we would really appreciate it," Justin said.

Mr. Samuel said, "My wife can be very persuasive, but if you're more comfortable in the barn, that's fine with us. But we're going to insist that you at least join us for dinner."

Justin accepted. Mr. Samuel told them he had a couple of hours to go before he could close the store, but had a young boy deliver a note to his wife saying they would be having company for supper, and that their guests would be staying overnight. In a little while, a petite, auburn-haired woman wearing a sunny yellow dress walked briskly up to the group.

"Hello! I'm France Samuel," she said as she extended her hand to the first person she came to.

Allie grasped it and said, "I'm Allie Blake."

"I'm so pleased to meet you, Allie," Mrs. Samuel said. "What a lovely dress you're wearing!" She proceeded to shake everyone's hands and said, "Please call me France."

Allie introduced everyone to France as she greeted them. Jimmy expected her to draw back when he offered her his hand, but she grasped it with no hesitation. When she came to Nah-kay, Allie introduced her as Justin and Jimmy's grandmother and said her name. Nah-kay awkwardly held out her hand, and Mrs. Samuel took hold of it with both hands and looked her in the eye.

"It's a pleasure to meet you, Nah-kay," she said, and then turned to Allie. "Does she understand me?" she asked.

Allie told her no.

"Well, then how do I say *hello* so that she would understand me?"

Justin said, "I don't know a word for *hello* in Apache, but *dant'e* means *how are you.*"

"Dant'e, Nah-kay," France said, still holding her hand.

Nah-kay smiled shyly at France's effort to speak. She asked Justin how to say a word in English that responded to France's greeting. Justin told her, "Good."

"Good," Nah-kay said in English, nodding her head.

Allie caught Justin's eye and then looked at Jimmy. They were amazed that this woman had so easily drawn Nah-kay into a comfortable place for her, even to the point of Nah-kay returning her effort to communicate in France's own language.

"I'm so pleased you all will be joining us for dinner," she said. "I need to step inside the store for a few minutes, and then I'll be back to take you to our home."

France came back out with a flour sack of items, and Justin stepped up to take it from her.

"Thank you, Mr. Taylor," she said, letting him take the sack from her.

"It's Justin, ma'am," he said. "We're sorry to be putting you out—if this is going to be too much trouble, we can make do just fine."

"Nonsense, Justin! It's no trouble at all," she said. "We're so happy to be receiving company, and to tell you the truth, it's handy to be married to a general store owner for times like this! Now gather up your family and follow me."

Justin put the sack on the travois and started to help Nah-kay back on her horse. France stopped him and asked him to ask her if she would like to walk with her.

"It's only a short distance from here," she said. "In fact, we could all walk, if you'd like."

They agreed, and the two older women led the entourage several blocks through town. People even came out of the businesses to watch them, and France seemed oblivious to the attention they stirred up. She told them something about the community, and mentioned, too, like her husband, that it looked like rail lines would be coming through in the next few years. She expected the town to grow substantially when that happened.

"We wouldn't feel so isolated out here on the edge of west Texas. A rail would connect us to the big cities. We heard that Dallas has over eight thousand people now, and Waco has more than five thousand," France said as she stopped in front of an L-shaped stone house. "Well, here we are! Please excuse my chattering—we just don't have company near often enough! The barn is out back to your right if you'd like to take care of your livestock. That sure is an unusual-looking horse, Nah-kay," she said as she seemed to notice it for the first time.

Nah-kay heard her name and saw France glance at her horse.

"She likes your horse, Nah-na," Justin fudged a bit—he had no idea how to say *unusual-looking* in Apache.

183

Nah-kay beamed.

"When you're ready, there's a well behind the house where you men can wash up. Allie and Nah-kay, you're welcome to use one of the bedrooms, if you'd like," France said.

That sounded heavenly to Allie, and she looked at Justin. He told her to go on inside—that he and Jimmy would take care of the horses. Allie grabbed her skirt and blouse from Nah-kay's travois where she had draped them to dry after washing them out that morning.

Nah-kay walked over and touched the stone on the wall of the house. Justin asked her if she would like to go inside with Allie. She nodded, seemingly curious to see how this woman lived in a house of rock.

France took them to the front bedroom and left to go fill the water pitcher. She came back in and filled the bowl on the dresser, and laid out several towels.

"Oh! I forgot the soap," France said, and turned to rush out.

"That's all right, France," Allie said as she pulled her bar of soap out of the pocket of her skirt. "I have my own."

She had become quite attached to her bar of soap.

"Feel free to nap, if you'd like. Guilt-free naps are allowed in my home," France said.

Nah-kay followed France out of the room, and Allie called out her name and pantomimed washing and napping. She came back and washed her hands and face, and then walked out again. Allie watched her go into the kitchen and sit down, watching France.

"I guess she wants to watch you cook in your kitchen," Allie said.

France laughed. "Isn't that typical of us women! And that doesn't take a language barrier to understand that."

"I'll leave you two on your own, then," Allie said.

"We'll be fine—you make yourself at home," France said as she poured some flour into a bowl.

Allie went back to the bedroom and undressed. She was determined to take advantage of a good washing when she had the chance. She folded up the leather dress, and put half her clothes back on before lying down. It felt so good to be in a bed up off the ground. She shut her eyes to the sound of pots clanging in the kitchen.

France stoked the fire and added wood to the cook stove. Then she made an apple pie and put it in the oven before cutting up a roast and potatoes for a quick hash. She put some squash on to boil and sliced some tomatoes—the last of her garden, she said to Nah-kay, who didn't understand a word she said. But she seemed to enjoy France's company. Justin and Jimmy came in about the time France attempted to open a jar of peaches.

"—in case someone doesn't like apple pie," she told them.

"Here, let me open that for you," Justin said, taking the jar from her.

Mr. Samuel came home a little after five o'clock, and Justin and Jimmy visited with him out on the porch for a few minutes while France finished cooking supper. Allie woke up and came in and apologized for falling asleep.

"I didn't realize how tired I was," Allie said. "Let me finish setting the table for you."

"Thank you! And remember—guilt-free naps are allowed here," France said, smiling. "Well, I think we're ready. George!" she hollered. "Supper's ready!"

The men came in and after everyone sat down, France asked George to say grace. Allie quietly thanked God, too, for bringing them safely thus far. And now they enjoyed the first sit-down meal they'd had in almost three weeks.

"Nah-kay's a wonderful cook," Allie said, "but they don't have general stores where she's from. I've had my fill of rabbit and deer for a while."

"I think this apple pie is the best I've ever tasted," Justin said. "I love peaches, but a person would have to be crazy not to like apple pie."

Nah-kay didn't like the apple pie. She wasn't used to eating anything sweeter than berries growing in the wild. She did like the hash and squash, though.

George asked the brothers what they did for a living. Justin told him he ran his uncle's cattle operation on his ranch south of San Antonio. When George looked at Jimmy and waited for his response, Justin spoke up and told him that his brother had been breaking horses for people around Central Texas and planned to raise them someday.

Jimmy looked at Justin, wondering how he knew those things about him.

"People are always in need of good horses," George said. "And you're good at breaking them, too?"

"Yes, sir," Jimmy said.

"And he can outride anybody I know," Justin said. "He's also good at training horses."

"And people, too," Allie put in. "He's taught me a lot about riding these past several weeks."

185

Jimmy looked at Allie and then his brother. They acted like he fit in—like he had a future and established plans ahead of him.

"Do you mind if I make a copy of your address from your letter?" George asked Jimmy. "People are always asking me for information like that, and I could refer them to you."

"You just met me," Jimmy said. "Why would you take a chance on passing on questionable information?" *from people who've done the things I've done*, he thought to himself.

"I've been around a lot of people during my lifetime, and I think I'm a pretty good judge of character," George said.

"I appreciate that, sir," Jimmy said.

France shared with her guests that their family would be growing soon. Allie couldn't help but glance at her mid-section, although she did think France seemed too slender and definitely a bit old to be having a baby any time soon.

France laughed when she saw their expressions. "George and I haven't been blessed with children of our own, but in a few weeks, three young siblings—two girls and a boy will be coming to live with us."

"Congratulations!" Allie said. "Are they kin to you?"

"No, but they lost both of their parents, and the church that's responsible for them wanted to keep them together, if possible. A friend in Dallas knew we'd always wanted children," she explained, "so she contacted us, and voila! We're parents!"

"Now I need to get busy and add another room onto this house," George said.

"Too bad we can't stay and help you, but we're in hurry to get home," Justin said.

"That's all right, we'll manage."

"You may need to build several rooms eventually, honey," said France, smiling.

"Now, France, slow down," George said. "I don't know why the Lord didn't give us a houseful of children—France has enough love and patience and stamina for a whole herd of kids."

Allie hated to see the evening end; they had enjoyed the dinner and conversation immensely. The Samuels' home was a safe haven for all of them, and Allie hoped to have a household just as welcoming and comfortable as the Samuels' some day.

They left the Samuels early the next morning after France fed them a light meal of coffee, biscuits and honey butter. And Justin had that last piece of apple pie.

Jimmy commented after they started down the road, "Maybe there are more decent folks around than I realized."

"Yeah, but scoundrels are out there, too," Justin said. "I just hope you've figured out which side of the fence you're on, brother."

Jimmy nodded and looked away.

Eight days of slow travel later, they came across the northwest road leading into Grace. Their apprehension grew the closer they got, and now the end was in sight. Jimmy stopped his horse when they came atop a rise that looked down over the town. They could just see a glimpse of the roof of the Taylor house through the trees at the south end of Grace.

"I can't do this," Jimmy said, getting off his horse and walking away from the others.

Chapter 16

*A*llie dismounted her horse and followed him.

"I don't think I can do this, Allie," Jimmy said. "I don't think they can forgive me, and I really don't blame them."

"If I can, Jimmy," Allie said, "then they can. I don't see how you can get on with your life without getting this resolved and behind you. I'll do anything I can to help you."

"And I will too, brother," Justin said as he walked up behind them.

Jimmy turned around and faced his brother.

"I didn't want to believe it at first, but you've changed," Justin said.

Jimmy nodded. "It happened back at the camp—no, that's not right—it began on day one, and by the time I stepped into the river that night you found us, I wanted to change, and I asked God to change me. I stood in the rain, and something just came over me and took away the anger and blame I had towards everyone."

"It's called *grace*, Jimmy," Allie smiled, "it was God's grace falling like rain on you."

"You've helped me believe that I have a future, Allie, and I want to thank you for that," Jimmy said. "And Justin, I'm really sorry for hurting you—I don't know why I felt like I always had to get back at you. You never did anything but try to help me, and I kept pushing you away. After we came back to Grace, I was always jealous of you—I always wanted to be you."

"You don't need to be anybody but yourself," Justin said. "Even though I was mad as hell at you, it felt like a knife went through me when

I thought I'd lost you back at the Schaferling Ranch. I've missed things being right with us, Jimmy. I don't want to lose this."

Jimmy nodded and grabbed him in a bear hug.

"You have a place in our family and a place in this world, and don't let anybody make you think otherwise," Justin said. "Now, let's go home."

The shadows were long when they walked their horses slowly through Grace. Justin and Allie rode their horses beside Jimmy, protectively flanking him, and Nah-kay brought up the rear. Jenny and Marcus came out of the store, and other townspeople stopped what they were doing and watched silently as the troupe passed by. Jimmy and Justin continued to look straight ahead, but Allie turned to look at Jenny.

Allie could see tears in her eyes, and Marcus put his arm around her. Both of their faces showed a mixture of relief and worry. Jenny caught Allie's eye and mouthed, *"Are you all right?"*

Allie smiled wearily and nodded, and said, "Come with us," motioning for them to come up to the big house.

But Jenny just shook her head, no.

"Why?" Allie asked, but Jenny just buried her face in Marcus' shoulder.

Allie knew there would be a confrontation, but she had convinced herself that they could all sit down and work it out. She took a big breath and let it out slowly when the Taylor house came into view.

Allie could see someone on the porch hollering to the rest of the house. More people came outside, and three of them ran down the steps and started down the road toward them. She was shocked to recognize her parents and brother.

"Momma? Daddy?" she said. "My family's here!" she said to Justin. "How'd they know?!"

But she didn't wait for an answer. She quickly dismounted and handed her reins to Jimmy and ran the rest of the way into her family's arms. Justin and Jimmy pulled up and waited, watching her greet her family. They were also trying to gauge the tension emanating from the porch. They could see Matthew holding Julia's arm, and they seemed to be arguing. Uncle John just stood there watching them. Justin couldn't see his expression, but his stance looked determined, and his face was turned toward them, not Allie.

Allie had not seen her family for almost fourteen months. Her younger brother Jesse now looked down at her, he had grown so tall. They all shed a few tears, and Allie asked how they knew she would be there.

"Mr. Taylor sent a wire to John saying you would be here in a few days, so we caught the next stage up here," her father said. We've been here since yesterday waiting for you.

"Oh, Daddy—the newspaper! Your record..." Allie said.

"...is not worth putting above seeing my daughter again," he said.

"We thought you'd died, Allie," Jesse said.

"What?" Allie asked.

"Worst day of our lives, honey," her mother said.

"Yeah, we even had a memorial service for you," Jesse said. "You should've heard all the nice stuff everyone said about you."

"A memorial service!" Allie said. "What for?"

"John came back to Dalton without you—he told us you had drowned," her father explained.

Allie paled. "I didn't know that—I just thought everyone knew Jimmy had taken me."

"That beast. Are you all right, Allie?" her mother asked her. "We've been worried sick about you. You're so thin—did he hurt you?"

"No, Mother, I'm fine—just tired and dusty," she said. "And I promise you, he's no beast, Momma. We have a lot to talk about, but I need to talk to Uncle John and Mr. and Mrs. Taylor first, if that's all right with you."

Allie glanced back to see Justin and Jimmy still sitting there waiting. She waved at them to come on up, and turned to walk with her family up to the house. She embraced Uncle John, and then Julia and Faith.

"What do we do now, brother?" Jimmy asked.

"Let's go around to the back of the house and put the horses up before we face everyone—we have to do that anyway; we might as well get it out of the way," Justin said. "We can get Nah-na settled somewhere, and then we'll go to the house."

Jimmy nodded. Justin turned to say something to Nah-kay, and then they started walking the horses up to the house.

Julia broke away from the rest of the group and ran down the steps. Matthew called after her, but she kept running toward her sons.

Jimmy and Justin both dismounted, and she threw herself in their arms.

"My boys, my precious boys," she cried. "I didn't know if I would ever see either one of you again."

"We're all right, Momma," Justin said. "Don't cry."

"Please take Jimmy away from here right now," she said, almost hysterically.

"But I want to make things right with everyone, Mother," Jimmy said.

Julia put a hand on Jimmy's face. "I want us all to make things right, but you need to leave right now, please—or you may not—"

"No! You can't do that!" Allie's screams interrupted her. She had tried to run down the steps, but her father and brother caught her and physically restrained her. "Run, Jimmy!"

Three men had come from behind the house and walked toward them with guns drawn. They wore badges.

"What is this, Mother?" Justin asked.

"Step away from your son, Mrs. Taylor," a man called out.

"Please don't do this," she said in anguish. She would have crumpled to the ground if Justin hadn't steadied her.

"Put your hands up where we can see them," he said to Jimmy. "I am placing you under arrest on the charges of kidnapping."

One of the other men stepped forward to handcuff him.

"Just hold on a minute!" Justin said, stepping in front of his brother. "How can he be charged with kidnapping when we brought Allie back? And she's fine, so you can't charge him with that. Who told you to do that?" he demanded.

"We did, Johnny," said his uncle as he walked up.

Matthew stepped up beside him.

"You can't do this, Uncle John... Dad," Justin said, looking from one to the other. "You don't know what all has happened."

"Jimmy's gone too far this time, Justin," Matthew said. "We've covered over his mistakes for years for your mother's sake, but I can't allow this reprehensible act to go unpunished. I'll never forgive myself for letting it come to this."

"And I'll never forgive you for doing this!" Julia sobbed, and ran back to the house.

"Please don't do this, Dad," Justin said. "Jimmy's not the same person now—tell them, Jimmy!"

Jimmy stood there in silence.

"No sarcastic comment, Jimmy?"

"I agree with you and my father, Uncle John," he said calmly. "I deserve to be punished."

John Stockton didn't expect that. And Jimmy had called him *Uncle John*, and he called Matthew *father* in a respectful way. He knew that was definitely out of character for Jimmy, but he refused to dwell on it. "You're just remorseful because you know you're in serious trouble."

"He didn't have to come back," Justin said. "He chose to come back and face all of you. He wants to make things right. That takes courage."

"And what kind of courage did it take to force himself on a young lady?" John said angrily.

"I didn't touch her, sir," Jimmy said.

"Do you know the hell you've put us all through? You led us to believe that Allie died—how could you do that?"

Jimmy put his head down. "That was inexcusable, and I can't tell you how sorry I am about that."

Matthew hadn't said a word since Julia left, but he had listened quietly to the interchange. Up to this point, he had no hesitation about handing Jimmy over to the law. He was ready to wash his hands of him once and for all. But something *was* different about Jimmy, and doubts began to creep into the edge of his thoughts.

"It's too late to travel back to Waco now," Matthew said. "You and your men have already stayed one night with us, Bill. Would you mind staying over one more? Everyone's tired, and we have another issue to deal with," he said, looking beyond Justin and Jimmy to Nah-kay.

She glared back at him.

The Ranger said they actually did have time to make it back before dark, but something in Matthew's face made him agree to wait.

Matthew told Captain Williams to take Jimmy and his men to the washhouse, where they had stayed the night before. He said he would have Vestal bring something out to them for supper.

"Don't handcuff him," Matthew said, "but don't let him out of your sight, either."

Nah-kay sat quietly atop her horse during the entire confrontation. She didn't understand what was said, but she could read the signs, and Jimmy was in serious trouble. She watched them lead him away.

"Let's go back to the house," Matthew said to John. "Justin, could you get Jimmy's grandmother settled somewhere? We'll deal with her later." He turned around and started to walk back.

"She's my grandmother, too, Father," Justin said. "She's the only grandmother I've ever known."

Matthew stopped and turned around. His face looked pained.

"I'm sorry, Dad," Justin said, "but you can't keep denying what happened to me and Mom. And it's not Nah-kay's fault that it happened, but she loved me as if I were her own grandson. And it's especially not Jimmy's fault what happened to us, so could you stop blaming him?"

"I've never blamed him, Justin," Matthew said.

"You never said anything to him, but he felt it, Daddy—we all did," Justin said. "You never accepted him, and he knew it."

"How could I? He's his father's son, and after what he did to Allie, that just proves it all the more," Matthew said.

"Maybe he's lived up to *your* expectations," Justin said. "He was just a little boy when he came here, Daddy—he can't even remember his own father. He just knows you, and because of that he's never known where he belonged."

"Why are you defending him, Justin? Look what he did to Allie—what he did to all of us? He has to learn to be responsible for his actions," Matthew said and shook his head. "I can't talk about this anymore." He turned around and started walking back to the house.

Justin looked at Uncle John. "Did he hear anything I said? Did you hear anything I said?"

John let out a big sigh. "It's a tough situation, son. We've all been going out of our minds about Allie—thinking the worst had happened to her. And you can't change the fact that Jimmy's responsible for this mess." He looked at Nah-kay.

"Well, aren't you going to introduce me to your grandmother?" John said.

Justin said something to Nah-kay, and she responded.

"I didn't know you could still speak the language," John said as he nodded toward her.

She just looked at him.

"She's upset about Jimmy," Justin said. "I could speak their language better than I could speak English when I came back."

"Well, let's get your grandmother settled somewhere," said John.

Justin said something to Nah-kay and grabbed the reins to his and Jimmy's horses, and Uncle John took control of Allie's horse. He put a hand on his nephew's shoulder as they started walking toward the house.

"We're going to get this resolved, Justin."

Justin looked at him. "Do you realize that's the first time you've ever called me *Justin?*"

John smiled ruefully as he said, "I have a feeling we're all going to experience a few more first time moments before this is over with."

Turmoil ruled the Taylor house. Jimmy's impending arrest marred the joyous reunion of Allie and her family. Allie was torn—she hated that everyone had anguished over her disappearance, but she couldn't make them understand that there had been a purpose in it.

This homecoming brought about no reconciliation like she thought it would. The family was even more divided. Julia locked herself in her room. Faith disappeared. Marcus and Jenny couldn't even make an appearance at their parents' house—they couldn't face what was happening. Allie couldn't bring herself to speak to Uncle John and Matthew Taylor after they had ignored her pleading with them on the porch. They thought her hysterics stemmed from what had happened to her. She was tired, and she couldn't stop crying, but she thought she made perfect sense. Why couldn't anyone see that?

Allie ran upstairs and grabbed some clean clothes from the items her mother had brought for her and headed back downstairs, almost running into Matt and Catherine talking to Matthew on the stairs.

"I think you need to come up with a different name for your town, Mr. Taylor," Allie said coolly as she continued to walk downstairs.

Matthew didn't respond.

"Allie! I'm so glad you're back," Catherine said, trying to get her to stop.

"I can't talk right now," she said. "I need to get out of here."

"Where are you going?" Catherine called out. "Allie!?"

But Allie walked out the dining room doors. A couple of men stood by the open door to the bathhouse. She paused when she saw Jimmy sitting inside. He looked up and met her gaze. A thought crossed her mind. She walked up to the door and asked who was in charge.

"I'm Captain Bill Williams, ma'am," he said.

"I just wanted to let you know you're making a big mistake," Allie said.

"Why is that?" he asked. "Kidnapping is a very serious offense in these parts."

"But no kidnapping occurred," she said. "I wasn't taken against my will."

"Allie," Jimmy said. "Don't... "

"That's not what we were told, Miss Blake," he said.

"Well, I don't know what you've been told, but before you leave, we need to clarify this. You wouldn't want to be responsible for arresting an innocent man, would you?"

"No, ma'am," the Ranger said. "But you wouldn't be trying to protect a guilty man, either, would you?"

"If he was guilty, then neither one of us would be back here right now, would we?" she said.

"How about we discuss this with Mr. Taylor and Mr. Stockton in the morning before we leave," he proposed.

"I think we need to discuss it with the whole family," Allie said.

"Fine with me, Miss Blake," Ranger Williams said. "We'll see you in the morning."

"Thank you, sir," she said as she turned to walk away.

"Where are you going, Allie?" Jimmy hollered out, noticing she didn't turn back toward the house.

"I made another choice," she said over her shoulder.

Allie passed the barn on her way to the river. As she walked along, she reached in her pocket and felt the bar of soap. She paused on the rise above the river before heading down the steep incline. *No demons here*, she thought. When she reached the big rock above the swimming hole, she dropped her change of clothes, stripped down to her undergarments, grabbed the soap, and let out a frustrated yell as she jumped off the rock.

Justin looked across the clearing when he heard the holler—and just caught a glimpse of Allie going off the big rock. His heart stopped.

"Allie?!" he said, dropping the long poles as he ran at breakneck speed toward the river.

Uncle John was working on the old brush fence when he heard Allie, too. He threw down the pile of branches and ran towards the swimming hole by way of the longer path by the springs. Justin could see Allie's head bobbing in the middle of the river.

"Allie!" he yelled just before he hit the water.

She turned when he yelled her name and saw Justin jump in, boots and all.

"Justin?!"

He swam quickly toward her and saw her watching him, wide-eyed. He reached her and grabbed her arm like she was drowning and started dragging her to the shallow side of the river.

"What are you doing!?" he demanded to know as he tried to pull her along.

"I was attempting to take a bath," she said, yanking her arm back. "What are YOU doing?"

"Sinking with these boots on—*please* come out of the river," Justin said, struggling to keep his head above water. "Follow me over here."

"Here, let me help you," Allie said as she got behind him and pushed him toward the dry part of the riverbed.

Justin crawled over on the gravel and sat down, breathing heavily, but Allie stayed in the river. "What are you doing to me? Please get out of the river."

"I'm not dressed, Justin," Allie said. "I didn't mean to scare you—I had no idea anyone else was around."

"Don't *ever* come down here by yourself," Justin said. "Look what happened last time."

"I wasn't by myself that day, Justin," Allie said, "and I wasn't in the river."

Justin braced his arms on his knees and put his head down. "I can't lose you again, Allie."

Allie could see him shaking. A jab went through her heart when she realized the agony he had gone through thinking she had drowned weeks before. She threw all convention aside and crawled out of the water to put her arms around him.

"You won't, Justin," Allie said. "I'm never going to let you go."

"Isn't it the man that's supposed to say that?"

"Whoever decided that?" she said, "or that it's the man that's always supposed to do this." She leaned over and kissed him lightly on the lips.

Someone loudly cleared his throat from the other side of the river. Allie looked up to see Uncle John standing on the big rock above the swimming hole, bending over to catch his breath.

Allie scrambled back into the river.

"What do you think you're doing, young lady?!" he demanded. "You just about gave me heart failure."

"I was just trying to take a bath, if that's all right with you!" she said.

"The bathhouse is a bit crowded right now. What are you two doing down here?"

"We're setting up Nah-kay's house," Uncle John said, "and fixing a pen for her... uh... steed."

"At the old hiding place," Justin said as he pulled off his boots to pour out the water.

"That's perfect for her!" Allie said. "If you would let me finish my bath, I'll help you."

"I'll stay, Justin," John said. "You can go on back."

"Sorry, Uncle, but I'm not letting her out of my sight. Well, let me rephrase that—" he said when he saw his uncle's eyebrows meet in the middle of his forehead, "I'll face the other way until she's dressed."

"Justin, I can't allow that," John said. "You barely know her."

"I plan to spend the rest of my life with her, Uncle John," Justin said, watching Allie's face, "if that's all right with her."

Allie's eyes grew wide; then she smiled.

"It's all right with me," Allie said, trying to sear into her mind every detail of that moment—Justin in his sopping wet clothes, the evening sun on his rugged face, the beautiful riverbed and trees behind him, those blue eyes...

"Well, you need to ask her father's permission for her hand, and you already have my blessing, but until you say *I do,* we're going to do this proper," John said. "Now get back over there and set up your grandmother's house. We'll be there shortly."

"Is that all right with you, Allie?" Justin asked.

She just nodded and kept smiling.

A little while later Nah-kay walked Justin and Allie through the process of setting up her tipi near the spring. They arranged the three main poles like a tripod, and began to fill in other poles around the sides. They weren't able to bring all of the long poles from the original camp, but Justin found several tall saplings at the side of the clearing that would suffice. He cut them down and quickly stripped their leaves and branches to use for filling in the rest of the poles that would support the leather covering.

Uncle John worked on the brush pile fence until darkness had settled in, but he didn't have enough time to finish it, so they kept the hobble on Nah-kay's horse for the night.

Faith had shown up early in the evening to help, and Nah-kay cried and fussed over her like she had with Jimmy and Justin. Faith said she still had a few memories of Nah-kay, but she, too, had lost most of the language.

A little while later Julia came down to the new camp, bringing some food from Vestal's kitchen. The reunion with the old woman was emotional, and Nah-kay kept saying her heart was full. Julia could remember some of the language, and with Justin's help, she apologized to Nah-kay for the unhappy circumstances that had greeted her earlier back at the house. Julia told her that she was welcome to live on their land as long as she liked. She said she couldn't stay long that evening, but promised she would be back the next day to talk more with her.

Nah-kay seemed to approve of the location, and it hadn't taken her long to clean up the area and build a fire. It amazed Allie to see that she already treated it like home. She had worried on the trip back to Grace that Nah-kay would have trouble adjusting to life here, but she could see that bringing Nah-kay's tipi and belongings made this place home for her.

Nah-kay set about preparing something for their evening meal along with what Julia had brought. Uncle John and Faith tried the corn cakes and pemmican, and Nah-kay seemed pleased at their reactions to her cooking. She even tasted Vestal's roast and butterhorn rolls, and nodded her head in approval.

Justin told Uncle John that he and Allie would be staying with Nah-kay that night, and at first he objected. Justin reminded him that Nah-kay would be their chaperone, so he agreed. The sun had set hours before when Uncle John and Faith walked back to the Taylor house together. Justin told Allie that it must not have occurred to Uncle John that they had all been sleeping side-by-side for days on the road.

"Along with my cousin, Chastity," Allie teased.

"I don't particularly care for that cousin of yours," Justin played along. "Now, when did you say she was leaving?"

"I think she plans to be around a while—probably until our wedding," Allie said.

"Dang it."

Allie giggled.

She, too, was relieved that they stayed with Nah-kay and away from the house. She couldn't face anyone that night, but she would be ready for them in the morning. She told Justin that she called a family meeting.

"Oh, you did, did you?" he said. "And what did my father say about that?"

"He doesn't know about it, yet," she said.

Justin snorted. "If anybody could convince him to change his mind, you could, Alexandra Blake."

"Well, maybe not me," she said, "but God can. I have some serious praying to do tonight."

Justin had pulled several of the buffalo hides out of the tipi for bedding, but they were too wound up to sleep. So for a while, they sat comfortably in each other's arms facing the fire. Nah-kay had already turned in.

"I can see why you and Jimmy loved this place," Allie said, listening to the running water and the sounds of the night.

Just then a twig snapped behind them, and Justin jumped up to face the intruder.

Chapter 17

"Jimmy?" Allie said, as she turned around.

But it wasn't Jimmy. An old man stepped into the light of the campfire.

"Castro!" Justin breathed a sigh of relief. "What are you doing here?" he said in his language.

Castro waited, watching for Nah-kay to step out of her tipi. She did, and she seemed pleased that he was there, but she didn't get emotional like when she saw her grandchildren. Castro sat down by the fire, and Nah-kay prepared him something to eat.

"Is she being coy with him?" Allie asked.

"She doesn't act like she's at all surprised that he's here," Justin said. He asked Nah-kay if she knew he would come, and she nodded, yes. She said that she knew Castro would find her.

"Well, I'll be," Justin said. "I wonder why she didn't let us in on that."

After Castro put something in his stomach, he was ready to talk. He told Justin that the hunters had returned to find their families gone, and they followed them for several days, trying to figure out a way to get them back. But he said there were too many soldiers. Castro assumed Nah-kay traveled with them, but when he saw that she hadn't, he backtracked to the camp and found shod and unshod horse tracks leading the opposite direction away from the camp. He said Nah-kay's heavy travois poles made an easy trail to follow—they led him right here.

"You can stay here, Castro, but no more raiding or war," Justin felt compelled to tell him, "—only peace with my family."

Castro nodded and said something about being too old to fight anymore. Nah-kay brought him a blanket to sleep on, and he rolled it out beside the tipi. He fell asleep in no time.

"How did he keep from being seen?" Allie asked.

"He's the best at being invisible when he needs to be," Justin said. "He taught me."

"He stepped on the twig on purpose, then," Allie said, remembering that Jimmy had done the same thing that day.

"Yeah, like knocking on the door," Justin said, watching him. "You know, it may be a good thing that he's here—I really didn't want to leave Nah-na down here alone to fend for herself. I don't know how much help she'll get from my family, although I know Mother will try to take care of her. But I have responsibilities to Uncle John in Dalton, and now to you, too."

"You do what you need to do, Justin," Allie said. "I can wait."

"But *I* can't, Allie," he said. "It occurred to me earlier that most everyone that we know and love is here in Grace right now. And I don't know how long it's going to take to get Jimmy out of this mess." He paused a moment before saying, "What do you think about getting married before going back to Dalton?"

Allie looked surprised, and didn't quite know how to answer that.

"Or would that ruin your dreams of having a big wedding back home?"

"Every young girl dreams about her wedding," she said, "but I doubt my wedding would ever be *big* in Dalton—I wasn't their favorite ingénue, remember? But you're right; both of our families are here. Do you think we could get it all together that quickly?"

"I know where we could borrow a wedding dress, although it may be a little long on you, but it seems to be a tradition to wear it in my family," Justin said.

Allie's mind started racing.

"What are you thinking?" Justin asked, watching her reaction.

"Let's do it," Allie said, grinning, but then as quickly, her smile faded. "But we want Jimmy to be a part of it."

"We'll figure something out," Justin said. "We'll make it work. Let's talk to your parents after breakfast tomorrow."

"And the family meeting," she reminded him.

"Right," he said. "Now let's see if we can get some sleep. The night's half gone."

"Now I'm *sure* I won't get *any* sleep tonight after this conversation," Allie said as she lay down. Justin protectively put his arm over her and pulled her close.

"When did you know about us, Justin?" Allie asked as she watched the embers burning low.

"I think I fell in love with you when I saw you hugging those dogs goodbye at Uncle Junior's," Justin said.

"And I was embarrassed that you'd caught me," Allie said.

"When did you start having feelings for me?"

"On the stage ride to Waco," she said.

"No doubts?"

"No doubts."

And contrary to what Allie said, they both were asleep in a matter of minutes.

* * *

The little boy stood there crying as the huge horses ran this way and that. He tried to walk one way, and a horse blocked his path. He turned and tried to walk the other way, and another horse ran in front of him. He walked back to the motionless figure lying on the ground and lay down beside him. He tried to find some comfort by pulling the lifeless arm over him like a blanket...

Matthew woke with a start; the vivid images hung fresh in his mind. He hadn't let himself think about them for a long time now, but for years after rescuing Julia the memory of the lost little boy haunted him. He remembered her screaming for the little boy when she thought the worst seeing him prostrate beside his dead father. Matthew remembered the visceral shock he felt course through his body when he saw the little boy's eyes—Julia's eyes. He felt such anger and shame at that moment, but he swallowed his pride and let her bring him and Faith home. He eventually learned to love Faith, but he had closed his heart to the little boy, and he had tried to close his mind to those memories.

Matthew sat up stiffly and remembered where he was—on a pallet in the parlor. He looked through the open double doors to the closed door of his bedroom, and a vise squeezed his chest. Julia had never locked him out of their bedroom before, but he had wounded her deeply. He thought about Justin's words, and he knew they were true. Jimmy *was* just a little boy when he came to them, and Matthew had piled the weight of his anger and blame toward Jimmy's father on him. What a burden for a little boy to have to carry. Matthew couldn't deny it any more; he had to take some responsibility for Jimmy's behavior.

"Dear Lord, forgive me. Help me make it right. Show me what to do," he whispered into the dark.

He looked at the bedroom door again.

"Julia," he said with a desperate need to make things right with his beloved. "Forgive me."

He started to get up and go to her when a hand reached out and stopped him. He turned, and in the gray light he saw Julia's face. She had slipped in sometime during the night to lie beside him on the floor.

"I'm right here, Matthew," she said quietly.

She pulled him to her chest as he wept.

* * *

The canopy over the hiding place provided such a good covering that it blocked out most of the morning sun, and Justin and Allie woke up much later than they intended. Nah-kay wasn't within sight, but they could see Castro working on the brush fence.

"What time do you think it is?" Allie said, pulling on her shoes and lacing them as fast as she could. "Do you think the Rangers have already left with Jimmy?"

"I don't know— but it's later than we think," Justin said. "Let's go."

He grabbed her hand and helped her up. They ran along the trail to the swimming hole, and he half dragged her up the steep incline to the path toward the house. They were out of breath by the time they reached the barn. Justin ran inside to look in the stalls—empty —and then he checked the outside pens. They only held horses that belonged to the Taylors.

"They've already gone!" he said.

"Oh, Justin, no!" Allie said as her heart sank.

"Let's go to the house," Justin suggested. But they found the house empty as well.

They found that Vestal had left out biscuits, eggs, and ham for them to eat, and that Julia had scrawled a quick note for them. *We're all at church—we'll be back soon*, it said.

"It's Sunday?" Allie said, running into the kitchen to look at Vestal's regulator clock. "The service has just started—we can still make it. The gall

203

of them going to church like nothing out of the ordinary has happened here! How can they live with themselves?"

"I don't think we're dressed for church," Justin said.

"Let's go—we don't have time to change," Allie said. "I think it's about time somebody gave a little testimony about grace—seems like folks around here haven't a clue what that means."

"Do you want me to saddle our horses?" Justin asked.

"That'll take too long—it's not that far to the church," Allie said. "Let's just go on foot."

They ran out the kitchen door and around the house to the end of the flower garden in front before Allie pulled up with a stitch in her side from having run all the way from the spring. "Maybe we should just walk for a while," she said, trying to catch her breath.

"So you're going to help the preacher this morning?" Justin asked.

"If that's what it takes to wake up our families," Allie said, "then, yes."

Less than ten minutes later, they walked up the steps to the church. They could hear the people singing the last verse to *Amazing Grace*, but Allie couldn't recognize the tune coming from the piano. She looked at Justin questioningly.

"Mrs. Mamie," Justin explained, and then noticed something at the side of the church. "Demon!"

Allie continued to march through the door, but she felt obligated to address Justin's remark. "Now we don't have to go in there name-calling, Justin," she whispered over her shoulder. "We're just going to convict them with the truth."

She was loaded for bear.

"No, I wasn't saying that—" Justin said, but Allie had already gone inside.

Justin walked through the foyer and paused at the doors to the sanctuary. Allie was halfway down the aisle when the congregation finished the song and began to sit down.

"Excuse me, sir, but I'd like to say something," she said, noticing the Taylors and her own family had chosen to sit on the first couple of pews.

Allie stood there in complete disarray: tangled hair, wrinkled clothes, and she reeked of campfire smoke.

"Miss Blake, welcome!" Pastor Jenkins said. "We would be happy to hear a testimony from you, but we've had several other requests to speak before you, so if you'll please take a seat, I'll let you know when it's your turn."

That let the wind out of her sails. Allie just stood there.

How could they act like nothing has happened? Did Jimmy mean so little to them? she thought to herself.

Justin came up beside her and led her to the nearest pew. "Let's hear them out," he said.

"Mr. Taylor, you're first," Pastor Jenkins said.

Matthew Taylor stood and walked to the front of the church. He nodded a greeting at Allie and Justin before addressing the congregation.

"A lot has happened in my life—I've experienced great joy, and I've experienced great sadness, and I don't have to go into all that—you all know what happened to my family. And we appreciate all your prayers, your help, and your friendship to my family and me during that time.

"For years I thought if I could just get my wife and son back, everything would be all right. But it hasn't been all right." He looked down to gather his thoughts before continuing. "My wife brought home with her a couple of reminders of the pain that I wanted to forget... those reminders were Jimmy and Faith." He paused again. "I never mistreated them; I let them live with us as our children; I made sure they were educated. I took pride in the fact that I was a big enough man to overlook their obvious lineage. I learned to love Faith as my own daughter, but I couldn't say the same about Jimmy.

"My son Justin told me some things yesterday that hurt me—it hurt because it was the truth that I had refused to face all these years. God help me, but I finally realized that I *had* been placing the blame on Jimmy for his father's sins. And no little boy should ever be given that big of a burden to have to carry through life. Jimmy has struggled for years not knowing where he belonged, and his frustration and the lack of acceptance by our culture have pushed him to behave in unacceptable ways, culminating in this last incident that broke the law as well as our hearts. I'm not excusing that behavior, and Jimmy has some penance to pay, but I realized that I have to take some responsibility for Jimmy's actions, too.

"He was just a little boy when we brought him here—Julia's son, not mine, but God placed him in my hands to love and care for, and I failed him. I recall that God gave a similar task to a man to raise and love a son that also wasn't his own, but in that situation and family, Joseph did it right.

"I have asked Jimmy's forgiveness privately, but today I want to ask his forgiveness publicly—in front of my family and my community. And I want to declare my devotion and loyalty to him as my son—morally and legally. That means if you don't accept him, you don't accept me." He looked at Jimmy, sitting on the front row. "Could you please come up here, son?"

The tears were already flowing throughout the church, but Allie choked back a sob when she saw Jimmy stand from the midst of his family. He was clean, and out of the torn and stained clothes that he had been wearing the day and weeks before. She grabbed Justin's hand as she watched Mr. Taylor place his hand on Jimmy's shoulder.

"Will you forgive me, Jimmy, for all the pain I've put you through?" Matthew said as tears began to fall unabashedly down his cheeks. "Forgive me for not loving you as a father should. I want to make that up to you, if you'll let me."

Jimmy swallowed hard, trying to hold back the tears. "I should be the one asking your forgiveness, sir."

"Not before I ask you," Matthew said, and then repeated the question. "Could you find it in your heart to forgive me?"

Jimmy nodded, overwhelmed and unable to speak. Matthew pulled him into his arms. Julia stood up and put her arms around them both.

"Jimmy, you asked if you could speak," Pastor Jenkins said.

Matthew and Julia continued to stand with him. It took a few moments for Jimmy to regain his composure, and then he addressed the congregation and his family.

"I used to hear some of you say that God works in mysterious ways, but I never understood that until recently. I always thought I was in control of my life, but God orchestrated some events that can't be explained other than they led me to Him. He brought a miracle into my life—her name is Allie Blake, and if I ever gave anyone reason to hate me, it was Allie. But she never did. She forgave me—not once, mind you, but time and time again. And she still walked in here today to try to defend me," Jimmy's voice broke, "in spite of all the things I put her through. If that isn't a picture of God's grace, I don't know what is. And I want you to know that I've accepted his grace, and because of it, I need to ask my family and Allie's family to forgive me for what I put them through. I don't know how, but I want to try to make it up to you." Jimmy looked at Allie's family and his own family members as he asked, "Will you forgive me?"

Justin and Allie were the first ones out of their seats to embrace Jimmy. The rest of his family followed and hugged him, and Allie's father came up and solemnly shook his hand and sat back down. Allie knew he was stepping out in obedience to forgive Jimmy, but she also knew her family still had a ways to go when it came to feeling that forgiveness after the grief he had caused them. But she knew her family, and she knew it would come eventually. She walked over and thanked her parents as she embraced them, and they all returned to their seats.

Pastor Jenkins spoke from the pulpit, "I couldn't have preached a better sermon on forgiveness than what we've witnessed today. Miss Blake, did you still want to share a testimony?"

Allie shook her head, no, but then on second thought, stood and addressed Matthew Taylor by saying, "You did give this town the right name after all, Mr. Taylor."

* * *

They all came back to the house after church, and Vestal cooked up some chicken and dumplings while everyone visited. Justin and Allie learned that Matthew had gone to the bathhouse before sunrise Sunday morning and thanked Captain Williams and his men for their service, and then asked them to leave—without taking Jimmy.

Matthew said he had a long talk with Jimmy, and had him actually use the bathhouse for what it was intended. When he came back with some clean clothes for Jimmy, he saw his scars, still red and in the process of healing, and shuddered when he realized how close Jimmy came to dying. He thanked God for protecting Jimmy and for giving him the opportunity to make things right with him. He also knew Jimmy had emotional scars that were just as deep, but he saw little evidence of them during their time together that morning. Something *had* happened to him during the weeks he was gone.

Between the Blake and Taylor families, all the tables in the dining room were full. Allie and Justin sat together, situated between their families, and Jimmy sat in-between his parents. It had been quite some time since he had attended a family dinner, and he didn't have much to say, but at the same time he didn't seem to be uncomfortable. Allie noticed he really listened to everyone and watched them like he was seeing them anew. She caught his eye and smiled at him, and he couldn't help but grin back.

What a beautiful face you have when you smile, she thought. *You're going to break hearts some day, Jimmy Taylor.*

He mouthed the words, *thank you*, to her.

She raised her eyebrows in question, *for what?* She mouthed back.

For not letting me go, he grasped his arm; *for bringing me home*, his lips said.

Allie nodded and smiled as tears filled her eyes. *Thank you, Lord, for bringing Jimmy home*, she said in her thoughts, treasuring the hard-earned bond between them. *Please take care of him when I'm gone.*

Toward the end of the meal, Justin suddenly stood up and asked for everyone's attention.

"I have an announcement to make," he said.

Allie raised her eyebrows and whispered, "Now?"

He nodded his head. "Now."

"But you haven't asked my..." she tried to say, but this time he put his fingers to *her* lips to shush her.

"I cornered Mr. Blake a little while ago and asked him for his daughter's hand in marriage," he said to everyone.

Startled gasps were heard around the table, followed by smiles. Allie hugged her mother next to her, and leaned over her to kiss her father's cheek.

Justin continued. "It took some powerful convincing, but he finally agreed, probably because I told him I wouldn't take his daughter too far from him and Mrs. Blake—that we would make Dalton our home, thanks to Uncle John. I just want everyone to know that I love Allie, and I'll do my best to make her happy."

Justin stood there for a moment before saying, "I'm not sure what else I'm supposed to say now."

Matthew spoke up. "Congratulations, son, but we're all a little curious to find out if you bothered to ask Allie, and what was her response?"

Everyone laughed as Allie stood up beside Justin.

"He did," she said. "And I said yes."

Everyone applauded as Justin hugged her, and then he pulled back and said, "Oh! And we'd like to get married before everyone leaves tomorrow."

Shocked silence followed.

"What did you say, Justin!?" Julia asked.

"Think about it, Mother," he said. "You know how hard it would be to get everyone together again. Both of our families are here. Allie could use your dress, and Pastor Jenkins could marry us, and..."

"I don't know, Justin—this is so fast. Do you know what you're doing?"

They both assured her they had no doubts.

Julia turned to Mrs. Blake. "What do you think, Mary?"

Mary turned to her daughter. "Don't you want to have your wedding in Dalton?"

"What's more important to us is having everyone we love at our wedding—not necessarily the place we're going to have the ceremony," Allie said.

"Then we're going to need more than one day to prepare for it," her mother said.

* * *

The wedding took place *two* days later. Allie wore Julia's dress, and her mother had hemmed it up for her. Allie asked Faith to be her maid of honor, and Catherine and Jenny her matrons of honor, breaking another traditional rule. Justin had Jimmy as his best man, as well as Matt and Marcus stand up for him. Julia even had the courage to play the piano for them, using her right hand. Invites were by word of mouth, and most everyone in the community attended since social gatherings were few and far between. Jenny insisted on decorating the church *and* the Taylor house again with lace and ribbons, and Allie told her that if they'd had a *whole month* to plan for this wedding, it couldn't have been any prettier.

Justin and Allie traveled to Waco with Uncle John and Allie's family on their way back to Dalton, but the newly married couple stayed almost a week in Waco before heading home. They treasured that time of rest and getting to know each other as husband and wife, and the time passed all too quickly.

When they arrived in Dalton later, just about everyone had heard the news of their marriage. Allie had been the talk of the town for some time with a death, resurrection, kidnapping, rescue, and now marriage. Uncle John and Allie's family met the couple at the stage office where they broke the news to them that they would be living in an old adobe house near the Nueces River on the Stockton ranch, about a half-mile from the ranch's headquarters. Allie invited everyone to come out to the house with them, but they all declined, insisting that Allie and Justin needed to have that time alone for their first visit to their new home.

Her mother asked everyone to come to Sunday dinner after church the following day, so Allie felt better about leaving the company of her family so soon. Uncle John lent them the use of his buggy to haul themselves home, and Allie's trunk was already loaded on the back of it. Uncle John had brought it home to her parents after her disappearance. Her mother handed them a basket, saying she had packed a meal so Allie wouldn't have to worry about cooking supper their first night home.

"We'll come prepared to start packing things up to take back to the house tomorrow, Momma," Allie said as Justin started the buggy forward.

Her mother just smiled and waved.

"I thought they'd want to spend a little more time with us when we got back," Allie said. "You'd think they were trying to get rid of us."

"We have our work cut out for us with this old house," Justin said. "Uncle John has been using it for storage. I don't know if we'll even have a bed to sleep on."

"Well, I do have a quilt packed in my trunk," Allie said. "I guess we can manage one more night on the floor if we need to. Do you have a lot of stuff at Uncle John's you need to pick up, too?"

"Just a few clothes and my horse and saddle," Justin said.

The house was about three miles out of town. Allie was glad it was close enough to walk if she needed to, but far enough away to have some privacy and space. She wanted to have her own dogs and cats and chickens and a milk cow.

"I don't remember ever coming out to this place," Allie said.

"Uncle John's ranch foreman and his family lived in the house for years, but it's been empty for a while," Justin said. "He told me that I'd eventually move in here, but neither of us had the gumption to come clean it up and make it livable."

It took about twenty minutes to get to the place, and Allie expected the worst. But surprisingly, she saw a rustic charm about it, and someone had cut down the weeds around the house.

Allie jumped out of the buggy, anxious to see the inside. Justin had to catch up with her and make her stop so he could carry her over the threshold of their first home.

"I almost forgot—how'd you know about this tradition?" Allie asked him.

"I'd never heard of it, but Mother told me I'd better not forget," Justin said as he threw open the door and swept her up in his arms.

"Lead on, husband o' mine," Allie said as she wrapped her arms around his neck.

They both laughed until Justin bumped into something as he walked into the center of the darkened room. He backed up, and Allie turned to see Uncle John's beautiful dining table, chairs, and buffet sitting in the front room. Justin set her down and Allie picked up a note on the table and read it aloud, *"Our gift and love to you both. May God bless your marriage. Uncle John and Sarah."*

"Oh, Justin ... I can't believe he did this," Allie said, moved by the generous gift. "I wish we could've known her."

Justin looked around. "Somebody's done a lot of work in here. This place was a wreck the last time I saw it, and there wasn't anything here but junk."

It looked like the house had been cleaned from top to bottom, and as they walked from room to room, Allie saw odds and ends of furniture with notes of congratulations on them. One of her favorite Sunday School teachers had given her and Justin a rocker. A small table was from the general store owner and his family. A friend from her school days had given them a coal oil lamp. Allie walked into the first bedroom and found her bed and hope chest from home. And on it went. The generosity of the folks in Dalton overwhelmed her when she realized that they hadn't forgotten her, nor had they shunned her.

"I can't believe this," she said, looking around.

"Allie, come to the kitchen!" Justin hollered.

She ran back to the front room and down a couple of steps into the small kitchen. Justin stood beside another table loaded with canned goods and other cooking staples—flour, sugar, spices, and such.

"It's from the Dalton Ladies Home Club," Justin said, reading another note, "welcoming us home and congratulating us on our wedding."

"They gave us a pounding, too?" Allie said, and then burst into tears.

"This is a bad thing?" Justin asked as he took her in his arms. "You just tell me who these evil people are, and I'll go pound them for you myself."

Allie pulled back and started to explain to Justin what a pounding was, until she saw the smirk on his face. Then she socked him.

He pulled her close again telling her, "I know what a pounding is, Allie, but I don't understand why you're so upset about it."

"I thought they all hated me," she said. "I was prepared to come home and live like a hermit, thinking no one would want to have anything to do with me. And here they are being so nice to me."

"Maybe you taught them something, Allie," Justin said, "or maybe there's a little grace left in this town, too."

* * *

Two weeks after coming back to Dalton, Allie and Justin went to town to get some supplies. Justin had to go by the blacksmith's first and agreed to meet Allie at Cranfill's Store. Allie had just about gathered up everything on her list when a familiar voice spoke from behind her.

"Let me help you with some of that, Allie."

Her breath caught in her throat as she turned to face Miguel. He smiled—a friendly smile. She couldn't help but respond in like manner.

"Hello, Miguel," she said, realizing the moment wasn't as awkward as she thought it would be. "How are you?"

"Very well, gracias," he said, "y tu?"

"Muy bien," she said, nodding her head. "Muy bien."

"Ah, you remembered," he said, obviously pleased.

"I had the chance to practice some of my Spanish recently," she said, "but you wouldn't have been too proud of me. I butchered it terribly. But the little I knew was a big help during a difficult time, so I appreciate your teaching me."

"I had heard something about that," Miguel said. "You gave everyone quite a scare. We thought we'd lost you."

"But everything is all right now," Allie said.

"I hear you are married now, too," Miguel said. "Congratulations."

Allie nodded. "His name is Justin Taylor—he's John Stockton's nephew."

"I'd seen him around a few times," Miguel said, "but I had no idea he even knew you."

"I hear you're getting married, too."

Miguel nodded and smiled. "She's an old friend. I think we will be very happy together."

"I'm glad, Miguel," Allie said. "I'd like to meet her sometime. I hope you know I wish only the best for you."

He nodded and said, "And I wish you every happiness, too, Allie. You deserve it."

At that moment Justin came through the door and paused to let his eyes get accustomed to the inside. He looked around and spotted Allie and Miguel.

"Come on," Allie said to Miguel as she placed her merchandise on the counter and walked over to Justin. "I'd like you to meet my husband."

Allie introduced the two men. They shook hands, sizing each other up. Justin had expected to feel jealous when he finally met this man from Allie's past, but for some reason he felt no animosity toward him at all.

"You are a very fortunate man," Miguel said, "to have Allie for a wife."

"That's what she tells me all the time," Justin said without cracking a smile.

"Oh, you!" Allie started to sock him, but he grabbed her hand and pulled her toward him.

"You are exactly right, Miguel," Justin said, putting his arms around her. "I am a fortunate man indeed."

* * *

Otto Schaferling rode up to the big house, yelling at his father and brothers working around the barn, "Come to the house! I think I have news of Jimmy!"

The whole family—men, women, and children congregated in the front room, anxious to hear word of Jimmy Taylor—their Jimmy. Otto held a small package wrapped in brown paper and tied with string.

"Is Jimmy all right?" Mrs. Schaferling said.

"The return address says *J. Taylor*, so I'm not sure which brother this is, but either way, we'll know what happened," Otto said.

"Well, son," Josef said impatiently, "open it!"

Otto's hands shook as he used his knife to cut the string. He unwrapped the paper to find a bar of soap.

"Soap?" Mrs. Schaferling said. "I don't understand."

"There's a note underneath it, Otto," Karl said. "Read it to us."

Otto handed it to his wife. "You read it, Lena. You're a better reader than me."

Lena unfolded the note and began reading.

Dear Mr. & Mrs. Schaferling & family,

I am writing on behalf of Justin and Jimmy Taylor. You don't know me, but I visited your home two months ago as I write this. My name is Allie, and Jimmy and I stopped there during a thunderstorm. We knew something was wrong in the area when we found no one around and signs that you all had left in a hurry. Our worst fears were realized the next morning when we were attacked and taken by a band of Apaches raiding your place. But God was gracious and allowed our lives to be spared, although Jimmy was seriously wounded before I had the chance to tell our assailants that he was one of them—the Indeh. We spent the next ten days or so traveling with this band until we arrived at their home camp.

I don't know how much you know about Jimmy and Justin's past, but this group of Apaches included some that were a part of the band they lived with when they were young. Jimmy and I were handed over to the care of an elderly woman who we soon learned was Jimmy's grandmother! She is the only other surviving member of his birth father's family, and we spent several days with her before Justin arrived to "rescue" us. Justin could still remember much of the language, and in spite of our circumstances, we enjoyed getting to know his and Jimmy's grandmother, Nah-kay. We also found out there were several others who remembered the brothers. The Apaches accepted us and protected us because of that bond from years ago. We were able to arrive back at Grace a week and a half later, and were able to bring Jimmy and Justin's grandmother with us.

Justin asked me to write you because he knew you would want to know about Jimmy. His wounds are healing, and he will be just fine. He has big plans to raise and train horses in Central Texas, and hopes to get down to see you soon.

And if you're wondering about the bar of soap, I used your soap on the back porch to leave a message on the window, and then I took it with me. I wanted to replace it, but more importantly, I wanted you to know that your soap was my connection to home and my life before, as I knew it. I still have a piece of it left, and have wrapped it up and placed it in my hope chest along with a beautiful leather dress that Nah-kay gave me. I'll have some special stories to tell my children and grandchildren some day about those treasures.

Jimmy spoke very highly of you all. And he was right, Mrs. Schaferling—you do make the best apple butter!

With Kindest Regards,
Allie
Mrs. Justin (Alexandra Blake) Taylor

Epilogue

Justin and Allie rode their horses up a grassy rise overlooking the river below. They dismounted and watched the cattle grazing peacefully in the rich bottomland on the other side. It had been two years since Allie's ordeal on the trail. But now Allie felt content. She felt safe. She felt loved.

Justin pulled her toward him, and Allie closed her eyes and lifted her chin in anticipation of a tender kiss. She felt his breath on her cheek. She felt his hand on the side of her face as he reached back and yanked the dickens out of her hair…

"Ouch!" Allie said as the dream disintegrated, and her eyes flew open. All she could see were the biggest blue eyes right in front of her face—beautiful blue eyes and curly blonde hair. And then came the biggest, slobbery-ist kiss right on her cheek.

"She *sure* loves her momma," Justin said, grinning.

"I think somebody put you up to that, baby girl," Allie said as she rolled her over in the middle of the bed and blew on her neck, causing a burst of giggles.

"Were you dreaming again?" Justin asked.

Allie nodded. "But they're good dreams now. And all that time with your brother made me realize some things."

"Like what?"

"Like… a bath feels best when you're at your dirtiest. And food tastes so much better when you're hungry. And I didn't appreciate some things until I was without them. And I realized that God's strength was greatest when I was at my weakest," Allie said.

"And you don't realize the depth of your love for someone until you've lost them," Justin added.

He leaned over and gently kissed her on the lips. Allie sighed with contentment and leaned her head on his shoulder.

"And you said you weren't a poet."

Justin leaned back a bit and looked into Allie's eyes. "You liked that? Well, how about this." He leaned over and whispered into Allie's ear, "We're gettin' sort of hungry."

Allie giggled. "You're so bad."

"Oh, right—the poet in me is supposed to look at food as if it wasn't food, right?" He thought for a moment. "I've got it. The flapjacks flopped across the plate like stones skipping across the water."

Allie groaned and then socked him. "All right, all right—I can take a hint; pancakes it is," she said, looking at her little girl and then up at Justin. "You look just like your daddy."

"And acts just like her momma," Justin said. "Oh, yeah—we've been practicing something for you."

"You have?"

Justin nodded and grinned. He pulled his daughter into his lap and said, "Now tell Momma—what's your name, baby girl?"

The blue eyes looked up at Allie and said, "Gwace!"

* * *

Dear Reader,

Grace is one of those old fashioned words that sounds simple on the surface, but we make it so complex because the meaning defies human logic. Human nature tells us that the grace of God is earned—that it is something we have to work for in order to gain. But grace is a gift that we simply receive from God through his Son Jesus. Grace is all about what *He* did for us because of his amazing love for each of us—not what we think we can do for Him. Some recognize the impossible task of being good enough for God, and use it as an excuse to avoid Him altogether. Others work themselves to the bone trying to earn favor with God or a place in heaven—and never have the assurance of that, which is such an insecure way to live. But the fortunate ones are those who recognize and accept God's grace as the gift it is—this *unearned* favor, mercy, and forgiveness— and extend it toward others. That is the greatest evidence that a person has experienced the grace of God.

I hope you enjoyed reading *Grace Falling Like Rain* as much as I enjoyed writing it. One of my pre-publication readers came to me after she finished the manuscript and told me she wanted to know what happened to Jimmy. Beth was right—there's another story in Jimmy, so I began writing the sequel several months ago. It promises to be as exciting a journey as the first. You'll be surprised to see who turns up on the pages of this story— old familiar characters and some new ones, too. The story is titled *Mercy's Face*, and I've included an excerpt on the following pages.

I would love to hear your response to the story, too. Email me at donna@donnavancleve.com with any comments or questions. My web site is www.donnavancleve.com where you can find more information and read other columns I've written. If you would like a signed bookplate for your copy of this book or a gift book, send an SASE to P.O. Box 482, Hutto, TX 78634 with your request.

With kindest regards,

Donna Van Cleve

For by grace we are saved through faith; and that not of ourselves: it is the gift of God: not of works, lest any man should boast. – Ephesians 2:8-9

Chapter 1

Fort Worth... 1877

*E*very head turned as the beautiful woman sauntered through the hotel lobby on the way to the stairs. She smiled to herself, basking in the attention she drew—especially when men seemed to forget their female companions when she entered a room.

She walked up the stairs, swaying her hips just enough to insure she had everyone's attention. She was sick of those stairs, and the hotels, and the gambling houses. Surely Eustace would be ready to settle down soon. She stopped at Room 204. She was sick of this room, too, and hoped they could eat somewhere besides the hotel tonight. She opened the door to find Eustace stuffing something in the new leather valise she had recently purchased for him, at his suggestion.

"What are you doing?!" the woman asked.

"Ahh, my lovely Reen, back so soon?" he said calmly as he pulled the buckle tight and secured it. "I was hoping to avoid this."

"Avoid what?!" she said, feeling the panic rising in her throat. "Why did you pack your bag? Are you... are we going somewhere? Why didn't you tell me? You know it's going to take me more than a few minutes to get my things together."

In the back of her mind she knew what he was doing, but she refused to let the thought venture forward. This couldn't be happening to her.

Eustace walked over to the chair and picked up his coat—the expensive coat she had also bought him. "You know as well as I do that this couldn't last," he said as he pulled his left arm through the sleeve, then the right.

1

"Couldn't last?" she said, shaking her head in disbelief. "You said you loved me!! You said we would always be together! I believed you!"

"I did love you, Reen," he said, "for a while. But all things come to an end eventually."

"We haven't been together three months, Eustace! I think the word 'always' means quite a bit more than three months!"

"You can always go back to *Daddy*," he suggested as he put on his hat—the hat she had bought him, no—that wasn't right—the hat was his. It was the new boots, the new shirt and pants she had also bought for him. "You told me you had him wrapped around your little finger."

"Don't you remember? You made me choose between my parents and you," she said, her lips trembling. "And I took their money—you insisted we had to have it to make a fresh start—that we would pay them back eventually. How am I ever going to pay them back? We've spent almost half of it!!"

"You're a smart girl—you'll figure out a way," he said as he walked towards her. "Now, if you'll pardon me, I have a stage to catch."

"You can't do this to me, Eustace!" she cried, the tears flowed freely now. "I gave you everything of me! I held nothing back from you!!" She braced her arms across the doorway. "You have to take me with you!!"

Eustace stopped in front of her, calmly put the valise down, gripped her arms and picked her up off the floor, turned and set her down behind him. He retrieved his valise and walked out the door as she started screaming and pounding his back.

Halfway down the hall he dropped the valise, turned and violently shoved her up against the wall.

"Don't push me, Reen," he said, through gritted teeth. "Why don't you try to act like the lady I hoped you would be instead of the spoiled little girl who always gets her way. If you want to humiliate yourself further and ruin your chance of bagging some other imbecile who's stupid enough to hook up with you, then just keep following me downstairs. There's a good-sized audience down there to see your performance."

"You're hurting me," she whimpered.

She shut her eyes halfway through his barrage of insults—she couldn't stand to see his handsome face snarling so close to her own. But she needed to tell him something, and she was sure he would take back everything he said and take her with him. She opened her eyes and looked straight into his.

"I'm carrying your child," she said, bracing for the worst. She wasn't completely sure if that was true, but she suspected it.

He let go of her and backed away as if she were a leper.

After a moment, he shook his head and said, "You're lying."

"I wouldn't lie about—" she tried to say, but he cut her off.

"You'd lie about anything to get your way," he said, "or to get back at somebody. I heard stories about you before we met—about a lie you told a girl that sent her to her death... just because she was interested in the man you wanted."

She shut her eyes again, feeling nauseous. "But she didn't die—why do people keep saying that? She was taken by that half-breed! I had nothing to do with that!"

"But it was your lie that put her in his hands, wasn't it, dear? You're a liar and a thief, and you're just trying to trap me," he said, grabbing the valise again.

"I'm telling you the truth!" she said, this time pleading with her eyes. "You're going to be a father."

"Well, in that case, I'm living up to my name," he said.

"What!?" she asked.

"*Eustace* means fruitful," he said, turning to walk away. "You aren't the first woman who's tried to trap me that way, and you probably won't be the last."

She grabbed the first thing her hand touched and threw it as he started down the stairs. The vase shattered behind him, along with all her dreams.

She ran back to the room, slammed the door, crawled onto the bed, and pulled the covers over her head before the deep sobs came.

Four days later...

"Where is she?" the tall, dark-skinned man asked the hotel clerk.

The clerk couldn't help but stare at his piercing blue eyes, seemingly out of place with his skin.

"Is there a problem?" the blue eyes continued, "You said she was here."

"Uh, yes sir," the clerk said. "We can't seem to get rid of her. She won't come out of her room, and her bill is passed due. She gets hysterical if anyone tries to go in there. I don't know what she's doing for food. We haven't heard a peep out of her today and were considering calling the doctor or sheriff or somebody."

"Do you have a pass key?"

3

He nodded his head. "We're ready to see her leave, but before I hand over a key to you, I need to know who you are and what relation you are to this woman," the clerk said cautiously.

"My name is Jimmy Taylor, and her father hired me to bring her home," he said as he took out a letter of reference stating his business. "And I'll be taking care of her bill, but before that, I need you to bring some food to her room, and she'll need a woman to assist her for a little while. Can you recommend someone?"

The clerk called to a young boy walking through the hotel lobby and motioned for him to come over to the desk.

"Tommy, go to the kitchen and tell Mrs. Connor to bring a tray of soup and a pitcher of water for Room 204."

"What about hot tea or coffee?" Jimmy suggested.

"I think water would be the best choice for your friend right now."

"I didn't say she was a friend."

"Your *charge*, then," the clerk continued. "She threw an expensive vase of flowers at her gentleman friend on the day he left—by the way, that'll be three dollars added to her bill. Anyway, hot liquid of any kind might mean an additional risk to you when you face her."

"Good point," Jimmy said. "Water, it is."

"Go on, Tommy," the clerk said, "do as I told you."

The young boy walked swiftly across the lobby to the dining area and then through the double doors at the far side. In a few minutes, a short, stocky woman carrying a linen-covered tray shuffled over to the two men. The clerk introduced her to Jimmy.

"He's here to take our *favorite* guest home, Mrs. Connor," the clerk said, with a hint of a smile.

"Praise the Lord!" she said, acting relieved, then quickly apologized. "I'm so sorry, sir. I didn't mean to offend you."

"No offense taken," Jimmy said, smiling. "Could you help her get ready to leave?"

The woman nodded, and turned to walk toward the stairs.

"Here, let me carry that for you," Jimmy said to the older woman as he reached for the tray.

"Thank you, young man," she said. "You're definitely not cut of the same cloth as our queen up there."

Jimmy snorted. "No ma'am. She's the daughter of a friend of my father's, and her daddy had a penchant for spoiling her. I have no idea what to expect when we walk through that door, other than I know it's not going to be easy."

"You're right about it not being easy. She's had us wait on her hand and foot up until her *friend*—" and she raised her eyebrows on that word—"left. Then after that, she's just holed herself up in that room for the past four days—allowing no one inside. She even stopped ordering food. I've had Tommy leave some bread and water by the door—I didn't want her to starve," she said, and then lowered her voice to a whisper. "We're a little concerned that she might've gone off her rocker, if you know what I mean."

Mrs. Connor stopped in front of room 204. She looked at Jimmy, took a deep breath, and then knocked on the door.

No answer.

"Miz Reen?"

Still no answer from beyond the door.

Jimmy looked at the woman. "Did you say *mis'ry?*" *How fitting*, he thought.

"No, sir, I said *Miz Ree-nuh.*"

"Are you sure we have the right room?"

The woman nodded her head and tried again. "Miz Reen? Someone's here to take you home."

"Nobody from home knows I'm here," a hoarse voice said from the other side. "Go away."

"Here," Jimmy said, handing the tray to her and turned and slipped the pass key in the lock.

"Mr. Taylor's come for you," Mrs. Connor said. "And we're coming in there with some food."

"Justin?" the voice asked.

Jimmy stepped into the darkened room and paused, waiting for flying objects.

Nothing.

He walked across the room to pull back the heavy drapery from the windows.

"Justin, is it really you?" she asked in a small voice, shading her eyes as she slowly sat up in bed.

Jimmy pulled the last drapes back, took off his hat and turned to face the woman.

"No, Florine, it's not Justin," he said. "It's me… Jimmy."

5

"No!! Not you!!" the woman said with a horrified look on her face. She let out a blood-curdling scream and promptly fainted.

Chapter 2

Mrs. Connor set the tray down on the table and walked over to the bed. "Oh, my," she said. "She doesn't seem to like you at all, Mr. Taylor."

"Yeah, I figured Florine wouldn't be too happy to see me," he said. "I'm a reminder of something she'd like to forget ever happen. And what is this *Reen* name you called her?"

"That's how Mr. Ashton introduced her—as Miz Reen. She tried to make us think they were married—but we knew better. He was a snake, that one. I knew he was trouble when I first laid eyes on him. But Miz Reen, she seemed to see only what she wanted to see, though, and not how things really were," Mrs. Connor said as she leaned over Florine. "Poor thing, she's thin as a rail. Her heart's been stomped on and she's afraid to face the world."

"You do realize it's the devil you are referring to," Jimmy said, "although she doesn't even look like the same snooty debutante I remember."

"She's definitely been knocked off her high horse," Mrs. Connor said, patting Florine's hand and then her face. "Miz Reen?" No response. She turned to Jimmy. "Dip that towel in the water pitcher and hand it to me."

He did as she asked, and the older woman began wiping Florine's face and arms. The younger woman came around and blinked her eyes. When she saw Jimmy, she opened her mouth to scream again, and Mrs. Connor jabbed the towel in it and grabbed Florine's right hand reaching up to grab it. Jimmy grabbed her other arm.

"You just hold on a minute, missy," she said. "We're both here to help

7

you, so we'd appreciate you not damaging our ears again. We'll let you go if you promise to calm down."

Florine's chest heaved and nostrils flared as she glared at them. But she finally nodded her head, and Mrs. Connor pulled the towel out of her mouth and let her go.

"Get your hands off of me," she spat at Jimmy.

"Gladly," Jimmy said, raising his hands and stepping back.

"What are *you* doing here?" Florine demanded. "Why are you in my room?"

"Your father sent me to find you and bring you home," Jimmy said.

"Do you know who this is?" Florine asked Mrs. Connor as she looked at Jimmy.

Mrs. Connor nodded. "Mr. Jimmy Taylor."

"No—not his name, simpleton. Do you know what kind of person he is?" Florine asked again. "I bet you don't know that he's a savage Indian, and a kidnapper, and a lying drunk, and my daddy would never have sent someone like *him* to find me."

"I'm sorry, Florine, but that's exactly what your *daddy* did."

"I don't believe you."

Jimmy pulled out the letter of reference Mr. Locke had given him and handed it to Florine. She read it, and read it again, and then dropped her hands in her lap as a look of hopelessness swept across her face. Then the tears came.

"Why are you crying?" Mrs. Connor asked. "Your daddy wants you to come home."

"He hates me," she blubbered. "He'll never forgive me for what I did. He's hired a half-breed kidnapper to punish me."

"Oh, good grief, Florine," Jimmy said. "That's the most ridiculous thing I've ever heard."

"But you did kidnap Allie," Florine said to him as she turned to Mrs. Connor. "He really did kidnap a girl two years ago, Mrs. .... what was your name?"

"Connor," the woman said. "Now, now, you don't know what you're saying. You just need to get some food in you, and we'll get you all cleaned up and ready for travel and—"

"Tell her, Jimmy!" Florine interrupted. "You can't deny it."

"I guess I can't," Jimmy said, "but that's all worked itself out."

Mrs. Connor looked at him with raised eyebrows.

8

"It's a long story, but I assure you, Mrs. Connor," he explained, "the kidnappee and I are on the best of terms. She's my sister-in-law now, and I even stood up for my brother at their wedding."

"Well, then," Mrs. Connor patted Florine's knee, "that settles it. Mr. Taylor must not be too bad of a man if he participated in the *kidnappee's* wedding. Now let's get some food in you so you'll have some strength for the trip home."

"He's an Indian, too," Florine said, disgustedly. "I can't believe my daddy would want me to be in the company of this... savage. Have you heard of my family—the Lockes of Waco? Our ancestors were very close to the British throne."

Jimmy rolled his eyes and said under his breath, "Inside or out..."

Mrs. Connor snickered, and then said, "No, I haven't heard of your family, Miz Reen, but my husband's family is the potato-growing Connors from Ireland; my family's Welsh, and according to Mr. Taylor's name, I believe his ancestors are British, too, but then the other side of his family probably has more claim to this country than you do, so I wouldn't go flaunting your pedigree like it means something around here."

Watch for it – Summer of 2007

Printed in the United States
72313LV00007B/82